The Building

by
Dmitri Gheorgheni

The Building
Dmitri Gheorgheni

Copyright © 2023
All rights reserved.
ISBN: 978-1-4467-4702-5

Just How Sacrilegious *Is* This Book?
Or,
What Were You Thinking?

This novella was conceived from a single image: a heavenly choir of angels. Literally a choir, since they're a musical ensemble, wings and all. Even Ophaniel, who is 'full of eyes round and about', has been known to emit a drone or two. The angels are busy making divine harmonies in their home, which is the penthouse floor of a very mysterious and skyscraper-y building, when one of their number decides, 'I am bored. And what's on the other floors, anyway?'

That was how the adventure began. It's taken me on an interesting elevator ride since then. Writing serial fiction with no other prompt than the ambiguous 'a crime has been committed' and no other audience than the loopy froods at h2g2.com turned out to be a more productive exercise than might be expected by the average university English department. The result, which you have before you, led its author to some unusual places and, I hope, to a few insights among what I really hope will be a lot of laughs.

The Building relies on two main sources of inspiration: the Old Testament and Sumerian folklore. While riding roughshod over the geography of the Fertile Crescent and cavalierly mashing together at least a millennium's worth of spacetime, I've tried not to do violence to the resilient spirit of the humans of ancient Mesopotamia. We owe them a lot: writing, for instance. Also beer. And some really terrible jokes. Have you heard the one about the dog in the bar? Read on: you will.

Do I expect to incur the wrath of Marduk and Inanna? I have named them but to praise, although I've been a bit flip about Nudimmud. The same goes for Prajapati, for whom I feel nothing but the profoundest love. Will monotheists object? Not if they read carefully and in the spirit in which this is offered. Milton took creative liberties with the Biblical material. So did CS Lewis, Constantine Fitzgibbon, Joseph Heller, Thomas Mann…the list goes on. Frederick Buechner's *Son of Laughter* enables a deeper appreciation of the original story, while making readers want to cross their eyes. I feel that I am in good company with my Biblical/mythological fanfic here. I hope readers will not take the snake business amiss. Ori the angel was pretty annoyed with me, though.

The h2g2 Post fiction writers' serial novel experiment took place in 2022-23. At the same time, AI art burst upon the scene. We were promised miracles. Dubious claims were made to the effect that if we could describe it, the computer could draw it. Just for fun, some of us illustrated our stories by this means - and got what we deserved. We had arguments with the engines as to just exactly how many fingers a human ought to have, and where angels' wings should go. Lessons were learned, though how many of these were by the AIs, we weren't sure. These bogus works of 'art' do not belong in a book, but if you're interested you can see them online. Just go to h2g2.com, unclick 'Guide Entries' in the search box, and type in 'Crime Has Been Committed'. You'll find all the weird illustrations in their natural setting. There are also snatches of scores and links to music samples.

Thanks as always to SashaQ for editing help, to Brian Larholm for keeping h2g2 running and responding to our cries for help, and to Robbie Stamp for keeping the dream alive.

Now go and explore. And remember to dance to Nudimmud. You might get a carp flood.

Chapter 1: The Penthouse

In the beginning was The Building. Nobody knew how long it had been there. Nobody knew – or, at least, remembered – who had built it, or where they went afterwards. Because they certainly weren't here now. There were even rumours, not reliable because, well, rumours, that whoever constructed The Building had retreated to another, more ethereal, Building that couldn't be seen with the naked eye. Or so it was said. You know how rumours are.

Opinions differed as to whether The Building was built from the bottom up, or the top down. Nobody knew exactly how many storeys it had, because the ones doing the speculating lived in The Penthouse. And The Penthouse, with its 360 elegantly pointed glass spires, reared up, reflecting the thousand suns in magnificent glory, above a perpetually rolling bed of celestially fluffy white clouds.

The inhabitants of The Penthouse knew that The Penthouse looked like this from the outside because they had been there. They had wings (some of them, more than two) and could fly around and see for themselves. They often did this – for exercise, not curiosity. Curiosity was in short supply in The Penthouse. Nobody up there (or hardly anybody, as we shall see) ever asked what was going on in the Lower Floors of The Building, or whether its inhabitants were happy or sad, or, in fact, what was holding the building up. Things were just fine in The Penthouse, and that was all that mattered to them.

When the Penthouse People weren't flying around, they liked to dance inside The Penthouse. Their robes and feathers were bathed in the light that filtered in through the myriad panes of glass that broke up the rays of the thousand suns into glittering rainbows. Their dances were stately, simple. And as they danced, they sang.

'Wholly sat-is-fact-or-y...'

In the midst of this glittering (and possibly fatuous) crowd was one feathered being who was not happy. The being's name was Orion, Ori for short.

Always the same song, Ori thought. Will it ever end? Ori tried to stay out of the celestial conga line, but kept getting swept along as the winged crowd danced in stately procession around the centre feature of The Penthouse: the column of light the others insisted on calling The Throne.

Everything here is a 'The'. With a capital 'The'.

The Throne was supposed to represent The Architect (Another 'The', Ori thought.) – the unseen Designer of all this splendour. Allegedly, The Designer was so splendiferous that even immortals' eyes could not gaze upon The Sight. A lot of Capital Letters get thrown around, too. This is Tedious. Still they danced on, singing. The 'wholly satisfactory' song could go on for hours. Or days.

'Whol-ly sat-is-fac-to-ry! We are so complete!'

'Sing it, siblings!'

Ori had Had Enough. 'Hey, feathered friends!' Ori called. The conga line stopped. All eyes turned to Ori.

This was disconcerting, because some of the dancers had more than two – hundreds, in fact – and it added up to a lot of eyes on Ori.

Ori ventured, 'This is getting a little repetitive. How about a call-and-response?'

Samya, the eight-winged leader of the Celestial Chorus, thought a second. 'Like half of us sing *Wholly* and the other half sing *Satisfactory?*'

'Er, I was thinking more along these lines…' Ori sang.

Somebody needs you, Lord, come by here…

Samya frowned a mighty frown. 'What is this 'need'?'

Ori sighed. 'When you don't have something you should have.' *Like melody, harmony, or a reason to go on existing in this bland eternity.*

'We don't have 'need' here. We are complete.'

'We are perfect!' the others chorused – in C major. Ori winced.

'We don't have needs! We are complete!'

Samya patted Ori on the shoulder. 'Don't you remember? We tried splitting our voices before. You know where that got us. There were Tone Wars!'

The feather crowd nodded sadly. They remembered the Tone Wars: immortal being against immortal being. It was a terrible fight. Feathers got ruffled.

'Fortunately, Good triumphed over Evil,' continued Samya, 'as it always does. But that's all dissonance is good for: a big fight, and we end up triumphing over Evil, and then we're back to the Celestial Tonic.' Samya smiled benevolently. 'So it's better to skip all that dialogue and stick to what we know.'

Ori yelled, 'That's not dialogue! That's dictatorship! It's a zero-sum game! I'm not saying have a fight! I'm saying, *talk* to each other! Or at least sing,' Ori added, more quietly. 'We need a few things around here. We need to find things out. Isn't that what we're for?'

Samya frowned. 'Find things out? What things? We already know all the answers!' The choirmaster beamed around the circle of immortals and was rewarded with another rousing chorus of 'Wholly Satisfactory'.

Ori had had More Than Enough. 'You don't know any answers! You don't even know the questions! Who is The Architect? What do They want? How many storeys does The Building have? Is there anybody else there? Are they okay? Is there something we can do for them? I hear things, you know – even up here in Hunkydoryland.'

The crowd gasped – and held their ears. 'No, no, no, no,' they chanted. 'Not again!'

In disgust, Ori sang loudly.

Come o thou Traveler unknown, whom still I hold but cannot see...

Further singing got drowned out in a chorus of protest. 'No-no-no-no-no, no minor keys, no questions! Blasphemy is what this is!'

'Yes,' Samya concurred. 'Blasphemy. It is blasphemy to insist that The Architect has not given us everything we need, and that The Architect does not see and hear us from behind The Veil, without our doing anything at all but sing hosannas.'

The chorus got agitated. Some tried to sing *Hosanna* in the key of F, and others tried to sing it in C. Another group went back to *Wholly Satisfactory*. The result was a sickening dissonance that only got worse as various Section Leaders tried to organise the sopranos, altos, tenors, basses, subbasses, woofers and tweeters...

Suddenly, there was a New Sound.

None of those in The Penthouse recognised it. But if you have a cat, you would have recognised it. It was the sound made by a fairly large kitty in the next room knocking over a piece of furniture – say, a small bookshelf, chair, or occasional table – and then leaping free. If there had been a cat – and there wasn't, because it had never occurred to anyone in The Penthouse to keep pets – the cat would just then be stalking around the corner with its tail in the air, pretending insouciance, as if to say, 'Who, me?'

That was the noise. But it wasn't a cat.

The noise was accompanied by an abrupt shake in The Penthouse floor. Something went *thump* and everyone's back teeth rattled. Then there was silence.

To the assembled crowd of feathered immortals, this silence was even more ominous than the noise. It meant something had changed.

And if there was one thing nobody wanted to see around The Penthouse, it was *change*.

All eyes – hundreds and hundreds of them – turned accusingly on Ori.

'YOU did it! You upset The Architect! Now we're going to be smitten! It's all your fault!'

Ori glared at them. 'Y'all won't have conversations. All you do is insist on this enforced unity. And now y'all are in a needless panic. I suggest…'

'I suggest you leave,' said Samya calmly.

Everyone stared.

'Leave?' asked Ori. 'How? And go where?'

Samya pointed dramatically (Samya practised in a mirror) to the far wall. Where something had appeared which nobody had ever seen before. It was a strange, gleaming opening in the wall.

Samya continued to point (majestically, this was a big moment) at the strange portal. The car within appeared to be moving in a downward direction. When it disappeared, there was a sort of moving wall for a bit, and then another car appeared. It seemed to be a conveyance of some sort. Each car was just big enough for two immortals to stand side by side, if they folded their wings politely.

Of course, Samya was only suggesting that *one* immortal take a ride in the mysterious conveyance. That someone was Ori.

'We think you should go,' Samya said in a voice that managed to mix solemnity, awe, and insufferable smugness. 'You're only disturbing everyone. You should leave so that we can get back to normal. Besides, you might find some of those questions you're looking for.'

Ori had absolutely Had the Most Enough a Person Could Have. 'All right,' Ori said. 'I'll do just that!'

Ori stepped into the vehicle, whatever it was. It kept moving – downward. As it did, Ori caught a last glimpse of the assembled throng.

They were staring with their mouths open. *At least they aren't singing* Wholly, Ori thought. *But what have I gotten myself into?*

Chapter 2: Going Down

Well, that was a grand gesture, thought Ori. *But very possibly an unwise move. I've never seen anything like this before. I mean, nobody has. It's moving downward, who knows where, and I don't even know what it's called.*

Call it a 'paternoster'. You won't get the joke now, but you will later.

The statement was accompanied by a deep chuckle – not exactly an unfriendly sound, but still unnerving, here in this otherwise empty conveyance henceforth to be known as a…

'Paternoster,' repeated Ori aloud, which seemed only polite, although, come to think of it, the Voice seemed to be coming from inside Ori's head, rather than outside. In fact, looking around the moving cabinet (which didn't take very long, after all), Ori couldn't detect anyone at all. Not bird or beast or flying thing with a thousand eyes, or upright being with two arms and legs and binocular vision. Nor, indeed, a loudspeaker of any kind, let alone one that could project a Voice inside one's head. So Ori settled for 'disembodied communication' as the most likely explanation.

Ori's speculation was greeted with another low chuckle. The chuckle was deep in pitch, and warm – avuncular, somehow. **You're getting it, child. Get off at the next stop and we'll talk.**

Stop? thought Ori. The open side of the Paternoster was showing more fluffy clouds. But as the box moved in a direction Ori could only think of as downwards, the clouds gave way to swirling banks of colour: vibrant hues of red, green, gold, blue alternating with paler shades of pastels. Here and there were splashes of unnameable pigments that Ori found downright threatening. Eventually the whole array settled down somewhat to a dull light-grey. It was at this point that the Voice in Ori's head yelled, ***Jump!***

Ori jumped.

At the same time, Ori spread wings and prepared to hover: this was just as well, seeing as how there was no floor. All around, all that Ori could see was a vast expanse – up, down, and sideways – of moving forms. It was noisy, too, with a sound like that of the Celestial Orchestra tuning up and utterly failing to find their 'A', while the Celestial Choir ran endless *solfeggi* in tragic mistiming.

The whole place smelled of lavender. Ori, who loathed the smell of lavender, sneezed and reached for a handkerchief. Then Ori sighted what was so far the weirdest apparition of all: a park bench, stationary in the midst of madness, for all the world as if it made sense for a park bench to be there. A bench just like the ones in The Penthouse gardens. Only it was sitting in a grey void.

Not knowing what else to do, Ori went and sat on it.

That's a good idea, said the Voice, soothingly. ***Sit there and rest for a bit while we talk things over.***

Ori wasn't finding this restful at all. It was nice – for a certain value of 'nice' – to be sitting quietly. As opposed to hurtling downward in a strange box encountered for the very first time only a short while ago. On the other hand, the vista in front of the bench was anything but restful: weird forms kept swooshing forward at eye level – round shapes, angular shapes, shapes that resembled a line one minute only to turn and reveal themselves as walls the next... Ori found them somewhat menacing. It was as if they were rushing up to the bench to show themselves and say, 'Nyah, nyah.'

'What are you all?' Ori wondered.

Oh, that's right. You haven't encountered mathematics before, said the Voice.

'Mathematics appear to be rather aggressive life forms,' replied Ori. The Voice laughed.

They are, actually. Ignore them. Besides, I have better things to show you.

With that, it seemed that an invisible hand had shooed the aggressive lines and circles and shapes away. Ori breathed a sigh of relief, especially since the smell of lavender seemed to have gone with them, leaving behind a faint odor of jasmine. Now jasmine, Ori liked.

The space all around the bench turned darker and filled with bright lights. Ori sat back and gaped: lights were born, fiery balls, out of multicoloured nebulas. Other bright lights arced across the space, trailing crystalline clouds in sparkling tails. Rocks the size of very large rocks collided, whizzed around, collided again, and formed balls that began to rotate. Some of the very large rocks began to circle – or rather, ellipse – around the bright lights.

'What am I watching?' asked Ori. 'And does it need an audience to happen?'

You're watching Creation, said the Voice, *or Evolution, depends on whom you ask. As to whether we need to be watching for it to happen? Ask a philosopher. But be prepared for arguments.* Again the deep chuckle.

'All this appears to amuse you,' commented Ori drily.

Yes. And no. It's serious, but a happy thing. A good thing, but you'll have to trust me on that. Anyway, doesn't watching a universe come into being beat singing hosannas any day of the week?

'Well, yes, it does. Er, what's a week?'

Laughter. *I like you. You ask good questions. What you're looking at is the first day or two (I forget, haven't read the book in a while and no, don't ask what a book is right now) of the first week. It's just Time. Everybody gets confused about it. Don't worry. It will all become clearer as you go along.*

…or more muddled, the Voice mused. *We'll just have to see, won't we?* The silence that followed seemed very much like a shrug to Ori.

'I guess 'we' will,' replied Ori. 'But while we're talking like this…just who, exactly are you? I can't keep calling you 'the Voice'. It's extremely inconvenient, not to mention needlessly portentous.'

Another imaginary shrug. **Hm. Tell you what. Just call me Prajapati for now. It means something like 'creator', and I'm busy creating. Look around you.**

'Yes, I'm looking. It's all very impressive, I'm sure. And it beats dancing the 101,111st gavotte to *Wholly Satisfactory*. But what am I meant to do about it? You didn't pull me in and out of a metaphysical elevator just to show off, did you?'

More laughter. **No, kid, I did not. Gaze over there.** Ori gazed as directed. A small, mostly-blue planet appeared. It was orbiting (the vocabulary was coming to Ori) a smallish yellow light (oh, yes, sun) that was out on the arm of a huge, swirling mass of lights (a galaxy, okay). It looked tiny, lonely, but somehow inviting.

'Is that where we're going?' wondered Ori and 'heard' Prajapati nod.

Indeed, that is where you and I are going. Well, you, because you have physical presence in all these dimensions. Me, I'll stay in radio contact. Inside your head. Whenever, er, possible. If you go where I tell you, we might learn something. For right now, I need you to head back to the Paternoster. Jump in and ride down to the next level that looks inviting. And lo, I am with you always, even unto the end of the shaft, or something.

Ori did as instructed, jumping back into the Paternoster – a little too hard.

'Ouch! I think I sprained a wing!'

Down went the Paternoster – direction, small blue planet.

Chapter 3: Ardi

Down, down went the Paternoster with Ori inside. The speed was dizzying. At times, Ori's feet didn't touch the floor as air from the open side ruffled Ori's feathers and lifted wings.

At first, all Ori saw were landscapes whooshing past – mountains, streams of water and, more alarmingly, lava, the occasional shower of rocks. Then creatures started to appear in flashes: writhing things, crawling things, lumbering things. Ori jumped when once a gigantic beak, attached to an even more gigantic head, thrust itself halfway into the open doorway before withdrawing with an angry hiss. Ori had absolutely no desire to disembark at any of these places and shrank back into a far corner of the conveyance as it continued its rapid plunge.

Being at the back of the Paternoster compartment was just as well, because now there came torrents of rain – massive drops from above falling on the earth beneath, causing rising waters. Ori worried for a moment that the Paternoster was going to experience flooding, but the rain seemed to trigger a defence mechanism in the lift: it threw up an invisible force field that repelled the water. That was something, at least. Ori wondered if there would ever be a sight out that doorway that looked the least bit safe.

Actually, Ori would have settled for 'not immediately life-threatening.'

And then Ori saw it: sun and cerulean. And an arch of lovely colours spanning the air. Ori didn't need an invitation from Prajapati, but simply jumped into that inviting sky.

The weather was great for soaring, and soaring is what took place. Ori was feeling cramped from being inside the Paternoster and enjoyed stretching wings. The angel climbed and dove and wheeled around for quite a while before remembering that there was probably some landscape below that might be worth looking at. So Ori did.

Wow was all Ori could think. There was a sea down there. Incredibly blue. Bluer than the bluest blue of the skies around the Penthouse. And that sea was extremely noisy, because water, gallons and gallons of the stuff, hundreds and thousands of gallons of the stuff, was pouring over a cliff into the basin and making, as we said, a lot of noise, more noise than the entire Celestial Host Massed Choirs singing *Wholly Satisfactory* at the top of their lungs with maximum amplification.

That's one noisy waterfall.

It was also a very effective waterfall: looking down, Ori could see the water level rising on the downside of the relentless cascade. You didn't have to wait long, either: that big sea was getting deeper by the minute.

Obviously, this creation business could take some surprising turns. *At least nothing's trying to eat me,* thought Ori, and decided to go in search of some land and maybe a fruit tree or two.

Ori had to fly quite a way to find land. This sea was really big. The wings were getting a workout. Finally, Ori spotted a shoreline, with a beach, and came in for a landing. The soft sand was warm to Ori's toes. Lots of interesting shells. Funny-looking creatures scurried along, in search of food, no doubt, before the next wave carried it away. Ori smiled: it was a nice day.

A whirring of wings overhead: Ori looked up as the sky seemed to become cloudy. Birds, hundreds of thousands of them, flying together. Small birds, much smaller than Ori, but impressive in such numbers. Ori smiled to see them, and stared upward, fascinated, as they performed patterns of murmuration against the blue sky. The birds were a light grey. Lots of food down here, he thought as they sped inland.

Then Ori heard a less pleasant noise: even an out-of-tune cherub section couldn't have matched that sound. Somewhere between a squawk and a roar and sounding badly out of temper. Ori turned.

That's an awfully big bird, thought Ori. *Looks like it has a nasty temper, too.* The big bird glided over the beach, obviously looking for prey. Its wingspan was impressive, even to Ori, who decided to let it go on its way.

That is, until it spotted the primate: about half Ori's size, upright, bipedal, binocular, forward-looking like Ori's species, and covered with brown fur. The little creature was picking up shells along the water line and didn't notice the huge bird bearing down on it. Obviously, the bird had spotted dinner. When the little animal looked up and saw the bird, it uttered a sharp cry and began running in the direction of the forest at the edge of the beach. It ran as fast as it could – but it wasn't going to make cover before the bird caught up with it.

Oh, no, you don't, thought Ori, and without thinking, flew after the nasty-looking avian.

The bird was a fast flyer, but Ori was faster. Circling around, Ori headed the bird off with menacing wing flaps.

'Ya! Ya! Go away, you! Shoo!' Ori shouted.

The bird, startled, veered off. It didn't seem to be sure what it had run into.

Probably used to being the biggest bird in the neighbourhood, thought Ori drily. *I'll show you big bird.* And Ori pursued the predator, doing the best imitation of a raptor possible for someone who had never, ever, been in a fight before.

'Ya! Ya! Go away, mean bird! Not satisfactory! Not satisfactory at all! Go peddle your wares elsewhere!'

Shouting seemed to help. It also made Ori feel better. Anyway, the big terror bird took its terror somewhere else. Out of the corner of an eye, Ori saw the small primate make an astonished dash between some trees.

Ori alighted on the edge of the forest. Chasing big birds was hard work, and Ori wanted a drink. Also snacks, if possible. It had been quite a while since Ori had last eaten or drunk anything and there was no sign of the kind of thing available in The Penthouse, such as an ambrosia fountain or water feature. Furling wings and adopting pedal movement, Ori locomoted into the forest, following the trail where the bipedal primate had disappeared.

The forest was a lot cooler than the beach, Ori noticed. And quieter. The ground underfoot was soft with mulch and old needles. The air smelled sweet. Ori drank in beauty: sunlight filtered through varicoloured leaves of red and brown and gold, as well as green from the needle-bearing trees.

'Ouch!' Something fell on Ori's head. Looking up, Ori saw that the tree above was full of some kind of green fruit. Ori bent to pick up the one that had fallen.

What are you? Ori thought. *Can I eat you? Hm…* Ori peeled off the outer husk, only to find a hard nut too solid to crack easily. I'd need really big teeth, Ori thought. I wonder what those little primates eat? Ori dropped the nut along the path for some better-equipped traveller to find and headed in the direction of the sound of water. Now water could be drunk.

Ori soon came to a stream that gurgled over rocks and flowed down in the direction of the beach. Finding a nice flat rock to settle on, Ori sat down – and was surprised at how good it felt to be sitting. Paternosters are fine vehicles, to be sure, but there's something to be said for resting once in a while. Ori scooped up water from the stream: it was icy cold, fresh, and tasted wonderful. Now, if there were only some fruit…

A quiet grunt interrupted Ori's thoughts. Ori looked up – straight into the brown, inquiring eyes of a friendly creature. It was the little primate. It regarded Ori without fear. And it was holding something in its hand: offering it to Ori, who took it.

It was a palm-sized round fruit, red and yellow, with a fuzzy outer skin. Ori nodded thanks and bit into it. The sweetness was astonishing. The fruit was incredibly juicy and tended to drip on one's chin. Ori shared the fruit with the little primate, whom Ori privately decided to name Ardi for no particular reason other than that the syllables sprang to mind. The fruit and the water made Ori feel a lot better. *This place is nice. I think I'll stay a while.*

Ardi tugged at Ori's hand, beckoning Ori to follow, and together, they hunted berries (also tasty) and collected some of those hard nuts. They also collected as many fruits as the two of them could carry.

If I had something to make a bag with... thought Ori, but nobody in The Penthouse ever carried things about: there was no need. However, Ori was inventive – which The Penthouse considered one of Ori's less admirable traits – and soon hit upon an idea. One of the trees by the water had really big leaves. Ori placed fruits, berries, and nuts on the leaves, rolled them up and tucked in the ends, and was able to carry a stack of them in two arms.

Ardi was delighted by this new discovery and danced a small dance of joy. Ori's small friend insisted on being given rolls of food to carry as well, and together the two of them followed the trail, carrying their spoils.

The forest was becoming darker by the time they reached the small clearing. Ori assumed the sun was going down and remembered the crash course in planetary movements from a few floors up. Ori wasn't really surprised to find more of Ardi's people in the clearing. They seemed to be unfazed by Ardi's turning up with a large bipedal bird, especially one bearing gifts of food. There were pleasant chattering noises and sounds of pleasure as the 'packages' were unrolled and food surprises found.

Some of the little primates had small ones with them, and Ori ended up holding a couple of them. Their fur was soft to the touch. Ori rocked and sang to them and soon had a cluster of little ones around, so Ori sat cross-legged on the ground and entertained them.

The adult primates, who were all of a size with Ardi, ate the fruit and berries, or masticated a few to feed the infants, and crooned to one another. A couple of Ardi's tribe showed Ori how they opened the nuts by cracking them with rocks. Ori was impressed with their skills.

As dark came on, the primates began to make nests of conifer branches in the trees. One by one, Ori handed back the babies. When they all seemed to be tucked in for the night, Ori went on a postprandial flight above the beach and forest. The sky was like a velvet backdrop to a dazzling array of sparkling stars.

Lighting in a tree near the clearing where it was possible to keep an eye out for nocturnal predators, Ori settled with a rustle of feathers. There was a sense of peace and belonging here that Ori hadn't felt for a long time in The Penthouse.

I think I'll stay here for a bit, thought Ori before drifting into a light doze.

You do that for as long as you can, said Prajapati, but Ori wasn't listening.

Chapter 4: Pain

Days, months, years passed by. Ori spent them with the primates as they wandered about, following the food and water sources. They spent an amazing amount of time playing, and Ori played with them. He minded children, delighting in them as they learned and grew.

From time to time, Ori did overflights to survey the territory. The angel noticed that the big waterfall kept filling up the giant sea. It was steadily getting higher. There were lots and lots of birds, mostly of the small variety. Ori enjoyed watching their flights. The occasional annoying terror birds got a nasty surprise whenever they challenged Ori: it was a big surprise to them to run into something large, flight-capable, and at least as smart as they were. Ori thought the terror birds were a bad idea and told Prajapati so. All he got in return was a mental shrug.

The days and months and years were full of tiny joys: discovering a new, fragrant flower. Following bees to find their hives and steal a bit of honey. Laughing, suddenly and for no reason. Taking Ardi and the others for aerial 'rides'. Playing with Ardi's babies when she became a mother. Ardi was a good mother, and her babies were beautiful.

Ori discovered feelings that had been unknown in The Penthouse: love for another, care for their welfare, anticipation of experience, a sense of belonging. Ori was happy.

As time passed, a few things changed. Familiar trees got taller. Babies grew up. The big sea grew. That was fine. But gradually, Ori noticed, Ardi's brown hair began to lose its lustre. Some of it turned white. Ardi herself began to slow down. She ran more slowly – and less frequently. She was still the same joyous creature as always, but in the mornings, she rose with less alacrity from her nest among the tree branches. In the evenings, Ori sometimes had to help her up the tree to join the others when she seemed to have trouble climbing.

One morning, Ardi didn't get up at all. Not even when the others called to her. Not even when the youngsters climbed the tree and playfully shook the branches. Alarmed, Ori flew to her nest.

Ardi's eyes were closed, but she wasn't sleeping. Her body, folded in the posture of sleep, wasn't relaxed, but stiff and unyielding. It was cold to the touch, not warm. There was no life left.

At first, Ori was unable to comprehend this change. How could this happen? Ardi was there, but not there. Carefully, afraid that she'd fall out of the tree, Ori scooped up the little body and flew down with it. Ori placed it gently on soft grass.

The others gathered around. They touched Ardi's body. They were much quicker to understand than Ori. They knew death.

They howled.

Forming a circle around the lifeless body, the primates linked arms and keened loudly. As they wailed, they pointed their faces first at the body, then at the sky, as if to ask the question that was repeating itself over and over in Ori's mind: why?

Who are they asking? thought Ori. In confusion, Ori flew away, to a nearby hillside where it was possible to think without the sound of weeping primates. For the first time, Ori deliberately called on Prajapati.

Oh, Prajapati, Ori thought. Why did Ardi...die? What's wrong here? How do I fix it?

Working as intended, I'm afraid, came the answer. *Why are you surprised? Haven't you noticed the leaves falling from the trees every year? The plants withering?*

'Yes,' said Ori aloud. 'But the trees don't die. And the plants come back again.'

Not the same ones. New ones. Even the trees die, eventually. They are replaced by new growth.

'Will Ardi come back?'

No. Her children will live on and have other children.

'Will I die someday?'

Of course not. You're an immortal. That means 'not dying'. You remain.

'I don't want to remain. I want to see my friend again.'

You will. Someday. But not here.

'Where? How?'

I know this sounds lame, but...I have a plan.

'A Plan?' scoffed Ori, in no mood for Penthouse games.

No, no, nothing so pretentious as A Plan. Just…a plan. But you'll have to do some more travelling, my friend.

Ori flew back to where Ardi's body lay beneath the tree.

The keening was over. The primates had moved on down the trail, leaving the body where it lay under the tree. Before they left, they had covered Ardi with flowers and branches. Ori discovered a bunch of sweet-smelling flowers – her favourite – pressed into her clenching hands.

Ori picked up the body and flew with it to a cave under the hill. Ori took every one of the flowers and branches. It took several trips. Ori rearranged the branches to make a bed for Ardi and laid the flowers over her. Before leaving, Ori leaned down and kissed the cold forehead.

Sleep, Ardi. Until we figure this out.

Ori didn't know where to go next and flew off in the direction of the big waterfall. On the way, Ori had an odd thought.

Prajapati didn't call me 'child' this time. Prajapati called me 'friend.' As I called Ardi 'friend.'

The big waterfall was still falling, thundering and roaring its way to filling up the sea in the middle of the world. Above the fall was a rainbow. And in that rainbow, Ori glimpsed a familiar sight.

As Ori flew into the Paternoster, there came other odd thoughts: *I learned a lot here. I gained a lot. But I lost a lot, too. Why does happiness come at the price of pain?*

Chapter 5: Different Worlds

The world Ori emerged into was inviting: green and blue, warm, with a mild sun, and surprisingly devoid of killer birds. Ori flew over mountains and valleys and forests, drinking in the sights.

A river looked inviting. It turned out to be teeming with fish and visited by all manner of wildlife: birds, deer, even rabbits. Ori sat down and enjoyed the view for a while.

Ori noticed the huge flocks of birds. Ori noticed the conspicuous lack of threatening megafauna. Ori noticed the beauty and calm and magnificently ordered perfection of the ecosystem. Ori sent mental thank-you notes to Prajapati for a job well done.

What came back was a dry chuckle.

You're putting it off, aren't you?

'Putting what off?'

You know what I mean. Going to see what Ardi's descendants are like. You're afraid of getting hurt again.

Ori sighed, deeply. 'Yes, I am. But you're right, I should go.' And Ori took flight, following the valley where the river flowed, upstream, until something appeared that looked like it might be where some primates lived.

Ori looked down in amazement. The houses were a far cry from Ardi's tree-branch nest. These were complicated structures of mud and sticks and woven straw. They were grouped in a clearing around the remains of a campfire. In other words, these primates had technology. At least, Ori assumed they had figured out how to start fires – there was smoke curling up from a hole in the middle of one of the houses.

Come to think of it, mused Ori, *how DO you start a fire? I mean, I could, by thinking about it, if I concentrated. But how does a primate start one?*

In Ori's head, Prajapati answered, **You have to understand causation. It's…a step.**

Ori landed, folding wings, and decided against disturbing the inhabitants of the house with the smoke. This was because Ori heard light voices, childish giggles, and babies crying. Ori had experience with mothers and didn't wish to startle them.

Wonder where the rest of them are? Maybe out looking for food? That's what I'd do on a nice day. Let's follow the path through the woods and see if they've found some berry bushes or something.

An initial search yielded plenty of fruit trees – Ori grabbed a juicy snack – but no primates. Angels can be silent, and Ori made no noise while weaving a path through the trees to the next clearing. Somebody was making noise, though: Ori heard whistling.

It wasn't birds.

The whistles had patterns, tunes, almost. No, not like the *Wholly Satisfactory* song. A more urgent message.

Ori could understand any language. And this was a language!

The whistles said, *Go over there. I'm over here. Circle back, surround him.*

Whatever the primates were doing appeared to require stealth. *Why are they sneaking around? Maybe I should be quiet, too.* Ori approached the clearing cautiously and hid behind thick greenery before peering out.

What Ori saw was astonishing. In the clearing was a large, four-footed animal, about as high in the shoulder as Ori's head. It was pawing the ground with sharp hooves and shaking its powerful head with its branched antlers. The animal was distressed and angry.

Ori could see why: several ropes were looped around the animal's neck. The ropes extended to the edge of the small clearing. And as Ori watched, primates emerged from hiding, holding the ropes taut. Their faces bore looks of determination mingled with fear – their bare faces, Ori noted, bare like Ori's, not hairy like Ardi's. Still holding the ropes taut as they reeled them in, the primates advanced on the animal.

The creature tried to rear in order to strike at its tormentors but was held down by the ropes. It shook its head, lunging in the direction of the nearest primate, who backed away. The others took up the slack. They whistled instructions to one another as they immobilised the animal.

Ori watched in wonder at this madness.

When the primates were at a distance where the lunging beast still couldn't reach them, but wasn't able to move or run away, the first primate struck – thrusting a long stick with a sharp end into the side of the captive animal. The creature bellowed in pain. The other primates followed suit, plunging their spears again and again into the animal's body – until it fell to its knees, roaring in pain and bleeding profusely.

Ori groaned inwardly along with the creature. Tears ran down Ori's face in sympathy as it fell, its sides heaving as it gasped its last breath.

Ori was completely unprepared for the shout of victory that went up from the primates.

They yelled. They pranced. They danced around the corpse. They reached handfuls of the creature's blood and smeared one another's faces with it. They spoke words in a language Ori had never heard before but now instantly understood, just as Ori had understood the whistlespeak. 'We are the best hunters! Good work, men! We will feast tonight!'

Ori suddenly grasped the purpose of this slaughter.

Prajapati! They intend to eat this animal, he thought. They've become predators, like the terror birds.

At least they can't fly, replied Prajapati.

Back at the village, there was the making of a big fire in the open space. The dead ruminant was skinned and dressed for roasting. The hide was carried off by the women. Ori noticed that these primates had very little fur – in fact, they were nearly hairless, like Ori. They had taken to wearing pieces of animal skin and fur, to keep warm, Ori guessed. That meant they had killed a lot of animals, large and small.

The primates roasted the big animal over the fire. Some prepared other dishes: tubers they buried in the ashes, vegetables in clay pots over smaller fires, fruits and nuts they ate raw. It was, indeed, a feast. As darkness came and stars came out, there was eating and laughter. Women fed children. Men vied for the biggest pieces of meat.

Ori felt sick. Ori watched them from concealment and also felt lonely. Missing Ardi and her tribe was like a dull ache deep inside.

As the fires settled down to glowing coals, the men, contented, began to reminisce. They told stories of their hunting adventures. They boasted and praised the most skilled hunters. They exaggerated dangers and what they had done to overcome them.

Go and talk to them, said Prajapati. Ori sighed.

Stepping into the firelight, Ori spoke gently in their language in greeting. 'Hello…' Ori began.

The entire group let out a horrified gasp.

There was shouting.

There was screaming.

There were wails of terror.

Ori had never heard anything like it. 'Don't be afraid!' Ori began again but could scarcely be heard above all the terrified noise. Several of the men grabbed up spears and hurled them in Ori's direction.

Ori caught two of the spears, one in each hand, and threw them to the ground. One of the men, braver than the others, charged at Ori, a flensing knife in his hand.

Ori stepped to one side and in exasperation raised both hands, releasing bright shafts of light and at the same time spreading wings as if to ward off a terror bird.

The entire group fell to their knees – except for the babies, who cried. One cried especially loudly because its mother had dropped it.

'Now, listen…' Ori said. 'I'm not going to hurt you…'

'It speaks!' the primates said to each other. 'It knows our language! It must be a powerful being from another world! Look, it has wings!'

'What does it want?'

'It probably wants to kill us! I mean, we want to kill it…'

'Stop throwing spears, you fool! It's too powerful!'

'Offer it something so it will go away! Here! Give it a piece of meat!'

To Ori's utter horror, this suggestion was followed up on instantly. Two men grabbed a slab of wood, stuck a disgusting, steaming haunch of roast venison on it, and approached Ori with a solemnity which would have been comical if it had happened in The Penthouse. Laying the 'offering' before Ori's feet, the two men backed away, their every movement bespeaking extreme caution and a fear that they might at any moment be utterly obliterated by this fearsome apparition.

Oh, brother, thought Ori. *I give up.*

Ori was the mildest-mannered of creatures, but this was too much. Throwing the makeshift platter, meat and all, into the nearest fire, Ori flew off into the darkness.

Not fast enough, however, to avoid hearing the sighs of relief from the primates – along with an alarming comment.

'See? The Otherworldly One has accepted our sacrifice!'

Ori spent the rest of the night in the highest tree around, too disgusted even to discuss the situation with Prajapati.

Ori didn't like this new kind of primate very much at all.

Chapter 6: In the Garden

So you think we have a problem? was the first thing Ori heard upon waking, stiff, in a tree.

'I'd say so! These primates are not an improvement.'

They're called humans. At least, that's what they call themselves.

'I'd call them a lot of things, none of them nice. I don't think they understand causation as well as you think they do, either. 'Sacrifice', my pinfeathers.'

Prajapati sighed. *Something's definitely going on in their noodles. Tell you what: I think we need to take a look under the hood.*

Ori thought quizzical thoughts in the direction of the psychopompic communicator. Prajapati chuckled in response.

Just hop in the Paternoster. I'll need your help for this.

Ori flew around over the river, just for the exercise. After a bit, Ori spied the Paternoster in a cloud bank. Ori hopped in…

…and got a surprise.

Instead of going down as usual, the Paternoster went *sideways*, to Ori's right. The ride was a bit bumpy. At first, all Ori saw were clouds. Then darkness, stars, and streaks of multicoloured light. After that, weird blobs and oddly-shaped unicellular organisms, huge, colliding with one another. Then more clouds. Dizzy, Ori decided this ride might be better with closed eyes.

When Ori opened them again, everything was very green.

'A garden? Like in the Penthouse? Odd,' said Ori, and started to step out of the Paternoster.

WAIT!

Ori stopped.

We're in their noosphere right now. The part where we find out what the humans think they're doing. It contains the projection of their thoughts. You need to be careful: interacting with it can have strange effects. You have to let it do its thing, so to speak. You may find it hard to recognise yourself in there. Things could get rather…counterfactual.

'Counterfactual?'

In the human noosphere, we're interacting with the mental models the humans have. Which may have little or nothing to do with reality per se. Matter of fact… Ori detected some hesitation on the part of Prajapati… *that's why I can't go in there. I might get stuck. The whole matrix could go south pretty rapidly.*

Ori didn't know what to say to that and so said nothing. 'Can I step out now?'

If you're ready.

Ori took a deep breath and exited the Paternoster.

This was weird. Ori didn't know what to expect but was still overwhelmed. A tingling, all over. A sense of contortion – of wriggling in anatomical places Ori had never been aware of having before. A sense of simultaneous shrinkage and expansion in mind and body.

Oh, and a loss of appendages.

Ori tried to flap wings that weren't there. To move arms and legs that were suddenly missing. 'What in the world...?'

Finally, Ori figured out a means of locomotion: by stretching the back muscles. And then contracting them. This worked better than Ori at first thought it would. At first slowly, then with increasing speed, Ori began to navigate the somewhat convoluted paths of the garden. Wriggling turned out to be kind of fun, if a little disconcerting when you'd never done it before. Ori varied wriggling with undulating, then a bit of a ripple...

And found a pool. A pool whose waters reflected. There, Ori beheld a disturbing sight.

The angel had turned into a snake: a very picturesque one, admittedly, but still...a snake. No wings. No legs. No arms. No...ears, for harmony's sake. By watching the reflection in the pool, Ori was able to work out how to move: forward, backward, sideways, up, down... after a few minutes it got easier. Ori even figured out how to use the usual impulses to raise an arm or flex a foot in order to move this or that part of the snake-self. This became more comfortable with practice. But it was still confusing.

'THAT'S what I look like here?' Ori wondered. 'Why?'

That's what we're here to find out, said Prajapati. **See if you can find any humans about in this fantasyland of theirs. We need to have some dialogue.**

Ori moved on, still working on locomotion. Ori slithered along the path in a zigzag motion, head up, tongue darting in and out. It was amazing how much information could be gleaned from a forked tongue: water was this way, some very fragrant flowers that way. It was warmer over to the right: Ori headed in that direction and soon detected the smell of fruit trees – and a human. Definitely worth pursuing.

Zigzagging along, Ori sang one of his favourite songs:

It's the gift to be simple, it's the gift to be free, it's the gift to come down where we ought to be...

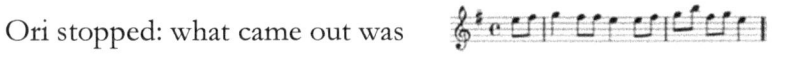

Ori stopped: what came out was

'Eww! They've got a warped sense of melody, these humans!'

Any species whose overwrought imagination could turn an angel into an oversized cobra was dangerous, so Ori moved cautiously (and silently) in the direction of a grove. Choosing concealment wrapped around the trunk of a fair-sized fig tree, Ori listened in as two humans had a conversation.

'See that tree? That's the one the insects go to. The Creator says we shouldn't eat from that tree. It's *special*.'

Ori peeked. The speaker was a male human. He didn't have any clothes on, unlike the humans Ori had seen before. *At least he hasn't killed any animals,* thought Ori. *Hey, Prajapati – did you tell these humans not to eat the figs in this tree?*

I did not, replied Prajapati. ***I don't talk to them. It would be bad for my mental health, and theirs, I suspect.***

The male human walked off in what seemed to Ori to be a self-important way, leaving a female human, also nude, alone in the grove. She combed her long hair with her fingers and hummed a tune to herself as she sat down under the fig tree.

Ori noted that the tune she was humming sounded exactly like the one that had come out when Ori tried to sing *Simple Gifts*. *This is strange,* Ori thought.

An insect buzzed around Ori's head. Ori flicked at it with a forked tongue. This annoyed the insect, which stung Ori.

'Ouch!' said Ori. Only it came out as 'Ssssss!' Ori undulated down the tree, using the bark to scratch the bite.

The young woman jumped. 'Oh!' she said, looking up.

'Hi,' said Ori in embarrassment. 'I'm Ori. What's your name?' It sounded lame, but it was the only thing Ori could think of to say.

The woman gave Ori a long, appraising look and shook her long hair. Then she batted her eyelashes coyly at the snake. 'Hello-o,' she cooed. 'I'm Kava. Pleased to make your acquaintance.'

Ori felt skin tighten under scales. This was an uncomfortable feeling. But the woman made Ori feel unsettled. Ori had the sense of being harassed in some inappropriate way. 'Er, this is a nice garden...plant it yourself, did you?'

'Idim and I did,' was the reply. 'Well, I did most of it. Idim just moves the big stuff. He says I'm supposed to be his 'help meet', whatever that is. That mostly means doing all the work Idim doesn't want to do.'

'I see,' said Ori, who didn't. 'Why did...Idim, is it? say you shouldn't eat these figs? They look perfectly ripe to me, and it's a sin to waste food.'

Her eyes got wider. 'You think we should eat them? Idim says not to. I think he's afraid he'll accidentally swallow one of those bugs. Of course, he has his own explanation for everything.'

So I heard, thought Ori, but said aloud, 'I imagine you could avoid swallowing a bug. Just wash the fruit. Fruit's a good source of vitamins and sugar. Much better than eating animals,' Ori added hastily, wanting to plant the idea of vegetarianism firmly in this human's mind.

Kava nodded. 'I'm sure vitamins and sugar will make you really smart, huh?'

Ori thought about it. 'Well, they're probably good for brain activity, I suppose...' Ori began. But that's as far as the thought went because Eve was way ahead of him. She'd heard what she wanted to hear.

'Yay!' she laughed. 'Now I know something that Idim doesn't! Won't he be surprised!' And, taking a leaf from the fig tree, she piled it full of figs and scampered off.

Ori slithered out of the tree and headed back to the pond. Talking to humans made Ori's head hurt. Also, Ori's throat was dry. The cool water tasted good after that. Ori decided to bask awhile in the sun and doze awhile.

Ori's restorative nap didn't last long.

'Oh, no! What have you done, woman?' Idim's angry shouting woke Ori with a start. The humans were coming this way – and arguing loudly.

'We have eaten of the Forbidden Tree! Now we're DOOMED!'

One thing you have to say about Idim, said Prajapati. **When he does a bit, he really commits to it.** The shouting got louder as the two humans approached.

'You just made that up!' yelled Kava. 'See! There's the snake I told you about! HE told me it was okay!'

I didn't say… thought Ori. And besides, I'm not a 'he'. Or a 'she'. I'm just a 'me'. Ori started to leave, but Idim stepped out and blocked the path.

'You are an evil snake!' Idim yelled. 'You got us both in trouble!'

This made Ori angry enough to rear up in an impressive display of cobra hood. 'I did no such thing! YOU made up silly rules! And then you broke them. And now you're trying to find somebody else to blame. Me, your…er, Kava…next, you'll be blaming Prajapati. Or the sun! Or the insects! Just…go away!'

Something strange happened next. It was probably the oddest part of the whole bizarre trip so far.

The sky got dark. Ori looked up: there were clouds in front of it, dark clouds, blotting out the light. There was a flash of lightning, followed by thunder and rain in large drops. The humans shuddered in fear and hugged each other.

'It's Prajapati! He's angry at us! Run away!' And the two of them dashed, not into the garden, but away from it, across a broad plain and toward the mountains in the distance. Ori hadn't noticed these topographic features before: it was as if the landscape had suddenly altered itself with their thoughts.

Ori remained alone in the path. Looking back through the pouring rain, Ori saw the grove of trees appear to shrink in the distance. A stone wall sprang out of the ground, separating the pond from the trees. In front of the wall glowed orange flames.

Those people have too much imagination, said Prajapati. ***I think you'd better head for the Paternoster. This could get even uglier.***

Ori undulated, slithered, scooted, as fast as possible under these conditions, in the direction of the Paternoster, which was rocking back and forth in rhythm to the thunderclaps. Ori launched the snake-body at the open lift, bouncing off the back wall and landing just in time for the Paternoster to take off again.

First sideways, then down a bit, then, to Ori's astonishment, diagonally. As the sound of thunder receded in the distance, and the Paternoster resumed more normal motion, Ori looked down and saw – with intense relief – a more normal angelic form.

That was no fun at all, thought Ori, and Prajapati agreed.

We're going to need to work on this, was all Prajapati said.

Chapter 7: Civilisation and Its Discontents, Part I

Ori straightened the folds of the ridiculous disguise and prepared to enter the city.

Remember, said Prajapati. *You're a male human. Don't talk to the women in private – or in a way that could be misconstrued as flirting. They're funny about things like that. And stay in the form we've chosen. No sprouting wings. We don't want to start any more mythology.*

Ori nodded. 'No mythology, be careful of the gender stuff. Got it. Remind me: why am I here?'

To get a read on what they're up to. We can't stabilise The Building if we don't know why it's gone wonky. Go on in and be careful about talking to yourself. Humans think it's a sign of mental instability.

Ori choked. 'They'd be the ones to talk.' Still, Ori resolved to talk to Prajapati on the mental frequency and continued down the road toward the city on the horizon. The sky was blue, the air was, frankly, too hot, and the landscape was flat and boring. Along the road, Ori saw families with handcarts, herders with sheep and goats, and the occasional pompous-looking male individual striding along in a long robe, funny hat, and weirdly trimmed beard, carrying a staff. These individuals turned out to be the local priesthood.

Ori inadvertently fell in with one of these. A stout and silly-looking fellow with a comically pompous manner apparently decided Ori looked like a good walking companion.

'Hello, there, young man, going to the big city for the first time?'

'I am, indeed, sir,' Ori said. 'I really don't know what to expect. I've never seen so many hum…er, people in one place at once.'

The priest chuckled indulgently. 'That's the usual experience of many of our country people. The great city of Warka is indeed impressive. This, of course, is due to our people's assiduous worship of the gods.' He looked very pleased about that.

'My name is Maruduk-bal-idinna,' he said. 'But everyone calls me Bidi.'

Bidi turned out to be a friendly guy – just a bit talkative, which suited Ori down to the dusty Mesopotamian ground. After all, Ori was here to learn. Bidi chattered on about the wonderfulness of Warka: its evidently central place in the cosmos, protected by all its gods and goddesses. Ori asked questions about this mythology, which made Bidi a very happy man, indeed.

Bidi: 'The gods were made by the Creator to tend the earth. But the gods were lazy.'

'So why worship them, then?'

'They have power. Get on their good side and you can have success, build cities, things like that. But you've got to flatter them.'

Ori thought about that. That might actually work if that lot in The Penthouse ever bothered paying attention to what was going on down here on the other floors. Aloud Ori asked, 'So how does this work?'

Bidi beamed. 'You have to figure out which god is good for what. Like Ea's the water god. You have to be nice to him so the water in the rivers doesn't come up and flood. Flooding is bad news…'

'…especially when the whole city's made of mud brick,' said Ori. Bidi shrugged.

'And then you have to take the power structure into account.'

Ori was confused. 'Power structure…? You mean there are unequal gods?'

Bidi went into storytelling mode. 'See, once upon a time, there was an evil goddess named Tiamat. She hated everybody, including the other gods. They were afraid of her because she was so powerful. But Ea had an idea.'

He continued, 'Ea picked Marduk as his candidate for leader of the gods. Marduk is a great warrior. To get the other gods to agree to the plan, Ea and Marduk invited them to a banquet.

'At the banquet, Ea and Marduk served lots of pancakes – the god's favourite food.'

Ori squinted. 'Pancakes, huh?'

Bidi nodded. 'Everybody knows that. They just *love* pancakes. And date wine. After a while, the gods were pretty mellow, what with the pancakes…'

'… and all that date wine.'

'You got it! So they agreed that if Marduk could defeat Tiamat, they'd elect Marduk king.'

'An interesting form of government,' was all Ori could say. 'So it worked?'

Bidi beamed. 'It worked like a charm! Of course, there was an epic battle up there in the heavens. Wham, bam, go away, ma'am! But Marduk was the victor – he rammed a spear right down her throat! – and now Marduk is the principal god. Which is why he gets the biggest temple.'

'Which you work at,' guessed Ori.

Bidi poked Ori in the ribs. 'You guessed it! You're a bright young fella. I believe you could be going places.'

By the time the travellers had reached the city, Bidi had made up his mind that Ori would absolutely have to become a priest-in-training at the temple of Marduk.

He squinted at Ori. 'You have something spiritual about you, you know. I think you'll fit in fine.'

Ori was a bit doubtful. 'Don't I have to have particular skills?'

Bidi thought. 'You have to be able to read and write well. Can you read this? It's a letter I'm delivering in the city.'

He pulled something out of his pouch. It was a dried clay tablet.

Ori studied it. Of course they write in clay, he thought. They make everything else out of clay, so why not? Ori could understand any language and read any writing, so he read:

> *Tell Ea-Nasir: You promised me high-quality copper. You did not deliver. You are a terrible crook!*

'Excellent reading!' said Bidi. 'You can start as a scribe and we'll teach you the rest.'

Oh, well, thought Ori. It's a way to learn. *And it's not like this is exactly celestial science.* So Ori agreed to come aboard as a scribe/apprentice priest.

The walk was long but not unpleasant. Still, Ori was glad when they arrived at Warka. Being with such an important man, Ori had no trouble being let in the gate.

The living quarters for the priests and their acolytes turned out to be in a house down a quiet alley behind the temple. It was dark by the time they arrived, and Ori was tired from all the talking. Supper was welcome – even if it did consist of pancakes and date wine.

The gods can have that date wine, Ori thought while falling asleep on a rather nice pallet. *But the pancakes were nice.*

Good night, said Prajapati.

Chapter 8: Civilisation and Its Discontents, Part II

He brought the pickax into existence, the day came forth,
He introduced labour, decreed the fate,
Upon the pickax and basket he directs the power...

Ori sat in the scriptorium practising combinations of wedges in soft clay. Bidi was very pleased with Ori: he'd never seen such neat writing. Ori found the process of combining vertical, horizontal, and corner wedges to make complex words and sentences fascinating. Ori found the content of most texts less interesting.

Lists, lists, lists. Ridiculous stories about imaginary gods. Customer service complaints. Liturgical texts. And fart jokes.

Ori found the Warkan sense of humour totally unappealing.

It's worse than that, Prajapati chuckled. ***4000 years from now, learned scholars from museums will be trying to understand those fart jokes. They'll write papers about them, with footnotes.***

I've been wondering about something, thought Ori in the direction of Prajapati. Ori had found that scriptorium work was conducive to discussions with the unseen travel guide as long as Ori remembered not to say anything aloud.

Prajapati, why do you keep referring to things that happen in the future? It's confusing.

Prajapati responded with something combining a chuckle and a sigh. It made Ori's head tickle. ***My problem, kid, is that I'm outside of time. It's part of why I can't get in there to fix things. I can see the whole thing at once, so I get more than a few doses of back-vectored irony. When I'm watching you, I can even tease out a few strands and see where this is going. But if we're going to troubleshoot the issue we need to play it out.***

Ori understood about half of that.

Around noon, Bidi let the scribes have the rest of the day off for the New Year's holiday. Since they had no duties to perform, not being 'initiated into the mysteries' yet, whatever that meant, they were free to go and have fun, whatever constituted fun in Warka. They even got pocket money. Ori decided to wander about the busy streets and see what he could find that might help Prajapati sort out this floor of The Building.

Ori bought some grilled vegetables on pita from a local stand and sat down on a bench to eat. The vegetables were yummy, served hot with just the right amount of spices and a cool yoghurt sauce. Ori watched the people passing by and the veggie stand owner's kids playing with hoops. One of them, a little girl about five with curly blonde hair, was in earnest conversation with a crow that hung around the stand picking up titbits to eat.

The crow peered up at the little girl. 'Bwaaack!'

The little girl spoke back. 'Caw!'

The crow seemed to think. Then it replied, clearly, 'Caw,' in a human voice.

The little girl's eyes got wide as saucers. Then, outraged, she ran to her mother. 'Mama, Mama! That crow is MOCKING me!!'

Ori almost fell off the bench laughing.

'Oh, Anunit,' laughed her mother, and to Ori, 'She's...got her own way of doing things.' The mother, whose name was Zimah, sat down with Ori and chatted. In spite of Prajapati's warnings, both men and women from the Warka working classes appeared to be outgoing, egalitarian, and friendly. Soon Zimah's husband Enlil joined them, leaving the booth in the care of his oldest son Dagan, who looked to be about eight. Ori learned the names of the smaller children: Zana, six, and her brothers Gibil, three, and little Zu, a one-year-old tied to Zimah's apron strings so that he wouldn't wander off.

'He's very friendly,' Zimah said. 'Sometimes too friendly.' The baby laughed and proved the statement by clutching Ori's knee and bursting into happy giggles. Ori laughed, too.

'What a lovely family you have!' Ori said.

'Are you new in the city?' asked Enlil. Ori nodded. 'Then you must come with us to see the festivities. As soon as the noon rush is over, we'll close up and go watch the parade.' Ori thought this sounded delightful. While the parents and Dagan attended to their business, Ori babysat Zu and let Anunit tell him many (possibly untrue) things about the gods.

'Gods eat pancakes,' said Anunit, and Ori agreed, yes, the gods definitely liked pancakes. 'And they get mad when Dagan doesn't play with me. So it's okay when I steal his toys and throw them in the goats' food so the goats eat them.'

Ori was less sure about that but decided to leave family politics to Enlil and Zimah.

'The boss god is Marduk,' asserted Anunit. 'His priest gets to hit the king today.'

Ori found this particular assertion extremely hard to believe, but let it slide. Ori and the kids played button buzz, whirling a clay button on a string until it made a buzzing sound. The children clapped in delight when Ori succeeded in making the sound. Then Enlil and Zimah called that things were all packed up and the family, with Ori in tow, headed for the centre of town.

The crowd was enormous. The procession was colourful: priests from all the temples dressed in their finest and most imaginative, carrying or pulling impressive statues of all the gods. The statues were of course very clean: even the household gods were well-washed three times a day after meals. There were no dirty gods in Werka. After all, there was plenty of water.

Speaking of water, the procession was headed in the direction of the Euphrates River. The crowds followed, singing along with the musicians. Ori thought it was a nice song. Prajapati said it sounded ***'a little like rebetiki'***, whatever that was.

The procession reached the river. Before they were ready to carry the statues onto the boats, the chief priest came out to bless the statue of Marduk, the 'boss god', as Anunit called him. The king was with him in his finest robes. The king got down on the ground and prostrated himself before the statue of Marduk. When he stood up, he faced the chief priest.

The music stopped. Everybody held their breath. It was so quiet you could hear a brass pin drop.

Ori couldn't believe what happened next.

Anunit was right: the chief priest slapped the king across the face — as hard as he could.

And the king just stood there.

The crowd was deadly quiet. But then the chief priest leaned over and inspected the king's face. He nodded in satisfaction. With a finger, he carefully touched the tears on the king's face and held his hand up to indicate that yes, there were tears. This was apparently a good omen.

A cheer went up from the crowd. Everybody cheered for the god, the chief priest, and the king. The ceremony was successful: there would be good crops. The loading of the statues onto the boats began. The priests and government officials followed onto the boats. The boats started their journey to the big temple downriver. The crowd began to break up.

O-kayyy, said Prajapati. **That was something new.**

Ori didn't know what to think about it all.

Chapter 9: Civilisation and Its Discontents, Part III

After the parade, Ori went home with Enlil and his family, who were remarkably welcoming – especially since Ori was a stranger and ostensibly from a higher class, being a scribe. They didn't seem to care. The kids in particular accepted Ori as a kind of older brother and wanted to play. Ori was touched: there was an odd feeling of disconnection to living in a city of 50,000 humans.

The family lived in a well-constructed reed house. Enlil and his cousins had done the work under instructions from Zimah, who had an eye for these things. Ori found out that women in Sumeria didn't usually learn to read and write, in spite of the example of the royal priestess Enheduanna, daughter of a king and the first named author in history. However, Zimah had learned from her brothers (who were glad to share what had given them no pleasure to acquire) and used her drawing skills to sketch out a quite attractive house.

'If we ever make enough money,' she told Ori, 'I'll design us one with sun-baked bricks like the rich people have. But this will do for now.'

Ori admired the work. 'At least your house won't melt in the rainy season.'

Dagan heard this and laughed. 'Yes, but reed houses leak, too. We have to do repairs every year.'

'You like to help,' laughed his father. To Ori he confided, 'The kid loves tools so much I'm thinking of sending him to my second cousin, the builder.'

In the centre courtyard of the house, Ori met the second cousin – and a lot of other relatives. It seemed the whole of Enlil and Zimah's families had gathered for the holiday. Ori was dazzled by the sheer volume of cheerfulness a few dozen humans could generate.

Ori enjoyed the dinner, which involved more vegetable dishes (Sumerians didn't eat much meat, thank goodness), homemade breads, and beer (also homemade, Zimah had serious skills). Ori watched Zimah feeding baby Zu on her lap.

'He will only eat from my plate,' she said with a laugh. 'He's afraid we will feed him something he doesn't like.' Zu chuckled happily as he munched on a fried slice of aubergine.

While they were eating, Ori noticed the children – Dagan, Zana, Anunit, and even little Gibil – whispering with their cousins. They ran into a room in the house. As the dishes were being cleared away and more beer brought out, the children emerged into the clear space in the centre of the courtyard. It was getting dark now, and Anunit was lit by the braziers in the courtyard as she called for attention. She was wearing a headdress the children had fashioned of pigeon feathers.

'Listen, people!' she said in her loudest and most solemn voice. Everybody listened, although Ori could hear a few adults chuckling in the shadows. 'We're going to tell you a Very. Important. Story. It's all about the gods.'

As Anunit told the tale, the other children came up to act out the story. The first was Dagan. He was wearing a crown made of reeds and dyed yellow with some sort of plant dye. Dagan stood with his arms folded, surveying the crowd.

'Oh, look!' cried an aunt. 'Dagan is Gilgamesh!'

'Quiet, peasants!' admonished Anunit the storyteller. There was more adult giggling.

Anunit began the tale.

> 'Once upon a time, there was a great king called Gilgamesh. This [*pointing*] is Gilgamesh, so you'd better be respectful. [*glowering by Dagan, giggling by relatives*] Gilgamesh was one-third god and two-thirds human, and all ANNOYING. He made his subjects VERY annoyed, so that SOMETIMES they snuck into his room and stole his favourite things and fed them to the goats. One day, Gilgamesh was bored and tired of annoying his subjects, which is what he did every day. He was a very annoying king.'

I can see where that would be tiresome, said Prajapati. But since Prajapati was talking inside Ori's head, nobody else heard and Anunit didn't shush the only actual 'god' in the room. The story continued.

> 'Gilgamesh decided to go into the forest. It was nice and cool there. There were lots of friendly animals. [*Several children made up to be deer and rabbits and such gallop across the*

'stage', to general applause. Gilgamesh waves his arms dismissively and they go away again.] Gilgamesh was still bored.'

'Gilgamesh' said, 'I know! I will go to the far mountains and seek the Tree of Eternal Life!"

Anunit turned to her brother. 'Hey! Who's telling this, me or you?' [General laughter.]

'Gilgamesh journeyed for 40 days and 40 nights. [*'Gilgamesh' takes huge strides around the open space.*] He fought monsters. [*The 'animals' return but this time wearing monster masks.*] Of course, being the great King Gilgamesh, he was always vict-, victor-, er, he always won!'

Zimah stuffed the corner of her apron in her mouth to avoid a guffaw.

'In the mountains, Gilgamesh found a beautiful palace. [*Two children hold up decorated reed poles, the 'pillars' of the palace.*] The king and queen made Gilgamesh welcome. [*A boy cousin and Zana come out wearing reed crowns and mime welcoming Gilgamesh. They all sit down to a pretend banquet using some of Zimah's dinner plates containing cookies. Gigil, who is serving, sneaks a cookie and gets a dirty look from Anunit.*].'

'Queen': 'I hope you're having a nice trip, King Gilgamesh.'

'King': 'Will you be staying long?'

> 'Gilgamesh': 'Oh, yes, it's nice and no, not long. Hey, I happened to notice your boat when I passed the river. It's a nice boat. Have you had it long?'
>
> 'King': Oh, there's a whole story about that, it's very interesting…'
>
> Anunit: 'I'M TELLING IT!'
>
> 'Once upon ANOTHER time [said Anunit loudly] The gods got tired of humans. They decided to make it rain really HARD. For, er, 40 days and 40 nights. AND they decided to make the Euphrates move over. It flooded all the houses. The reed houses fell apart and the brick houses MELTED. And the people DROWNED. It was AWFUL.'

There was a dramatic pause so that everyone could appreciate just how awful it all was. When she was satisfied that enough awfulness had been comprehended, Anunit continued.

> 'But the king and queen – the ones Gilgamesh was talking to – [*waving by participants*] were warned ahead of time by a friendly god. The friendly god didn't agree with the flood idea. So he told the king and queen to build a boat and put their family and animals on it. That's what they did. And when it rained for 40 days and 40 nights and everything washed away, the boat floated. They floated until the water went away. Then they built a new palace in the mountains. The End.'

Anunit bowed to much applause. Then she grabbed a cookie from Dagan's plate before she sat down with her parents.

Dagan stood up. 'But WAIT!' he boomed in his Gilgamesh voice. 'That's not all of the story! I'M going to tell this part.' The audience murmured agreement: obviously they knew that there was more to the story.

> 'The king and queen thought that Gilgamesh was a good guest. After all, he was very polite and… [*dirty look at sister*]… didn't interrupt people when they were telling stories. So they decided to share their secret with him. Their very BIG secret.'

> 'We are immortal,' said the 'king' in a stage whisper.

> 'That means we don't die,' said the 'queen' in a stage whisper.

The audience pretended to gasp in surprise. (Some giggled.)

> 'Now,' said the 'king', 'because you are such a good guest, we will tell you how to be immortal, too. Here is a map to show you how to get to the Tree of Eternal Life. You have to take our boat and dive into the deepest part of the ocean to find the Tree. Just take a branch from it and eat the leaves and you will be immortal. But first, you have to defeat the giant octopus. Good luck, and please bring our boat back in good condition.'

He took a clay tablet out of the folds of his waistband. *It probably contained his homework,* thought Ori, who knew about writing teachers by now. But the kids pretended it was a map. Gilgamesh' promised to take good care of the map and the boat, and they all shook hands on it.

Ori was finding this fascinating: more interesting, even, than the Dance of the Seven Wonders back at The Penthouse.

'Gilgamesh' took up the tale again.

> 'King Gilgamesh journeyed for a long time in the boat. When he got to the deepest part of the ocean, he dove in and swam to the bottom where the Tree of Eternal Life was growing in a magic cave. But before he could go in, the giant octopus showed up!'

The Giant Octopus did indeed show up. Ori suspected there were several children inside it, holding up tentacles under the painted reed mat.

They are very creative with these reeds, said Prajapati. **Glad I thought of them.**

The fight against the Giant Octopus was epic. Gilgamesh had a (reed) sword. The Octopus had way too many arms. More than eight, even. Every time Gilgamesh hit one, the child representing that tentacle 'died' spectacularly, to massive cheering. Finally, it was over. Gilgamesh snatched a branch with what looked like a pomegranate on it from a wall sconce and exited stage left.

Zana took up the narrative while Dagan caught his breath by pretending to sleep.

> 'Dagan…er, Gilgamesh was very tired after the big octopus fight. After he returned the king and queen's boat (in good condition), he went back to his own home. He decided to take a nap before eating the fruit of the Tree

> of Eternal Life. That way, he wouldn't be tired when he became an immortal. His bed was very comfortable. He was so tired he didn't even talk to himself before he fell fast asleep. [*snoring noises from the 'bed'*] But while Gilgamesh slept, an evil enemy crept into the room…'

Oh no oh no oh no thought Ori. Because what appeared next was…

A child. Dressed like a snake. Slithering into the room to grab the branch of the Tree of Eternal Life. And slither away with it, giggling.

Ori was mortified. **You're in the collective unconscious now,** commented Prajapati.

But I don't want to be, thought Ori.

Zana continued the narrative, which had turned needlessly theological.

> 'When Gilgamesh woke up [*Gilgamesh wakes up and stretches ostentatiously*] and found the branch missing [*he mimes doing this*] he wasn't worried. After all, he could go back and get another one anytime. But Gilgamesh got busy and forgot. That's why he isn't here today. But we are. So we hope you enjoyed our story.'

There was more laughter, wild applause, and at least six curtain calls before the kids were packed off to bed. After that, the adults poured more beer and brought out the musical instruments. Ori joined in the dancing, which was much more enjoyable than the choreography in The Penthouse.

Mentally, Ori could hear Prajapati humming along as they danced.

Chapter 10: Civilisation and Its Discontents, Part IV

A man finds something while walking around. A woman loses something while walking around.

Ori was getting tired of compiling proverbs for Bidi's collection. Ori was beginning to think Bidi was an obsessive collector of useless trivia, a...

'There should be a word for that,' Ori mused aloud, there being no one else in the room.

A nerd, said the Voice in Ori's head. **Bidi is a big nerd. I love him, but that's what he is. The future will be full of such people,** chuckled Prajapati, **and they will adore Bidi and all collectors who leave treasure for them to find.**

'Like rude proverbs that say "My gender's better than your gender, nyah, nyah",' scoffed Ori.

The fox, having urinated into the sea, said: 'The whole of the sea is my urine!'

Ori did an eyeroll while copying this. Prajapati chuckled. **Really wise, huh? Reminds me of a certain science fiction writer...**

'Science fict-? Oh, never mind.' The gong sounded for lunch break. Ori decided to go out for a walk.

The streets were less busy than usual because it was hot. Ori didn't go to Enlil's vegetable stand: the family was on vacation in the hill country, picking fruit and staying with rural relatives. Ori found a shady spot near the temple wall and sat down to eat wrap sandwiches and fruit. Also to admire a particularly interesting relief statue. It showed a temple guardian called a lamassu – a winged creature with a human head and the body of a lion. It made a good guardian. Nobody would mess with anything that looked like that, in Ori's opinion, at least not without wings like Ori's. When Ori wasn't in humanoid disguise.

That Thing has five legs, observed Prajapati. Ori sighed and nodded, mouth full. **You know, in the future, that could lead to Conspiracy Theories…**

Ori didn't answer. One, Ori's mouth was full. Two, Ori was busy listening to two women sitting on a nearby bench.

'Well, I think she's just awful!'

'My dear, you're so right! Have you seen her NOSE? It's positively Assyrian! You know she's Larsan on her father's side. Not really royal, you know, like our real princesses!'

'Oh, yes. You can tell she isn't true quality! That skin tone! And her clothes. Who designs them, Omar the Tentmaker?'

Who are they talking about? asked Prajapati.

Ori chuckled – quietly, so as not to alert the gossipy biddies. *Something you don't know? Ori thought back. That's new. They're trash-talking the new princess. You see, the king's younger son married a princess from another kingdom to the west. She's really beautiful and accomplished – she can sing and dance and read and write in two languages, and she plays* the harp well enough to perform in The Penthouse. Her sister-in-law is dead jealous.

I can see why the other princess would be jealous, said Prajapati, **humans being what they are. But why do these women care?**

It's a puzzle to me, too, Ori shrugged. *It isn't as if they benefit from the doings at the palace. It's more as if the whole thing were some kind of a show for their personal entertainment. They seem to revel in being unkind and making differences that aren't there between humans.*

And this from people who put up statues of winged, human-headed, five-legged lions, Ori thought privately. Prajapati, who heard everything, agreed.

'You just know she's an agent for that foreign government.'

'And have you heard? The son has her nose! It's a scandal. What if he were to inherit?'

'Small chance of that, I'd say! You know,' in an even more conspiratorial voice, 'I've heard she's planning to make the prince move back home with her.'

I wouldn't blame her, thought Prajapati and Ori at exactly the same time. This made Ori laugh out loud. The two women looked up suddenly. Their eyes narrowed when they saw Ori.

'What are you laughing at, young man?' one of them demanded suspiciously.

Her friend straightened her headdress nervously. 'You aren't from the palace, are you?'

'It isn't nice to listen to other people's conversations,' said the first woman pompously.

Ori thought quickly and replied in a loud monotone, 'In Eridug, built in abundance, the monkey sits with longing eyes in the singer's house.' Then, rising from the bench in (hopefully) a dignified and other-worldly manner, Ori sauntered away in the direction of the scriptorium.

'Oh! A sage!' said the second woman. 'That's all right. They are very spiritual, those sages.'

'But not very involved in current events,' said her friend.

Quick thinking, commented Prajapati.

'Sumerian proverbs have some use,' replied Ori and went in search of a fruit juice stand. Listening to nasty gossip made Ori thirsty.

Chapter 11: Scared Geometry, Part I

After the kingship descended from heaven, the kingship was in Eridug. And Alulim ruled 8 sars.

Ori sighed while copying. **What is this nonsense?** asked Prajapati.

'The King List,' said Ori.

And how long is 8 sars?

'28,800 years.'

Oh, brother.

The list went on, from antediluvian to postdiluvian monarchs, containing names of absurdly long-lived kings with names like Ubara-Tutu, which made Prajapati giggle for some reason. Prajapati also muttered something that Ori didn't get: it sounded like 'Darmok and Jalad'. Ori got down to Mesh-He, father of the current king.

What does 'Mesh-He' mean?

'Smith.' This set off another round of Creator-giggling.

The gong sounded for lunch. Ori went to Enlil's stand to get food and chat with his friends. The three oldest children, Dagan, Zana, and Anunit, came to sit with Ori while they watched the goings-on in the marketplace square. Ori was glad to see that there were no gossipy ladies around to talk about the palace and its princesses. Instead, there was a minor procession announced in honour of the king's second cousin, the renowned big-game hunter Nimrod.

At least, he thinks he's 'renowned', Ori explained to Prajapati. *Nimrod is sort of a legend in his own mind. He has a great genius…for self-promotion.*

Prajapati chuckled. **Must be one of those people who think that if they tell you how important they are, enough times and loudly enough, it will become true.** Ori agreed.

'Oh, look!' Anunit pointed. 'Here comes the parade! Mama! A parade!'

The parade approached. First came trumpeters making a lot of noise and Ori's ears hurt. **Don't quit your day jobs,** said Prajapati.

That IS their day job, Ori pointed out, sighing. *You have no idea what practice sounds like.*

The trumpeters were followed by chariots. The charioteers were well-dressed and bore the haughty looks of all chauffeurs everywhere – the look that broadcasts the fact that they, the chauffeurs, are important by association with noteworthy people, and that besides, they get to drive the latest in technology and you don't, so there. Prajapati's laughter in Ori's head almost drowned out the out-of-tune trumpeters, for which Ori was glad.

The passengers behind the smug charioteers were quite busy flinging things at the crowd: sweets and flowers and tiny trinkets made of woven reeds with bits of coloured ribbon. The children squealed with delight and ran to scoop up treasures.

'Be careful!' called Ori. 'Don't go too near the chariots!' But the children, surefooted, dodged wheels and hooves to pick up toys and candies from the cobblestones. They entrusted their first haul to Ori's keeping and ran back for more. Zana dutifully gathered an armful of blossoms for her mother.

After that, the children had to vacate the street, being shooed away by officious officials. They came back to sit with Ori and suck on boiled sweets – and watch the next part of the parade with awe.

For here it came, the *pièce de résistance*. The reason for all this pomp and show-offery: a gigantic male lion, the largest anyone had ever seen. It was dead, of course, victim of 'Nimrod, the mighty hunter before the gods,' but it had been expertly taxidermied so that it ferociously menaced the crowd as it passed. Onlookers yelled in mock terror as yet more trumpeters, walking behind the cart, did their best imitations of a lion's roar. It was so realistic that Dagan and Anunit wanted to run out and fight it.

That's disgusting, thought Ori and Prajapati simultaneously. ***What had the lion done to him?***

Last of all came the man of the hour: Nimrod himself, waving to the crowd and showing every sign of thoroughly enjoying all the attention.

'He's not nearly as tall as I thought he would be,' said Zana with a frown. Ori agreed with her: from all the hype, Ori had expected at least a seven-foot giant. Instead, Nimrod was about medium height and unprepossessing, not muscular at all – in fact, rather flabby – and pale, not sunburned as would befit an outdoorsman. He looked like he spent most of his time in his countinghouse tallying up his grain stores and writing customer complaint letters, Ori thought.

But right now, Nimrod was waving expansively to his adoring audience. To make doubly sure they kept on adoring, with every second wave he cast more sweets into the crowd.

'Hurrah!' yelled the crowd. From within the teeming mass of people another shout started:

> *Mesh-He has slain his thousands – and Nimrod his ten thousands!*

I suspect that shout was worked out by Nimrod's PR team, thought Ori. Prajapati agreed. But sure enough, some people in the crowd took up the shout. Soon everyone was cheering loudly for Nimrod, who looked insufferably pleased with himself.

The parade passed by, followed by a cleanup crew with brooms. Children dashed between the workers picking up the last of the sweets. Life went back to almost-normal.

On the way back to the scriptorium, Ori picked up bits of gossip.

'Did you hear? Nimrod has big plans!'

'Yes! I hear he's selling shares in his latest venture!'

'He's going to build his own city!'

'Where?'

'Somewhere out on the Plains of Shinar! It's going to be the biggest, the newest, the best!'

'There isn't going to be a ziggurat. Instead, he's building a giant tower! People will live and work in it! It's going to be the biggest building in the world!'

'It will make its own weather!'

'The top floors will attract rain clouds!'

'Eagles will nest in its parapets!'

'I heard...' conspiratorial whisper, 'that the tower will reach into Heaven. And challenge the gods themselves!'

'Oh, that Nimrod. He's crazy.'

Scoffing. 'Yeah, crazy – like a fox! He's smarter than everyone else.'

Ori went back to the Kings List with a shrug and a shake of the head, thinking about self-promoting humans and 28,000-year reigns.

Prajapati sang:

> *I was born about ten thousand years ago,*
> *There ain't nothing in this world that I don't know,*

> **I saw reed boats out of Hades floating down the wide Euphrates,**
> **And I'll whup the guy who says it isn't so.**

I'm glad you're having fun, thought Ori, pushing stylus into wet clay.

Chapter 12: Scared Geometry, Part II

Ori was on the road again. After confirming that Enlil and his family had too much common sense to follow the Nimrod bubble, Ori had got leave from Bidi to make a field trip over to the new project to see what was going on. Bidi was promised a report. The road was just as dusty as Ori remembered it. At least this time Ori had a picnic basket packed by Zimah, with lots of nice veggie wraps, sweets, and bread for the journey.

The people on the road were extremely cheerful, even though many were pulling (or pushing, techniques varied) handcarts full of belongings for the move. Obviously, they were all-in for Nimrod's new venture, sight unseen. Some of them were singing:

> *O you youths, Sumerian youths,*
> *So impatient, full of action, full of manly pride and friendship,*
> *Plain I see Sumerian youths, see you tramping with the foremost,*
> *Pioneers! O pioneers!*

> *Have the elder races halted?*
> *Do they droop and end their lesson, wearied over there beyond the rivers?*
> *We take up the task eternal, and the burden and the lesson,*
> *Pioneers! O pioneers!*

> *All the past we leave behind,*
> *We debouch upon a newer mightier world, varied world,*
> *Fresh and strong the world we seize, world of labour and the march,*
> *Pioneers! O pioneers!*

Sounds kind of like a dirge, thought Ori, and Prajapati agreed.

That Nimrod is dangerously persuasive, said Prajapati.

Ori fell into conversation with a man pushing a handcart. Ori took turns with him to give him a rest, and asked what he was looking for in the new city that he didn't have in Warka.

'Freedom!' the man said. His name was Shemash. 'In Warka, the elites take everything! Nimrod will give us new opportunities!'

'Isn't Nimrod part of the elite?' asked Ori. 'He seems pretty rich to me. And he's related to the king.'

'Yeah, but he's an outsider like us. He's not like them. He lets us vote on everything. He's a man of the people!'

As long as the people vote for what he wants, thought Ori, but didn't say that. Instead Ori asked, 'What river is the new city on?'

The man shook his head. 'It isn't on a river. That's the beauty of it. All rivers do is flood! Who needs that aggravation? Babel is right in the middle of the plain. No water hazard. That's the genius of it! Oh, that Nimrod is clever! Everybody else built on a river, but not him!'

Ori squinted at the horizon, which was shimmering in the heat and bore no sign of a tree. 'Er, where will the city get its water?'

'Wells, silly! We'll dig wells!'

Ori thought about the problems of digging wells in an arid plain: how deep they would need to be, how many they would need for a city the size of Warka, or even much smaller...

'Do any of you know anything about digging wells?' Shemash shook his head impatiently.

'We'll let Nimrod think about that. Besides, how hard could it be?'

Ori shrugged and looked up and down the column to see if anybody had thought to bring along some donkeys. Donkeys were good at finding water and could dig as deep as four cubits[1] in search of it. But Ori didn't see any donkeys, at least not of the equid variety.

Ori helped push and listened to Shemash talk about his big plans for a new start in Babel. It seemed he planned to open a fashionable furniture shop.

'All the good locations in Warka were already taken,' Shemash complained. 'Beside, I couldn't join the guild without paying exorbitant dues. In Babel, I can start my own guild and people will go crazy for my new designs! I have great ideas.'

'I'm sure you do,' said Ori soothingly. 'But where will you get the raw materials? Don't reeds grow mostly near, I don't know, water?'

Shemash waved his hand. 'There you go again, seeing the downside! My friend, if you don't let go of this negativity it will

---

[1] Two cubits=1 meter.

choke you. Take it from me. I don't do negative. I'm always positive!'

'Yes, but…reeds. And glue. And varnish, and…'

'Oh, pish! Once they see how great Babel is going to be, the traders will rush all the necessary goods right to our doorsteps! Mark my words, this is going to be the most central location of all!'

Save your breath, advised Prajapati. **You may need it.** So Ori concentrated on the road.

That night they all camped along the road, lighting fires to discourage predators. Ori shared his food with Shemash. They bought some fruit juice from a vendor who went up and down the column and who, at least, was making money out of this exodus.

Staring up at the stars, Ori thought about how far the Paternoster journey had taken one lonely angel – and wondered how much farther it would be before Prajapati had manage to 'stabilise' the structure of The Building.

In the dark, Ori saw glowing eyes, but they kept their distance.

****

The next day went much like the first one. Shemash discovered some friends from his old neighbourhood, so Ori walked from group to group, listening to their chat. It seemed almost all of the migrants were looking forward to life in the new city with a great deal of optimism. Ori feared they had exaggerated expectations.

'I hear every new citizen will get a plot of land with a house and garden!'

'Well, *I* heard that we can also buy shares in the Tower! We'll all be rich and have servants! Special conveniences in every apartment there! Balcony gardens, maid service, all included!'

The expectations grew with the telling. It helped to pass the time, Ori thought, because the road was really wearisome. Full of stones and not a tree or spring in sight, just scrubby bushes everywhere. Occasionally a wild goat was sighted in the distance, darting away before anybody could chase it.

It was late afternoon when the pilgrims came over a rise and saw...

Ori wasn't sure what they were looking at. It was the strangest building anyone had ever seen.

Round and round the Tower went, levels...no, that wasn't right, the floors weren't level, they were at a slant, rounding up and up and up, the structure narrowing slightly the higher it grew...made of mud brick, not fired, as far as Ori could tell...not terribly stable, either, but huge, enormous, rising from the plain like a challenge to...well, something...

Oh, heck.

Prajapati's exclamation was so loud in Ori's head that it actually hurt.

This is going to be a problem, was all Prajapati would say.

Chapter 13: Scared Geometry, Part III

It was evening. The migrant horde had dispersed eagerly to various inns, taverns, and hostelries, there to pump the locals for information on the new city, its amazing Tower, and all the latest Nimrod-related gossip. In turn, the locals were busy pumping the newcomers for coin and barter items. Ori was shocked at the inflated prices they were charging for food and lodging.

'If these people don't find their own shelter soon, they won't be able to afford to start their own businesses as they planned,' Ori commented to Prajapati.

That may be part of Nimrod's scheme. If they're out of money and trade goods, they'll be willing to join the Tower work gangs for low wages – or even to sell themselves into slavery. It was a sobering thought.

'I'd like to get inside that Tower and take a look for you,' said Ori. 'But I think they're closed to visitors after dark.'

That's good! I don't want you inside that thing yet. First, we have a lot to talk about.

So Ori waited on a bench in the 'park' – a pitiful sandbox with two sad-looking potted figs – until the city had settled down for the night. By midnight, there was nothing to hear except snoring from house and hovel, punctuated by the occasional howl of a dog, snarl of a cat, or exclamation of a night watchman as he stubbed his toe on a random bit of irregular paving.

When it was clear that nobody else was around, Ori sprouted wings and took off.

The view of Mesopotamia was, as usual, uninspiring. Under the canopy of stars spread the winding rivers to the east. Here, beneath Ori's gliding wings, was a wide, level stretch of scrubland, now dotted (Ori had good night vision) with prowling nocturnals: wolves and small-but-deadly cats, hopping rabbits, browsing deer, and other creatures looking for food away from the hot sun.

The Tower ranging out of this desert made Ori distinctly uneasy. It didn't fit, somehow. Even at night with no one clambering about on it, the giant conical structure seemed menacing. Ori ignored the anxious feelings and used the air currents generated by the building itself for lift. Reaching a considerable height, Ori began to trace lazy circles in the sky above the city. It had been a while – Ori was enjoying the exercise.

We need to talk, came the soothing voice in Ori's head. ***I'm afraid I'm going to have to ask you to make a difficult decision.***

Ori, thoughtful.

'I'm listening.'

Do you somewhere to sit while we discuss this? I'd rather you didn't sit on...that. But it might take a while.

'Oh, no, I'm fine flying. It's relaxing. Also, this building has great thermal updrafts.'

Okay. Now, you have questions. I would.

Ori circled the Tower thoughtfully. 'All right. Why did you say oh, heck when you saw the Tower of Babel? It's ugly, sure, but what's alarming about it?'

Prajapati sounded unhappy. *It has to do with sacred geometry.*

'Sacred geometry?' (*More like scared geometry,* Ori thought.)

Sacred geometry involves proportions and shapes that affect spacetime. Look…what makes humans different from other animals?

Ori laughed. 'Where do I begin? They make messes. Instead of following their species' programming, they run all over the place. They have plans. They have *agendas*. Worst of all, they lie. To each other, for cheap advantages. Worse, they lie to themselves. They make up crazy stories about 'this means that' and 'I'm doing this for a good purpose' when what they really mean is, 'I did it because I wanted to and now I'm making up a good excuse.' They're wearisome.'

Prajapati laughed, a sad laugh. *All of this is true. But have you ever heard them say they're made in the image of the gods?*

'Absolutely. I thought they were bragging. Or else trying to blame somebody else for when they mess up.'

Like blaming a certain red-headed snake for the debacle in the noospheric garden?

'Yeah. Like that.' Ori was still cross about that garden.

You're partly right. But that isn't all of it. Humans are made in my image, in a sense. I seem to have set them on an evolutionary quest for sentience…it was part of the design, the pattern…

'Like the scared geometry?'

Sacred. But yes. The short version of what this means is that humans can generate spacetime. They're supposed to be helping us fill in The Building and stabilise the structure. But…

Ori stopped circling and hovered over the hideous Tower. 'But instead of helping, they're hindering.'

Exactly.

'Instead of doing constructive things, they fight among themselves. Each one wants to be the cleverest. Or the richest. Or the prettiest. Or the most talented. They're always trying to be popular.'

That's true. This warps the spacetime out of shape. The geometry's all wrong. I try to fix it from my end, but I can't. Especially… Ori detected a hesitation, as if Prajapati was afraid of saying too much.

'Especially…? Come on, I won't tell them. Promise.'

Especially because they…won't talk to me!

'You mean they could? And they won't?'

Yes, my friend, that's what I do mean. I try. I talk at them all the time, just as I talk to you. I call to them in their sleep. I shout when they wake up. When they're happy I try to sneak in a word of congratulation. No response. Happiness is all for them, you see.

When they're sad or in trouble, sometimes they'll yell for me. But once I've helped them they go back to ignoring me totally. I try to contact them and it's crickets.

Some of them, like those priest friends of yours…

'Not exactly friends. More acquaintances I copy tablets for.'

I wasn't blaming you. Those priests will pretend they talk to me. But they're just making it up.

Ori was agitated and showed it by flying some more. 'That must be incredibly frustrating.'

Oh, it is. Especially since, if we worked together, we could fix a lot of this. Or at least get the players out before the whole spacetime crashes and burns. Which is what this one is going to do in short order if we don't intervene.

'Seriously? There's going to be trouble down there?' Ori surveyed the sleeping town.

Trouble? You don't know the half of it. Famine, violence, ecological disaster. You name it. We need to intervene, you and I.

'What can I do? I'm ready.'

Bless your heart, I know you are. But there are consequences to this one. Worse than being turned into a snake.

'Yes, but…if there's violence and famine and an ecological disaster, Enlill and Zimah and the kids won't be safe. Whatever it is, we've got to do it.'

Prajapati sighed. **You're right. Even if the whole world turns inside out and upside down, it has to be done. They won't like it, and you may not enjoy all of it. But, Ori, we've got a world to save.**

You'd better find someplace to land. I need to send you a major upgrade and it might interfere with your navigation.

Ori understood not a word of that other than 'find someplace to land,' but settled with a flutter of wings on a brush-covered knoll to the west. A furtive bunny, startled by the arrival of the biggest bird it had ever seen, hopped rapidly away. Ori sat quietly and waited for the 'upgrade.'

It was a long one. Ori sat as if in a trance until the first streaks of dawn in the east announced the arrival of a new day in Babel. Then the puzzled angel headed for town and, hopefully, a cold drink.

Ori had the mother of all headaches.

Chapter 14: Scared Geometry, Part IV

It was daytime in Babylon. Merchants were hawking wares in the marketplace. Buying was desultory: most could not afford the prices. The new arrivals had settled over in the big makeshift tent colony outside the city walls. They preferred to face the dangers of night predators – four-legged as well as human and for all they knew inhuman – than pay the high rents that were the going rate in Nimrod's new kingdom.

Workmen were scrambling up and down ladders carrying hods of brick. Occasionally, one would fall: the sharp cries were unsettling to newcomers, but those who had been there a while merely ignored the shouts and the sickening thuds that followed. Teams of what Ori presumed were at least nominally medical men ran with stretchers, to render assistance in rare cases – or, more commonly, to take away the corpses.

Ori had ceased to be surprised by anything these people did. Ori walked across a fairly empty square on the other side of the marketplace. The clock pillar cast its shortening shadow over the mud-brick plaza; it was late morning, said the sun. Ori refused to hurry to the appointment with Babylon's CEO.

'Let Nimrod wait,' Ori said inwardly. Still, Ori was on time arriving at the portal to the HQ Palace, a spacious high-ceilinged structure adjacent to the ever-growing Tower.

Servants met Ori at the door, where Ori was frisked to make sure he wasn't carrying anything more lethal than a cuneiform stylus (they allowed the 'scribe' to keep that, after all, this was supposed to be an interview), and then escorted the disgusted angel into the Nimrodian presence.

The 'conference room' was typically modern and designed to impress. Ori stood around waiting. If Ori had learned anything about humans it was that sitting down before the 'most important' person had arrived was considered very bad manners.

Ori didn't have long to wait. Nimrod burst into the room like a pudgy sandstorm, surrounded by attendants waving tablets at him, all talking at once to get his attention. The busy little executive nodded, shook his head, waved this one off and that one closer, muttered replies like 'yeah, okay' and 'not on your life' and 'tell him to go peddle his wares in Arabia,' and generally sorted out his personal universe on the fly. He settled down in his ergonomically designed reed chair with a sigh and ran the stubby fingers of a heavily-beringed hand through his stiff, unruly hair. He turned a beaming smile on Ori, who had also taken a seat and was waiting to ask questions.

'Mister Nimrod…' Ori began.

'Tell your bosses they have nothing to fear from me,' Nimrod said abruptly. 'We're in the same business.'

'Er, what?' Ori was nonplussed.

'Gods-bothering. The priests and I. Only,' he grinned mischievously, 'I'm better at it. I'm really going to bother those gods. Better than they've ever been bothered in their miserable lives.' Nimrod looked eerily triumphant.

Ori didn't know what to say. *This is alarming,* Ori thought in the direction of Prajapati. Prajapati didn't say anything, which was even more alarming to Ori than Nimrod's manic grinning.

'Your priests have tried everything to get the attention of those lazy deities. Music!'

Ori thought of what The Penthouse would have said about Sumerian music. Ori imagined the hours-long, nay days-long lectures on contrapuntal theory that would follow and winced. Nimrod saw this and took it for agreement – as, indeed, he took every form of response to his utterances. It was the secret of his business success: just charge along as if everyone agreed with you. They'd be too surprised to stop you.

'Sacrifices and ceremonies! They pay no attention!' Nimrod leaned forward in mock-conspiratorial solidarity. 'Those *shabarras* aren't into negotiation. What we've got to do is…' his grin became wide enough to engulf the long table, 'storm the castle!'

'Storm the-? Er, surely you don't mean…?'

Nimrod pounded the table with a small, round fist. 'I DO! And I know how to do it!'

To cover confusion, Ori pretended to take notes, hoping Prajapati was listening.

'The secret, of course, is sacred geometry. Oh, your priestly employers think that's a trade secret of theirs, don't they? But they're wrong! I know all about it! And my space programme here is going to exploit it to the fullest to fulfill human destiny, bigly!'

'Bigly?' Ori wasn't sure how to spell that.

'Bigly!' Nimrod leaned back in his chair, which tilted comfortably so that the mini-dictator could cast his gaze impressively toward the ornate ceiling. Which he did. 'Those gods won't know what hit 'em when thousands of Sumerians show up on their doorstep with Big Questions.'

Ori felt a sense of panic imagining the Sumerians loose in The Penthouse. Ori was trying not to think about an encounter between a Warka cobbler and one of Ori's thousand-eyed colleagues.

Ori managed a question – not that Nimrod needed much encouragement to go on. He could apparently talk all day. He probably talked in his sleep and used words like 'bigly.'

'Uh, Mister Nimrod, is this tower connected to your plan to, er, storm Heaven?'

Again the grin. 'Oh, yes. Don't you see? The Tower is our spaceship! That's why I secretly call it The Dragon. It's going to give those gods quite a fright when we start opening doors into their pancake-banquet room!'

Oh, dear, thought Ori frantically. Still no response from Prajapati.

Nimrod warmed to his subject, jumping up and pacing the cavernous room, gesticulating. 'The trick is to generate a wormhole in spacetime. And I've just about done it! Of course, I had a proof-of-concept model made out in the desert. It wasn't big enough to send anything through, but we're sure it works. This time, we'll send everyone through! I'll be the greatest innovator since Whatshisname the Ark Builder. Only they'll remember my name: Nimrod the Great!' He raised his arms as if acknowledging invisible accolades.

Ori tried to bring the interview back down to brass tacks. 'Er, exactly how does a giant apartment building turn into a wormhole? Forgive me, but I'm not conversant with the science.' Oh, harmony, I'm beginning to talk like them now.

Nimrod was confident. 'I'll show you.' He snapped his fingers and an attendant handed him a tablet. He sketched the following with a knife:

'You see, the staircases constantly go up, never down.' Nimrod beamed at the cleverness of it.

Ori studied the drawing. 'You mean a person walking up the staircase never goes down.'

Nimrod scowled. 'That's what I said.'

It wasn't, but Ori ignored this. 'But that's not possible in this frame of reference. It breaks the laws of physics.'

'I know! Isn't it brilliant?' The ever-mercurial Nimrod forgot his pique in the sheer pleasure of contemplating his own cleverness. He flopped back in his chair, steepling his hands, and proceeded to lecture.

'You see, there are two kinds of people. The sheep, who follow the rules, like the workers out there, these guys…' he indicated his attendants, 'and…well, you.'

You don't know the first thing about me, thought Ori, but merely nodded for Nimrod to go on.

'And then there are the geniuses like me: the rule-breakers. The chaos-creators. The disruptors.'

The stealers of others' ideas, thought Ori. *You don't have the first idea how that staircase works, do you? You're just mimicking some design you stole from someone.* Ori wondered where the person he stole it from was. Or if he or she was still around.

'I know we're breaking the laws of physics!' Nimrod crowed. 'That's the beauty of it! By putting these staircases in we're forcing the universe to move into the fourth dimension! Once all the people start moving in – and climbing those staircases – it will generate one *haramen* of a wormhole! We'll sail right through to the garden of the gods! Won't they be surprised?'

Ori took notes, all the while thinking, *Can he do that? Would that work? That could get messy.* Still from Prajapati, in Prajapati's own words, 'crickets.'

'So you see,' concluded Nimrod, 'With my visionary leadership I have accomplished what countless generations of priests have failed to bring about: the chance to confront the gods. Challenge them about their mismanagement and malfeasance. And make Earth Great Again!'

'And you famous,' Ori said aloud without thinking. Nimrod wasn't at all displeased.

'Of course!' he said expansively. 'After all, I am the innovator who brought this about. I imagine people will be talking about me for centuries to come.'

Millennia, said Prajapati, but not until Ori had left the building. Apparently, Prajapati didn't like any of Nimrod's structures. ***They'll be talking about him, but not in a good way.***

Ori flew off to an oasis in the west – to rest up for the next day. That, he informed Prajapati, was when Nimrod had promised the 'priest's scribe' a tour of the Tower.

We'll have to act then, decided Prajapati. Ori ate dates from the trees, sipped water from the spring, and gazed at the stars, perplexed. Ori still didn't know what exactly they were going to do, but there was a buzzing in Ori's head.

Chapter 15: What's the Sumerian Word for Dictionary?

The next day dawned bright and clear – because it was the Plain of Shinar, where every day dawned bright and clear. The sun beat down on the flat, scrubby landscape. The temperature, depending on how you measured it, was either 100° Fahrenheit, or 38° Celsius, or – since nobody had been born yet to whom those measurements would have made the slightest bit of sense – roughly, same as usual: hot. And dry. The chance of precipitation would have been calculated by any of Sumer's sages as zero.

Sumer's sages would have been wrong. Rain wouldn't be the problem, though.

Again, Ori walked across the open square. The clock pillar said it was about eight in the morning, the time Nimrod had set for his big inspection tour of the building site. Ori wasn't looking forward to this. That building was beginning to get on Ori's nerves, especially after Nimrod's boast about 'confronting the gods.'

Ori was pretty sure that Tower was already warping the air currents around it. *Could it really bend spacetime?*

I'm afraid so, said Prajapati in Ori's head. **Which is what we need to do something about.**

Ori stopped by the clock pillar, pretending to fasten a sandal strap. *Er, Prajapati?*

Yes? Go ahead and ask. I know you want to. The voice sounded avuncular, like an indulgent older relative amused by a child's query.

If this Tower can actually threaten creation, why didn't you intervene before? For that matter, why didn't you plan the universe differently, so this wouldn't be possible?

(Chuckle) Good question. I wish I had a good, simple answer for you. But it's…complicated.

Prajapati sounded rueful. **Intervention has, er, rules, just like anything else.**

Rules? Ori was surprised. *Who's making these rules? I thought you were in charge.*

Being in charge doesn't mean there aren't rules for how things work. If you compose a piece of music, you can choose what you like. But…

….there are still rules, they thought together.

I see what you mean, thought Ori, who had run out of excuses for standing around by the clock pillar and thinking, so now went on to attend Nimrod's inspection tour.

You know what to do were Prajapati's last words as Ori joined the small crowd of reporters, minor officials, and attendants who were following along in Nimrod's wake. At least this time Ori didn't have to talk to the guy.

****

Nimrod was in top form, nattering on about his great project and pointing out its features, such as they were, to everyone who was listening and those who were just gawking.

'See these stair rails? Latest design. I brought them in, all the way from Ur. Adds a touch of elegance, don't you agree?'

As if he led the camel train himself, thought Ori as the gaggle of followers trailed along in the mini-mogul's wake, up the outside staircase and round and round the Tower, ever higher. Workmen barely paused in their labours: for one thing, they had obviously been told not to. For another, the Boss was there so they wanted to look busy. They were busy, though: construction was obviously behind schedule. There was lots of brick-toting, mortaring, and ladder-moving going on. The inspection team dodged between piles of fired brick.

Fired brick was expensive. Ori wondered where Nimrod was getting the funds. *Who's backing this boondoggle? It's definitely not the priests. They're actually worried about this thing.* Ori said nothing but watched for the opportunity to do what Prajapati had told him to do.

The group had reached the top of the mezzanine level and Nimrod was expansively touting the interior features that they would see during tomorrow's tour. That smug voice was getting on Ori's nerves. Ori spotted a couple of workmen who, now that the parade had gone past, were leaning on the wall for a surreptitious snack break. As they munched on sunflower seeds, they chatted about this and that – quietly, so that Nimrod wouldn't hear. One of them noticed Ori but, when the stranger didn't seem to be likely to report them, went back to his conversation. Ori leaned over and whispered in his ear:

'Pistrast bike ku nêrdewan rast e.'

The workman looked at Ori in surprise. His eyes widened. Then he nodded.

'Ez ê bê guman wiya bikim, ezbenî.' And he hurriedly began to straighten the ladder, as Ori had told him to do.

His coworker looked on in astonishment and turned to Ori. 'What did you say to him?' he asked, his voice full of suspicion. Ori leaned over and whispered:

'Ainqal alsulm 'iilaa almustawaa altaali.' The workman stared at Ori for a moment, his eyes wide with astonishment at what was happening inside his head. Apparently, it wasn't painful, exactly: more like…enlightening. The workman nodded and began to pick up the ladder to move it to the next level, as instructed.

This move was stoutly resisted by the first workman. A conversation ensued.

'Tu çi dikî ehmeq?'

' 'Aetini alsulm 'ayuha al'ahmaqu!' Neither workman could make head or tail out what the other was saying. A struggle resulted in which the ladder was an unfortunate casualty. Ori left them struggling and hurried up the stairs behind the inspection group.

At the next level Nimrod was busy praising his own foresight in the selection of location and explaining how 'strategic' it was.

Some onlookers in the back were muttering about its only being strategic to onager migration. Keeping to the fringe of the group, Ori spied another workman and beckoned to him.

'Can I help you, sir?' Ori whispered in his ear. Again the moment of disorientation followed by a sense of 'Aha!' The workman began to gather up buckets of water and throw them over the parapets to the ground several storeys below.

There was yelling.

'What are you doing, you oaf? Stop that!'

'Mn sfarsh daram!'

'What the heck does that mean? Cut it out!'

From below came a shout: 'Te derenceya min xist xwarê!' There was scuffling and more incomprehensible shouting.

The inspection group hadn't noticed anything because…Nimrod was talking. When Nimrod talked, nobody noticed anybody but Nimrod. Ori decided that if there were a book of words with their explanations and pictures, Nimrod's image would feature next to the word 'exhibitionist.' And Nimrod was in fine form today.

All the better for Prajapati's plan, thought Ori, calmly picking the next linguistic victim.

Up the winding staircase the group went. Nimrod talking about profit, prestige, and interplanetary glory. Reporters taking notes in cuneiform. Courtiers looking bored. Acrophobic courtiers looking nervous. And behind, Ori the angel sowing chaos.

On level four Ori whispered: 'Où sont les neiges d'antan?'

On level five came: 'Warum bauen wir nicht einfach eine Dattelweinstube?'

On level six: 'Ga op een zandduin springen, idioot!'

Up and up they went, unconsciously trailing confusion in their wake. That is, Ori was conscious of it, but Nimrod and his toadies were blissfully unaware – until they got to the top-floor-in-progress, that is. It wasn't until they turned to go back down that the tour group realised the dilemma they were in: what they had taken for harmless background noise of a constructive nature had been, in fact, the beginnings of a full-scale industrial riot fueled by mutual incomprehension.

'La astutie fahmk!' 'Yunaani nemifahmam!' 'Je ne comprends pas!' 'Ich versteh' nur Bahnhof!' 'Govoriš mi na patagonski!' 'Daar kan ik geen chocola van maken!'

In other words: it's Greek to me, or Chinese, or Hebrew, or whatever-it-is I can't make head or tail of, why can't you talk sense? All of this frantic babbling was accompanied by hand-waving, yelling, throwing things, and industrial accidents.

The Tower's frontiers, where the ladders were, began raining bricks. People below cursed (in many languages, the plague was spreading) and dashed madly about, trying to get out of the way of whatever might come down next. Emergency services, such as they were, were summoned. Unfortunately, as soon as they got close to the Tower, the language plague hit them. Arguments broke out, machinery got broken.

For his part, Nimrod was beside himself. Still on the staircase at the top of completed construction, he danced about in frustration as his orders were not being followed – because hardly anybody understood them. Oddly, Nimrod himself seemed unaffected. He was still speaking Sumerian. The problem was, almost nobody else was.

The Chief Disruptor was being disrupted, and he did not like it one bit. 'Who's behind this sabotage?' he yelled. Nobody listened: not only could hardly anyone understand him, but they were also too busy rushing down the stairs to escape the Tower and its quarreling workers. Fist fights had broken out and crockery was being flung.

Standing well out of the way in a niche, the cause of all this mayhem observed things with a surprising equanimity. It hadn't been at all clear what was going to happen – at least, not to Ori. Now Ori understood: it was going to take a long time for the people of Babel to sort out the language issue. Long enough for factions to develop, interest groups to organise. Opposition to Nimrod's megalomaniacal scheme was likely to grow. The Tower project would most likely be abandoned. Indefinitely, Ori hoped.

Nimrod was growing more and more frantic. He stamped his feet in anger and shook his pudgy fists at the sky.

'This is a plot of the gods!' he thundered. 'I'll show them! I won't take this lying down! They won't stop me! They can't outwit Nimrod the Mighty Hunter! I'll become Nimrod the Terrible, just see if I don't!'

Ori didn't have a message for Nimrod, and so slipped out through the crowd fleeing the Tower. The murmuring, chattering, uncomprehending, babbling crowd.

The last thing Ori heard while exiting the gate was, 'Ga een kameel kussen, gekke buitenlander!'

Chapter 16: Swaying the Masses

All night, the verbal virus had spread from Sumerian to Sumerian. By dawn they were grouping according to language. Interpreters were few and far between: a few of the younger people had managed somehow to snag two languages and were doing their best to mediate. By mid-morning there was a huge crowd in the main square.

Some of them were holding signs. The fact that the signs were made of clay tablets on poles and not very big made it hard to read them. The fact that the signs were attempts to render hundreds of languages in cuneiform that had never been written down before (and some of which didn't even exist yet) rendered the protest signs even less effective than they might have been.

Knots of dissatisfied citizens were trying to organise chants. This, again, was hard to do since nobody could understand what the others were chanting. Ori, who could understand them all, noticed that they were more or less all chanting, 'What do we want? Communication! When do we want it? Now!'

Communication isn't going to come anytime soon, thought Ori, who was beginning to regret all of this.

Don't, said Prajapati. **They brought this on themselves. Besides, we're trying to save them from making a terrible mistake.**

Ori noticed trains of families carrying their meager belongings. They were forming up to return to Warka, or whatever city would have them. Ori felt sorry for them, but at least they would be away from the influence of Nimrod and his idiotic Tower.

Nimrod had noticed the growing number of would-be expatriates preparing for an exodus and he did not like this at all. He ordered his men to bring out his party piece: the stuffed lion.

The lion was still pretty impressive, although bits of it had started to shed. Some trumpeters were ordered to play in the hope of gathering a crowd so that Nimrod could address it and reassure everyone that the Tower was fully as wonderful as advertised and that all was going according to plan.

Unfortunately, the trumpets had been stored in the same place as the lion. All of Babylon was dusty, to be sure, but that particular storeroom was badly chinked, and the wind had been blowing. So when the hastily-assembled trumpeters raised their instruments for a heralding fanfare, what came out was an unpleasant *SQUA-a-a-awwwk!* accompanied by a shower of desert sand.

It reminded Ori of the time Samya had tried to stop the Tone Wars with a particularly threatening song called *Entropy*. The brass section had required therapy after that one.

The crowd jeered, but Nimrod was not to be deterred.

'Friends! Babylonians! Fellow adventurers! Listen to me! This is just a minor setback! My user-service team will have this problem sorted in no time!' He raised his pudgy hands in what he obviously imagined was an elegant and commanding gesture to underscore his mastery of the situation. Ori thought he looked like a bantam rooster trying to intimidate a barnyard full of Orpingtons.

If Nimrod's theatrical gestures failed to have an effect on the crowd, his words were worse than useless. Only a small minority of his listeners could still understand Sumerian. To the rest his speech, as one member of the audience put it, 'sounded like Chinese – whatever that is.'

Nimrod wiped away tears of frustration. 'Don't go! We haven't got to the good part yet!' But a fair number of the people in the square – about one in three – were in fact about to do just that. They headed for the city gates in a long queue of family groups.

There they were stopped by Nimrod's guards. The guards had orders to keep everyone inside. They refused to open the gates. The crowd refused to disperse. There was pushing and shoving and multilingual shouting. Finally, some of the burlier men in the crowd managed to wrestle the restraining bar off one of the gates – and the crowd began to pour through. Guards put up a show of resistance but were overwhelmed by sheer numbers. Soon, most of the men-at-arms had to scramble to one side to avoid being trampled underfoot.

Other gates were soon opened. The victorious crowd streamed out of the city in all directions. They formed caravans of humans, carts, and beasts. They marched determinedly away. Songs drifted back to the ears of those remaining in the city. The songs had different tunes and different words – but they all told one story: we're going home. The way may be long and hard but we will rejoice when we get there.

It would seem Nimrod has given them a purpose after all, commented Prajapati wryly. Ori agreed. But what about those still in the city?

I think it's time for you to do some talking, said Prajapati. ***If I were you, I'd put on a show.***

'All right,' replied Ori. Shifting form, Ori unfurled what were after all an imposing set of wings and flew to the platform where Nimrod was standing.

Nimrod stared, open-mouthed.

The crowd stared, open-mouthed.

A child shouted, 'Look, Mommy, that's the biggest bird in the world!'

You'd better be glad for that, kid, chuckled Prajapati. ***Those terror birds really were a bad idea.***

Ori turned to Nimrod. 'I think you'd better close your mouth. It's undignified. Besides, there are flies about.'

Nimrod closed his mouth. He glared at Ori, his beady little eyes trying to bore holes of malice in something – preferably this angel who had shown up to steal his thunder and spoil his fun.

'See, my people!' began Nimrod.

'My' people, in a black hole, snorted Prajapati.

'See, my people!' Nimrod repeated. 'See the lengths the gods will go to in trying to stop me, your friend and leader, from accomplishing this major milestone, this historic launch of the biggest thing ever! They're even sending their feathered minions to try to stop me! Me, Nimrod! I laugh at gods!'

This speech was pretty good for off-the-cuff, thought Ori. It might have been persuasive if enough people had heard and understood it. Alas for Nimrod: simultaneous translation hadn't been invented yet. Only a small percentage of listeners had a clue what he'd just said. He might as well have been shouting, 'Last one in the reflecting pool is a rotten egg!'

Ori spread wings and hovered a few feet above the platform. Ori knew this would drive Nimrod bonkers, and it did. The little dictator danced from foot to foot, shooting Ori looks that he only wished could kill.

'People of Sumeria!' called Ori loudly. 'Friends! I mean you no harm!'

Unlike Nimrod, Ori could be understood. By everyone. That was because in addition to the gift of language-shifting, Prajapati had given Ori the gift of universal comprehensibility. Each listener heard Ori speaking in their own language. This was a handy trick, and Ori was determined to use it.

Ori could tell that the words – the first announcement that had made sense all day – were helping people to calm down. Time to press the advantage.

'As you all can tell from what's happened, this Tower isn't a really good idea. It's bad for the environment. There's no good water source out here. The structure is unsound and likely to put you in serious danger…'

That part, at least, was true. Ori was determined to avoid needless metaphysical explanations – but determined to keep people out of that gravity-trap.

'Please go back to your groups for your noonday meals. Talk among yourselves. Make your own decisions. If you want to go back home maybe I can help organise something. If you want to strike out for new territories I can draw you a map or two. But let it be your decision. Take your time. And in the meantime, please stay out of the Tower.'

In any group of people, about one out of three will do the reasonable thing if it's put to them clearly. This third now began to reflect that, yes, there was a water shortage. That Tower didn't look safe. In fact, there had been more than a few fatal accidents among the construction crew. Come to think of it, this whole city was beginning to seem like a bad idea: too many strangers, now even more alien because you couldn't talk to them. High prices, a lack of meaningful work, no cultural activities to speak of and the falafel stands at home were much better… They decided to break for lunch and discuss things with their clan members.

Another third of any group will dig in their heels and double down on whatever silly activity is the latest thing, even when it's reached its sell-by date. These are the late mullet-wearers, the tragically diehard disco fans. There was a murmuring in this group next. An attempt was made to shout renewed support for Nimrod. Nimrod might have been encouraged by this if he had understood them. But since they were shouting in random languages, he thought they were threatening him. He signalled to the guards, who chased the confused supporters out of the square.

That left the remaining third – the hopelessly indecisive. These would be waiting for a winner to emerge among the warring factions. Thus it has ever been. This bunch decided that for now, nothing had been decided. And since it was lunchtime, they'd break for food. Time enough to resolve major issues on a full stomach once the next act of this highly entertaining drama started in the afternoon.

Ori could tell that this was the best that could be expected under the circumstances.

Nimrod wasn't having any. He eyed Ori balefully. 'This isn't over! Just you wait!' He stalked off to confer with his 'team'.

Ori flew to the top of the clock pillar, perched there, and waited for what came next.

Chapter 17: Up the Down Staircase

Ori woke at sunrise, a bit stiff from perching all night atop a pillar. A quick overflight of the city got some of the kinks out. Avoiding the Tower: not only was it beginning to make Ori uneasy but it was giving off a low-level hum that the angel didn't like at all.

Buildings were not supposed to hum.

Also, the Tower's entrances and exits were protected by armed guards. Some of them had crossbows, which looked suspiciously like anti-aircraft weaponry. Ori went back to the pillar in order to maintain an overview of the action and avoid Nimrod's guards.

The sky lightened on the sight of people dressed for travel. Singly and in groups they approached the city gates. On their backs were their portable belongings. Some carried small children. They weren't asking for anything. They weren't trying to negotiate with the Nimrod regime. All they wanted was Out.

The sergeant-at-arms in charge of the main gate came out and spoke to the group there. Ori had very sharp hearing and so picked up 'not here, this gate is closed…go with the guards here, they'll show you the exit…' The instructions got translated from group to group, either by the bilingual or through improvised sign language. Ori saw that this routine and pantomime was being repeated at the other gates. The groups of would-be emigrants obediently followed the men-at-arms to the designated 'exits'.

Which turned out to be the entrances to the Tower.

Ori watched with horror as the guards at the Tower entrances flung open the doors and herded the people inside. Some, realising the deception, tried to turn away – but were forced roughly through the doors with batons and spear handles. There was shouting and dismay, but the soldiers who were armed, burly, organised, and unencumbered by baggage, prevailed.

The guards were aided by Nimrod's supporters in the city – civilians who for some reason were still entranced by their leader's extravagant promises. Ori could tell who they were: the Nimrod fans had tied red cloths around their heads and were clearly visible to each other and from above. They crowded in behind the reluctant others, pushing and shoving to get in the Tower and sweeping the crowd in front through the portals.

'This is a disaster,' moaned Ori. Up to this point, Ori had harboured hope that the Sumerians would simply abandon Babel and its cursed Tower and return to some semblance of normal life. Now it looked as if Nimrod's ridiculous scheme was doomed to run its course. At the very least, the sheer number of people flooding into the unfinished structure would strain its capacity. At worst…there might be Geometry, if what Ori had been told was true.

I hate to ask you to do this, said Prajapati in a regretful voice, ***but would you mind following them in there? It's really a matter of life and death. Or existence versus entropy.***

Ori didn't hesitate. 'You got it!' And with a downward rush of wings, the angel dove for the nearest entrance, over the heads of the struggling crowd and soldiers alike.

The last thing Ori heard before flying through the open doors was a faint call from Prajapati: ***Stay off the floor!***

****

The inside of the Tower was the most baffling thing Ori had ever seen – and Ori had seen some very baffling things. A wide foyer encircled the entire Tower on the inside. Its high, curved ceiling gave an unhindered view of broad stairways leading from each entrance into the massive stairwell. Theoretically, the stairs led to different storeys where there were apartments, but Ori could see that the apartments were largely unfinished. All the construction effort had gone into this monstrous network of interlocking staircases.

Obeying Prajapati's last instruction, Ori hovered high in the vaulted stairwell. The sight made the angel's eyes water. Even from above it was impossible to sort out exactly where these stairs went. One seemed to dovetail into another, completely fooling the eye.

These were the stairs up which the people were being forced. Scared, panicky people. Wailing and shouting people. Shuddering and trembling people. They were inside now, and they didn't like it. This place inspired nothing in the heart but fear and confusion.

Babies cried. Somewhere in the midst of this moving wall of humanity a dog began to howl. The sound sent shivers down Ori's spine. Even the red-scarved Nimrod supporters were frightened.

Herded into the building in droves, the crowds by their sheer volume forced those in front of them, albeit unwillingly, forward and upward. But as Ori followed the movement of particular groups, they didn't seem to be making much progress: the staircases twisted and turned and seemed to double back on themselves. It was almost as if…

'They're moving in and out of other dimensions,' said Ori aloud to Prajapati. But Prajapati said nothing. Ori remembered that Prajapati stayed away from the Tower. But it would have been nice to hear a word of encouragement right about now.

The building's hum grew louder and changed pitch. The hum was now so loud that it could easily be heard above the lamentations of the people – who were still marching up, down, and sideways on the maddening stairs because they had nowhere else to go. They wept, and hung on for dear life to their few belongings and their family members, afraid to lose them in the pointlessly moving mass.

A shout made Ori look up – and curse.

'Flatted FIFTH!'

The curse wasn't what made all the people pause and look up. Instead it was the amplified aural assault of a tinny trumpet played by a tiny megalomaniac. In the cavernous stairwell, the squeaky sound reverberated like a Day of Judgement summons from the universe's most niggling accountant. It was Nimrod, of course: he grinned as if he'd just played a horn solo in the greatest symphony in history. He was standing at the very top of the staircase, near the ceiling.

'My people!' the grating voice rained down at them all like a shower of sparks from a mistimed firework – fragmentary and dangerous. 'My people! You are witnessing history!'

For some reason, everyone seemed to understand him, language or no language. *Could it be that the Tower has the same translation abilities as I do?* wondered Ori. Maybe that was part of what the humming was about.

Nimrod's manic grimace grew wider. 'No! I tell you what! You are witnessing the END of history!'

Ori stared. The people on the staircases stared. The guards, who had followed them inside to push more people around, stared. Even the Nimrod supporters stopped shouting slogans and stared. The end of history? What is he talking about?

The smug little monster was positively beaming. 'Just keep moving, people! You're doing fine. As soon as we reach escape velocity the portal will open – and I, Nimrod the Great, will ascend to the heavens! I will get to the centre of where the real power is! There will be changes, believe you me!'

The dictatorial statement echoed down the stairwell – and there was silence. Even the Nimroddies forgot to cheer. There was a collective catching of breath as it finally dawned on even the dimmest Sumerian that they had been had.

Tricked. Bamboozled. Led around by the nose. Sold a bill of goods, a pig in a poke, a cat in a sack.

A collective howl of outrage went up that filled the stairwell with such cacophony that Ori clapped hands to ears.

'He's been using us! He isn't on our side! We're out of here!' And they turned to go back down the stairs.

This was more easily said than done: no matter which way they started the fleeing crowds couldn't seem to get any closer to the exits. The stairs seemed perversely designed to keep them going up and bit, down a bit, around a bit, back and forth…it was maddening and futile. The wailing grew louder.

So did the hum in the structure. Now the sound developed overtones, broke into individual notes, formed a chord.

It was not a pleasant chord.

It was, in fact, a flatted fifth. The building began to vibrate.

The vibration reached into Ori's mostly hollow bones. Ori looked up and gasped: the top of the stairwell was swirling. And in the vortex generated by that circling spacetime, a gate was being opened. Just a crack. Slowly.

Nimrod saw it and rushed toward the portal. As far as he was concerned, immortality was within his grasp. He crowed in anticipation of triumph.

'Oh, no, you don't!' said Ori.

Grabbing a loaded crossbow from a startled soldier, Ori swung it upward, aimed, and fired.

Nimrod was caught in the shoulder. 'Wha-?' he grunted in surprise. He fell, head over heels, down the empty space of the stairwell.

At the same moment several other things happened.

The portal closed abruptly, as if a connection had been broken.

The vibration of the Tower increased in frequency. The annoying chord became louder and jumped up an octave.

The confused crowds gazed openmouthed at the plummeting dictator.

And directly in front of Ori, another portal opened. It was the Penthouse Paternoster.

'Get in!' yelled a voice from inside.

The Tower had begun to warp and change shape, as if the walls were attempting origami on themselves. The sound reached a pitch that could only be heard by dogs and angels.

Below, the dog howled.

Ori jumped into the Paternoster.

Chapter 18: All Hell Breaks Loose, and Then It Doesn't

Ori was glad to be inside the Paternoster but had no intention of leaving the Tower just yet – not until it was clear what was going to happen to all the people inside. Fortunately, the Paternoster showed no sign of departure. With difficulty, Ori averted eyes from the chaotic scene outside the haven and looked at the panel that had appeared, for the first time, beside the opening of the Paternoster.

Ori activated the STOP button just to be sure. And looked outside to see what was happening.

Nimrod's fall had been broken when he caught his robe on a low-level newel post. Unable to extricate himself, the little dictator was loudly cursing and calling for help – help that was not forthcoming. The guards, as panicked as the rest of the crowd inside the roiling Tower, were rushing about madly seeking exits.

Exits that had completely disappeared.

The Tower itself was shuddering, its walls expanding and contracting with a periodicity that kept increasing and decreasing with the fluctuations in tone of the sound it emitted – a sound which was not pleasant to Ori's ears. The people didn't seem to like it, either: some tried to cover their ears, others covered their children's ears, still others hastily wrapped cloths around their heads, trying vainly to shut out the persistent whine as they continued stumbling about in search of a way out of this madness.

Guards had dropped their weapons, although not before a few had fired arrows in random directions. The arrows hit no one and went nowhere: they seemed to lose velocity almost immediately. Some fell down the stairwell, a few raining down around Nimrod's head, much to Ori's satisfaction. Others, curiously, hovered in the air before being sucked upwards (outwards? Inwards?) into the vortex. Everywhere Ori looked, there was shouting and confusion and panic.

All hell has broken loose here was Ori's thought.

Then something even more inexplicable happened.

The hum in the Tower changed pitch again, to about 1050 Hertz. It got louder. The sound was disturbing, but – incredibly to Ori – it had the effect of slowing the people down. Instead of rushing about in a panic, they were now proceeding in orderly lines toward the nearest door.

The doors themselves were lining up just this side of the Vortex.

The whole procedure was chilling. A glimpse of the faces passing by the entrance to the Paternoster showed why: they didn't look frightened anymore. In fact, their faces bore no expression at all. They seemed to be sleepwalking.

'Hey!' Ori shouted to them above the whine. 'I'm over here! Anybody want a ride?' Two people turned to look at him, their faces blank. Showing no interest, they turned their gaze back to the staircase and continued their slow movement toward the nearest portal.

'This is madness,' said Ori aloud. 'Where are they going?'

'You wouldn't believe me if I told you,' said Prajapati's voice audibly. Ori looked around for the source of the sound: the voice appeared to be coming from a loudspeaker located in the ceiling of the Paternoster compartment.

'Where in creation are they all headed?' Ori said again.

Prajapati chuckled. **'Where in creation, indeed? I'll explain, but let's get a better view of things. Mash me a couple of buttons, please: first press 18, and then GO.'**

With a shrug, Ori did so. *What have we got to lose?*

To Ori's alarm (but not much, this was an alarming day), the Paternoster started to move, not up, down, or sideways, but diagonally, the way it had after the brouhaha in the Garden. The Paternoster went to the right and slightly upwards. The unexpected motion threw Ori against the wall, where, fortunately, there were convenient handholds. Emergency movement, for the gripping of, during, or something. Ori held tight, with involuntarily closed eyes.

When Ori opened them again, all was utter silence. At least, that insistent whine had stopped. Ori looked out the Paternoster opening and saw…

…space. Or something like it.

'Are we still in the world? Creation, I mean?' Ori found the view from the Paternoster alarming. Out among the stars – or whatever the stars looked like at this level of reality – were blobs of murky light, irregular in shape. They didn't look stable, those blobs.

Prajapati answered, **'Yes. Only it wouldn't have been in creation if you hadn't helped me by relocating the Paternoster inside the Tower. Thank you for that.'**

'Glad to do it,' replied Ori. 'Especially if that keeps all the people in your world rather than some half-baked exo-reality of Nimrod's. That man couldn't even engineer a city, let alone a universe.'

In reply, there was a sigh from Prajapati. **'You're getting the idea, kid. We've got to save them from themselves. At least we have temporary holding facilities.'**

'Temporary doesn't sound very reassuring,' said Ori doubtfully.

A deeper sigh. **'It isn't. We've got them in our world, sort of. But those spacetime matrices you're looking at? They won't hold. They're made up of half-baked ideas and general hubris, and held together with stubbornness, and driven by desire. Not a good combination. Like I said, temporary. Right now, they're in stasis. They'll collapse, eventually, once we let them run again.'**

Ori looked at the blobs in spacetime. They looked…lonely, out there among the stars. 'We've got to rescue them, haven't we?'

Prajapati's voice sounded as sad as Ori felt. **'Yes, my friend, we have. And all we have to do it with is you and me. And the Paternoster, of course. And a few tricks I'd have up my sleeve, if I had sleeves. Let me tell you what I have in mind.'**

Ori, wings folded, legs crossed, chin in hands, listened while Prajapati explained how. It took quite a while.

But then, they weren't going anywhere in a hurry.

Chapter 19: Decision Time

Ori and Prajapati talked for a long time. At least, Prajapati talked, and Ori mostly listened, occasionally interjecting comments like, 'Oh, wow!' and 'Wait a minute, how does that work?' Mostly, Ori just nodded.

Ori was any deity's ideal audience.

Of course, the 'long time' business was relative, too. There weren't any clocks where they were. Water wasn't flowing. Sand wasn't running. Suns weren't casting shadows. Even atoms weren't oscillating. Just two friends talking, mind to mind, about the problems nobody else was thinking about, but should have been because, let's face it, those problems were the ones causing spacetime to collapse all over the place.

And when you considered that spacetime was the only place most of the sentient beings in the universe had to live in – in fact, all of the sentient beings in the universe other than Prajapati and Ori – it was kind of an urgent problem. Of course, Prajapati could have just started over: wrapped the whole mess into a ball of pre-causal dough and tossed it out in a big bang of reinvention. But Prajapati wasn't willing to do that – and neither was Ori. So with the two friends in agreement, the only thing left to do was rescue the other x-billion sentient beings from the consequences of their own hapless folly.

That, as Prajapati explained, would involve getting them extricated from the collapsing spacetime matrices in which they were entangled – so that he could relocate them to models based on a saner rationale.

'Hopefully without Nimrods,' was Ori's comment.

Prajapati chuckled. 'Totally without Nimrods. Or better put, with Nimrods in their proper places. You'll see. At least, I hope you will. But that's where you come in.'

There followed another round of explanation and more nodding, coupled with a lot of 'you don't say' and 'seriously?'

Prajapati's voice grew wistful, almost sad. 'I can't make this decision for you, my friend. You'll have to work it out for yourself. So I'm going to leave you alone for a bit. Take all the time you need: the universe isn't going anywhere until you do.'

And Ori sat at the doorway to the Paternoster for what seemed a long time and studied the worlds.

As Ori sat thinking, sounds drifted upwards (outwards? inwards?) from the various muddled spheres.

'Μολων λαβε'

'Veni, vidi, vici!'

'Deus vult!'

'L'Etat, c'est moi!'

'Liberté, egalité, fraternité!'

'Gott strafe England!'

'Hell no, we won't go!'

Plus a discordant chorus of conflicting music, from *We Shall Overcome* to *I'm Proud to Be an American*, mixed in with cannon fire on the beat. It made Ori's head hurt.

How can I deal with it all? Ori thought.

A new sound reached Ori's ears, and a new sight appeared: another Paternoster. And standing in it, another angel. Ori stared.

It had never occurred to Ori to look in a mirror – not since the unfortunate snake incident. But there was something eerily familiar about this new angel. It looked a lot like Ori: two wings, thin build, red hair. But the new angel carried itself (himself? There was something rather human/masculine about the figure) with a bit of a swagger. And the face…bore a definite sneer. Overall, this person demonstrated a sort of knowingness that proclaimed, 'I am cool. I am the very definition of cool. Also, I know all your secrets. And I'm not impressed.'

Ori took an instant dislike to this person.

'Hi, there,' said the newcomer. The voice grated on Ori's ear. There was an unpleasant edge to it. The kind of edge that warned Ori: *Do not buy a used chariot from this guy.*

'Hello yourself,' replied Ori sharply. 'Just who in the universe are you?'

The figure in the other Paternoster gave a bow, at once more elegant than anything Ori could have managed, and at the same time mocking. Ori frowned.

'My name,' said the newcomer as if making a stage pronouncement, 'is Noiro. I am the Crown Prince of the Multitude of Worlds. I know, you're pleased to meet me.'

In a pig's eye, thought Ori, but said aloud, 'Hi. Just who made you a prince of anything? The only princes I know of are in Sumeria, and they aren't terribly useful.'

'I am worshipped throughout these worlds,' claimed Noiro with a sweeping gesture that took in the vista of planets before them. 'I am compounded of all their desires – peace through conquest, safety through paranoia, plenty through greed, knowledge through espionage, popularity through gossip… You name it. I know all their little tricks, you see, and yet…' he winked, 'unlike you and that stick-in-the-mud Prajapati, I accept them for who they are. In fact, I encourage them. You see, I want them to be happy. And they are. So…' he spread his hands in an expansive gesture, 'I am their prince.'

Ori's eyes narrowed. 'I'm sure you're very popular. But I've got a boatload of problems to solve and I don't think you're helping.'

The response was a big, booming laugh from Noiro. The sinister-but-handsome angel (even Ori had to admit he was handsome) stepped boldly out of his Paternoster, wings spread. Looking around, he whistled to a small passing asteroid, which obediently scuttled over so that he could sit on it, which he did, rather regally.

'Here, have one yourself,' offered Noiro. With a sigh, Ori stepped out of the Paternoster (the original!), and reluctantly sat down on the proffered space rock. It wasn't soft, but Ori wasn't fussy.

'What do you want?' asked Ori, ready to hear this strange creature out.

Noiro smiled. It was not a really nice smile: more a 'have-I-got-a-deal-for-you' smile. Ori was reminded again of the used chariot dealers in Warka.

'I want to offer you a deal,' Noiro said in a voice obviously intended to be persuasive.

Can't read my mind, anyway, thought Ori and said aloud, 'Go ahead.'

'First of all, you want to solve the problem of these collapsing worlds, right?' Noiro gestured at the worlds. 'I know what these people want: enough to eat, shelter, consumer goods, plenty of plenty of.' He leaned forward as if imparting a great secret. 'Just give them what they want. They'll be happy!'

'And the spacetime will collapse the following Tuesday!' snorted Ori. 'What one wants in order to be happy makes ten others utterly miserable. And when they have what they want today, tomorrow they want more. Some can't be happy unless they're making somebody else miserable. And all this getting tears great gaping holes in the spacetime continuum. Try again.'

Noiro sighed dramatically. 'I can see you're a sharp customer. Well-reasoned, that! Tell you what I'm going to do: I'll let you in on some inside dope. The big secret to spacetime management is – power! You gotta have it. You gotta use it. Make 'em fear you. Make 'em do what you want. Need to curb their acquisitiveness? Just set up some boundaries…and penalties. Enforce your will.'

Noiro's eyes lit up as he leaned forward confidentially, 'Between you and me? An angel can run these places with one wing tied behind their back. Fella, we've got superpowers! Compared to these puny mortal nitwits, we are gods! The genuine article. That's why they're always trying to find us. Name us. Make statues of us – okay, not very good ones, I've never seen an angel with the head of a fish, have you?' At Ori's involuntary headshake, Noiro went on, encouraged, 'See? Show 'em what's what. Do some flying around. I recommend a very public place, like the city's main square. Leap off a temple, or something. You'll have them eating out of your hand. What do you say?'

Ori's eyeroll would have been the envy of every teenager in Warka. 'You're a nincompoop, is what I say. We don't want to micromanage spacetime. We want to *participate* in it. The name of the game is interactivity. This being-a-god-and-setting-rules stuff is completely useless. As long as people can't work with each other, as long as they think of life as 'us-versus-them' rather than 'us-all-together', they aren't ready for their world to be self-tutorial. And they aren't ready for Prajapati to come live with them and make it a forever world.'

Noiro nodded in pretended comprehension. 'You're a tough sell, Ori. I can tell you know what you want. And you drive a hard bargain. So I'll tell you what I'm gonna do. I can't believe I'm saying this – I'm crazy for making this offer – but here goes…'

He leaned so close Ori could feel his breath. It smelled like mint. I'll bet he sucked on a lozenge before he showed up, thought Ori.

Noiro grinned, showing pearly teeth. 'The real secret, of course, isn't power. You were right to be suspicious of that. That's just what we tell the punters. The real key to manipulating humans is…desire. They all want. Constantly. That's all they ever do. They want, and want, and want some more. And nothing is ever enough. They get what they want, tomorrow there's a new want. They get a house? Great, they want a bigger one. A better one. One that's more imposing than the neighbour's. You get me.' He clapped Ori on the shoulder.

'The way we can interface with them is to grant their wishes,' he said, 'but only once they do what we want. It's a win/win, really. So, so simple. And here's my offer, friend, today only and a real bargain.'

Once again the mint breath as Noiro whispered in Ori's ear, 'Let me take over. You let me do the steering. You don't want to be their god? No problem! Let me take over the job. I'll hand them over to you, signed, sealed, and delivered. Just let us have our fun first.' He'd finally finished talking, had Noiro, but he didn't sit back on his rock. Instead, he pressed his advantage, squeezing Ori's shoulder harder, hoping to 'close the deal.'

Ori could hear Prajapati, who whispered something in Ori's ear. Ori nodded and turned to Noiro.

'You're right about desire, you know,' Ori said quietly. 'And about power, and need and appetite, too. But you're wrong about how to use these things to fix the problem.'

Ori stood up, grasping Noiro's arm with a strength that seemed to surprise the other angel. 'What I really need from you, friend, is knowledge. An understanding of how humans act and react. Of what's going on in their noggins. That's what Prajapati and I need to help them out of the dilemma they're in. We know what to do once we stop reacting to all these counterintuitive bits of mass drama. We just need the map. And…'

It was Ori's turn to grin. 'You are the answer to our prayers, you overinflated mass thought form!'

Noiro's eyes grew wide as he sensed danger. He tried to pull away, but Ori held him fast. And then Ori did a very surprising thing.

Ori sang.

The song wasn't terribly long – about a three-minute record's worth. It was loud enough to be heard from one end of creation to the other. And the notes were very, very pure, as if rendered by the purest quadriphonic equipment in all the universe.

The notes caused the worlds to dance, changing places with each other. The song made the stars twinkle and shine brighter. The melody drew the two Paternosters together, where they whirled in their own private dance and morphed through 42 dimensions at once – which would have made even an angel's eyes water, if any angel had been looking.

Instead, the angels – the real one and the fake construct with the sick grin – were staring at each other. As Ori sang, Noiro seemed to shrink, and then expand – like a balloon, growing thinner and thinner until he became completely transparent and almost totally round. As Ori sang the last, lingering note, Noiro simply went poof! In his place, in Ori's hand, there was a small, round thing, like a pill. Or a piece of candy.

Ori tasted it. Chocolate, Ori thought, and swallowed.

Chapter 20: The Shape of Things to Come

The taste of chocolate was accompanied by a burst of activity in Ori's head. Worlds opened. Aha moments exploded with light, sound, and satisfactions of clarity. Things good and bad and in-between made sense in ways completely unanticipated and unanticipatable. Connections were made so fast Ori couldn't keep up with them all. For an immeasurable space of time, the dizzy angel reeled, turning winged cartwheels in the vastness of stars and swirling worlds.

Then Ori's head settled down. It was time to go back into the Paternoster. It, too, had stopped dancing around. It hung there, waiting for occupancy.

The first thing Ori noticed was the back of the shiny lift. It had changed, its gleaming metal replaced with a rather ornate wooden door that seemed at once quaint, out-of-place, forbidding, and inviting.

Ori accepted the invitation. What was on the other side surprised Ori in spite of previous experience in travel in this odd conveyance. Not another forest, or desert, or garden. No towers or terror birds or snakes. Instead, a long, ornate corridor stretched from the portal: a hallway with many doors. Ori decided to take a walk.

There seemed to be nobody around. *There's so much room in here,* thought Ori. *A body could get quite lost. I wonder what's behind all these doors?* Ori walked along, fingers trailing over the polished, carved surfaces of the intricate wooden doors. A sign on one door caught Ori's eye: Library. Ori opened the door and went in.

Cavernous, ornate, imposing. Spacious and cluttered at the same time. A good kind of clutter, Ori decided. Lots to read here, lots to learn. Ori plucked a book at random.

Julius Caesar de vita et temporibus suis: quid facere se putaret, quid alii facere putarent, quid faciendum sibi videretur. Appendix ad Indicem gravioris aetatis C. Iulii Caesaris, inde a Felice Sutore.

'Julius Caesar, his life and times,' Ori translated (although there was nobody around to translate to, it was just a habit), 'what he thought he was doing, what other people thought he was doing, what we know he was doing. Appendix list of Julius Caesar's more important contemporaries, starting with Felix the Shoemaker.'

'This is really useful stuff,' said Ori. That whole stack of shelves held books on Rome, from its republic through the imperial period. Maps were included, from giant foldout atlases to a handy set of road maps (Via Appia, Via Aurelia, Via Egnatia, et cetera) conveniently made of vellum, artfully folded for pocketing.

A closer inspection indicated that these books were not limited to contemporary accounts. In addition to what a Roman of a particular time might have expected to read – say, Suetonius or Tacitus – there were books written centuries later. Even more interestingly, some of these books weren't written by humans.

Hannibal: My Part in His Story by Elufil the Elephant. The author even included a self-portrait. 'Elephants are good artists,' commented Ori. Obviously the Library (Ori had already started thinking of it with a capital L) offered a very diverse set of perspectives.

Ori spent a long time wandering the Library's stacks and sampling the works, that covered aspects of history (human) and culture (mostly human) around the blue-marble planet and from age to age.

Learnèd tomes with copious footnotes. Monographs and academic journals.

Novels, collections of short stories and poetry. Voice recordings of oral-formulaic epic poetry. Films.

Volumes of music. (Ori almost got lost in that section.) Recordings, too.

Newspapers, the good and the trashy. And then the utterly trashy.

Graphic novels. History lessons in graphic novel form. Propaganda in graphic novel form (which made Ori slightly nauseous).

Posters. Paintings. Coffee-table volumes of art. Films of art historians explaining art that put Ori to sleep.

After a refreshing art-historian-induced nap, Ori decided to leave the Library, a bit reluctantly, and do some further exploring. Pausing only to give the giant floor-mounted globe a playful twist, Ori headed out the ornate doors and back into the mysterious corridor.

After peeking through doors marked 'Dining Room' (sumptuously decorated) and 'Kitchen' (so fully equipped Ori wasn't sure what half of those things did), Ori came to one that said 'Bedroom'. It was…amazing.

'Just what I needed for a restful night,' decided Ori. In addition to a bed, there was a tall perch in the room, perfect for sleeping with wings folded.

Further investigation revealed other rooms, other purposes. But to Ori, the pièce de résistance was the one labelled 'Dressing Room'.

Ori explored the outfits on offer: togas, djellabas, robes. Pantaloons, hose, trousers, blue jeans. Suits from every era.

Dresses, too. Ori puzzled over farthingales and hoop skirts.

Then Ori discovered a codpiece and had to go back to the kitchen for water and a spoonful of sugar to quell the hiccups that followed a prolonged fit of laughter.

Back to the Dressing Room. Ori surveyed what seemed like miles of human costuming.

'The way I figure it,' said Ori, 'I can either open a theatre with the planet's largest repertoire, or…'

'…do a LOT of damage to their history.'

Now it was Prajapati's turn to laugh. The room shook with the sound of it.

Chapter 21: Of Fig Trees and Other Parables

The sun shone down on Sumeria, just as hot and merciless as it was before the great Tower collapse – which, apparently, nobody in Warka had heard about. On its busy streets, people were going about their business as usual. Near the five-legged lamassu the same women were sitting and gossiping.

'Did you hear the latest? The foreign princess is actually opening a new school for the palace children!'

The other one sniffed. 'Well, I never! *Our* schools weren't good enough, I suppose. How does she get away with it?'

'She's got some kind of degree in school-running, or whatever. Anyway, I wouldn't let my children go there.'

'I don't suppose you'd get invited, anyway. Probably just the nobility.'

'Well, even if I did, I wouldn't say yes. Things used to be better. She didn't have any influence at all when Prince Nimrod was around. But he's disappeared and the palace is going to pieces.'

'I wonder what happened to him.'

'Well, I heard…' conspiratorial whisper, '…that it was *aliens*.'

A loud laugh interrupted their whispering. The two women looked up in alarm to see Ori, back in Sumerian scribe costume, walking past them. Ori bowed ironically in passing.

'Oh! It's just that weird young sage. I swear they get stranger every day.'

'Maybe he knows what happened to Prince Nimrod. But I'm not going to ask him.'

Indeed I do, thought Ori, *but I wouldn't tell* you. Leaving the gossip klatch to work out their own salvation, if not with fear and trembling then with titbits of third-hand calumny, Ori proceeded to the market square, there to purchase a mattock, a bucketful of manure, a potted plant, and a box of sweets. Ori kept walking, toward a familiar residential neighbourhood, humming quietly, 'My lord, what a morning...'

At Zimah and Enlil's house, Ori was welcomed by Zimah, who said Enlil was at their food stand for the breakfast customers. Ori gave Zimah the potted plant – a lily – for her garden. The sweets were for the children, who were happy to see Ori (and to receive the sweets). Their mom let them have 'one apiece for right now, I'll hold the rest so you don't spoil your lunch.' They all went out to play except for Zu, who stayed with his mother, and Gibil, who followed Ori out into the garden out of curiosity, chattering all the way.

'They don't do things right, you know,' he was saying. 'There are rules.' Gibil was a very orderly boy and concerned with proper procedure. Ori nodded sagely while setting down the bucket of manure. Ori directed Gibil's attention to the family's fig tree, which wasn't doing too well.

'What do you reckon is wrong with this fig tree?' Ori asked the little boy.

Gibil stroked his chin in solemn reflection. 'It didn't grow any figs this year,' he replied.

Ori studied the unhappy foliage. 'Why do you think that is?'

Gibil shrugged. 'Maybe because the dog peed on it too many times. Or we didn't get enough rain at the right time.'

'What ought we to do with it, do you think?'

Gibil thought hard. Ori could see how hard he was thinking. Then he sighed. 'I guess we could dig it up and plant another one.'

Ori nodded. 'We could do that. But fig trees are expensive. And they take time to grow. Let's give this one another chance, why don't we?' And Ori picked up the mattock from the marketplace and began digging around the tree. Seeing what Ori was doing, Gibil ran to the garden shed and returned with a small digging stick. Together, the two friends loosened the soil, removing weeds and breaking up clods of earth.

'That's good,' said Ori finally. 'Now, this part may be a little smelly.' Ori scooped up some of the manure and began spreading it around the fig tree.

'What is that?' Gibil made big eyes.

Ori laughed. 'It's animal poop. But we can call it fertiliser. It will make the soil around the tree better. The nutrients will feed the tree. Can you help me mix it up?'

Gibil went to work with the digging stick and helped Ori mix the fertiliser into the soil. It was hot, dusty work and took quite a while. When they were done, Zimah called to them both to come and get cool drinks.

'And wash your hands, you two! I don't want that stuff in here!'

Ori and Gibil washed their hands and walked through the house into the cool inner courtyard for lunch with Zimah, Enlil (back from work), and the rest of the kids. Gibil proudly explained what they'd been doing all morning.

'And that's the right way to do it!' Gibil explained, somewhat patronisingly, which made the older children laugh.

'Never mind, you did fine,' said his mother when she saw Gibil frown.

Dagan asked Ori, 'Will we water the fig tree now?'

Headshake from Ori. 'No, not yet. The sun's too high now. If you water the plants when the sun is high, the water will evaporate too quickly. This is bad for the plant and will leave it thirsty. Wait until the sun goes down. Water it in the evening. Remember to pour the water at the base of the tree so that it soaks down to the roots.'

'Will you come back and show us?' Ori looked at Zimah, who nodded.

'We'd like it if you came for dinner,' she said.

Ori smiled. 'I'd like that, too. I have something else for the children and it will take some time to tell the tale.'

'Hurrah!' shouted the kids, both because their favourite 'grownup' (how grown up are angels, anyway?) was coming back, and because the purpose of the visit was to talk to them, not boring grownup stuff.

After lunch, the family went off for a nap (it was too hot to be messing about this time of year), and Ori, who didn't mind the heat, headed back to the temple scriptorium. There, Ori spent some time writing and copying a new text ('one without any fart jokes') and having a long, intense conversation with Bidi. Ori swore Bidi to temporary secrecy by the most solemn oaths of the gods, and somehow managed to keep a straight face while doing it. Bidi bound himself by powerful vows of honour to follow Ori's instructions to the letter and to make sure that the cuneiform tablet with which he had now been entrusted would never be altered or interfered with in his lifetime.

Of course, Bidi was in seventh heaven about all this. After all, this was BIG. How many Sumerian priests got to be the bearers of revelatory, even prophetic, texts like this? This was a career high for Bidi, and he began to carry himself with extra added dignity after this.

Ori, chuckling, went back to the apprentice priests' quarters to wash up and collect a few things. Ori looked around the place for the last time, thinking how surprising this particular part of the journey had been.

'Thanks for everything,' Ori whispered. 'I wish I could take a picture for those future archaeologists, but it wouldn't be fair.' There was a quiet chuckle, which only Ori heard.

Evening came to Warka. Ori sat with Zimah and Enlil and the children around a brazier. They'd had a tasty dinner and watered the fig tree. Gibil felt that it already looked healthier. Now it was time for Ori to give the children their present.

Ori took out a cuneiform tablet. Zimah and Enlil looked interested but the kids looked disappointed. They were hoping for something more exciting, like maybe a camel.

'I have a legacy for you,' said Ori solemnly. 'You're going to be the story-bearers for your generation.'

This sounded more important: the kids perked up. 'Do we get to read it to people?' asked Anunit. Ori nodded.

'You have to learn to read first,' scoffed Zana.

'I can read!' protested Anunit, 'and I can write my name!'

Ori smiled. 'You can take your time,' said Ori. 'And in the meantime, Dagan can read it for you. Would you like to read it to us now, Dagan?' Dagan took the tablet and frowned over the text. Clearing his throat, he began to read.

> *And the whole Earth was of one language, and one speech....*

'Wait!' protested Gibil. 'You can't tell it like that!'

'Why not?' asked Ori mildly.

'That's not the way it's done! You have to say things like, King Hashemi, ruler of the five waters, defeater of enemies, beloved of the gods, ruled long and wisely in the lands of the plains, 400 years he ruled, feared by his foes, worshipped by his people...'

There was a groan from Dagan, who heard this sort of thing in school. The rest of the family laughed. Ori smiled.

'Gibil, you will make a wonderful scribe one day. But let me tell this my way. I want even the uneducated to understand this tale.' There was general agreement that this was a good way to start the story. Eventually, even Gibil was convinced – well, sort of – and Zu started chanting, 'One language, one language...' until his mother gave him a sweet.

Then everybody had to take a sweet break before Dagan could continue.

> *...the whole Earth was of one language, and one speech.*
> *And it came to pass, as they journeyed from the east, that they*
> *found a plain in the land of Shinar; and they dwelt there.*

Gibil approved of 'and it came to pass' as a suitably official-sounding phrase. Enlil commented, 'I'm beginning to see where this is going.' Ori nodded encouragement at Dagan.

> *And they said one to another, Go to, let us make brick, and burn*
> *them thoroughly. And they had brick for stone, and slime had they*
> *for mortar.*

'Go to!' giggled Anunit and Zu said, 'Go to!' until he got the hiccups. Zimah rubbed his back.

'At this rate, I'll never get finished!' complained Dagan, and Zana agreed. 'It will be way past our bedtime if we don't let Dagan read.' So everybody settled down.

> *And they said, Go to, let us build us a city and a tower, whose top may reach unto heaven; and let us make us a name, lest we be scattered abroad upon the face of the whole earth.*
>
> *And the Builder's Messenger came down to see the city and the tower, which the children of men builded...*

(Ori had done some creative wording here.)

> *And the Messenger reported to the Builder and said, Behold, the people is one, and they have all one language; and this they begin to do: and if they keep this up very long, they will make an unholy mess out of the universe;*
>
> *And besides, they won't learn anything, because they don't have the right words. Also, they don't know the answers because they haven't figured out the questions yet. And people are getting left out of their stories. What we need here is more diversity.*

There, they'd said it.

> *Go to, let us go down, and there confound their language, that they may not understand one another's speech.*
>
> *So the Builder scattered them abroad from thence upon the face of all the earth: and they left off to build the city.*

'That's all,' said Dagan, and bowed to his audience, who applauded. They were quiet for a long minute as each one tried to absorb the import of what they had heard.

'So that's what happened,' said Zimah softly. She squeezed her husband's hand.

Ori nodded. 'More or less. But don't worry, all the people are safe. The non-Sumerian-speaking ones have, er, migrated elsewhere.'

'I'm glad we didn't go,' said Zana. 'I would miss my friends.' The other children nodded.

Ori hugged them all. 'I'm glad you didn't, too. There's plenty of time to go wandering when you're bigger. In the meantime, please keep this tablet for me. You can tell the story to all your friends.'

They promised.

After that there were snacks, and a bit of singing, and a lot of laughter. All too soon, it was time for the kids to go to bed. Ori and the adults sat around the fire, reluctant to end the evening. Ori explained that there were errands to run, and places to go, but promised to try and return if possible. Enlil and Zimah wished their friend safe travels.

There were tears at the door.

Walking through the now-quiet city, looking up at the stars, Ori thought, *Let the party begin…*

At the end of a blind alley where no one was looking, the Paternoster waited. Ori got in.

Chapter 22: One is the Loneliest Number

For a long while, Nimrod hung helplessly from the newel post in the madly pulsating Tower. He shouted orders – after all, that was his job, right, to give orders? But nobody paid any attention. The stupid guards were too busy firing arrows that went nowhere.

Well, not exactly nowhere: as soon as they lost velocity the arrows dropped like…something that drops, he guessed, and fell down. Mostly on him. He got several scratches.

'Idiots,' he muttered as he concentrated on the main task before him, which was to extricate his robe from the newel post so that he could deal with the crisis. The agenda appeared in his mind's eye, pressed into fresh clay, as

1. Free self.
2. Assess situation vis-à-vis populace.
3. Round up guards.
4. Fire half of them, put the other half to work.

Nimrod lived by plans and schedules. He'd always been organised: even as a toddler, he'd astonished his nannies by announcing that he, and not they, would henceforth be in charge of his daily routine. He had made charts with his own homemade symbols.

'Sunup, I get up. I eat breakfast. I go poop. We go walkies. I say hi to Mama and her new boyfriend.'

There was always a new boyfriend. Nimrod's Mama was a 'power behind the throne' type of woman, adept at using her personal charm and considerable skill at insider politics to navigate the Sumerian power scene. Princess Enheduanna was a mover and a shaker, and Nimrod was mostly an inconvenience to her, as her late husband had been. Nimrod knew this. It would have been an understatement to say that his childhood had influenced the direction of his life. His first experience of his mother's indifference had engendered in Nimrod a howling rage so deep that it encompassed the whole planet – and reached to heaven itself. Nobody would ever reject Nimrod again, he vowed, because nobody would ever get the chance. *He'd* control the narrative. And he'd organise his life. Organisation was one of his two great strengths.

The other was boldness. In Nimrod's view, everybody on Earth was a coward and a hypocrite except him. They knew what they wanted, only they didn't go after it. They played by the *rules*. They were afraid to seize the moment, grab the limelight, push themselves forward. Not him, not Nimrod: he had the nerve to do what others only dreamed of.

Want that vineyard? Who do I have to bribe? Want to build here, and not there? Who do I know on the zoning board, and what's his weakness?

See that attractive woman? What's her price? Everybody has one. Anything can be bought, sold, negotiated: anyone can be persuaded. You just have to find their pressure points. Nimrod was good at pressure points. He never had to fight – let's face it, in spite of all that 'mighty hunter before Marduk' stuff, he didn't even hunt. He had *people* for things like that.

Tired of worrying about the approval of the gods? He'd figured out where they lived – and led the charge up there. Now, finally, relief was in his grasp: relief from the gnawing sense of being unloved that he'd had all his life. If he owned the gods, he owned the world, right? He could *give* people things. Lovely, shiny things. And everybody would love him, forever…the plan was working nicely, too: look at this magnificent Tower, look at all the people doing what he wanted them to…look at…

'Hey, where did everybody go?' His voice echoed in the cavernous stairwell. Nimrod looked around: the place was completely empty…almost.

'They've all gone to the places they will be from.' Who was that?

Oh, no, that smartass emissary from the *Annunaki*, the council of the gods. Didn't wait for him to come to them, showing up to interfere. Must be responsible for all this.

'Who the hell are you, angel? And what do you want from me?'

The angel smiled a crooked smile. It was unnerving, that smile: it started out sweet and then went sad and wistful, only to leave the observer with an aftertaste of vague menace. Nimrod disliked it and fiercely envied it in equal measure. 'I don't want anything from you,' shrugged the celestial being. 'You've already done everything nicely, as far as I can tell.'

'What is that supposed to mean? I wasn't doing this for you lot!' The truth slipped out before Nimrod could catch himself. No: he did this for himself. How dare they lay claim to his great act of rebellion?

The angel chuckled wryly. 'There is a divinity that shapes our ends, rough-hew them how we will. And,' the gesture took in the vastness of their mad surroundings, 'you've been doing some interesting rough-hewing, I'd say.'

Nimrod was tired of being jerked around. 'I'm tired of being jerked around!' he shouted, pointing his finger imperiously at the heavenly messenger. 'I want a straight answer! Where did everybody go?'

The god looked pensively into imaginary distances, blue eyes unfocused as if seeing scenes that weren't there. 'Some here, some there. They all went wherever they most desired to go. Don't worry,' again that smile, 'they'll be okay. Once they work it out. They've chosen their paths: the rest will sort itself.'

Nimrod practically exploded. 'They aren't supposed to be somewhere else! They're supposed to be in your living room! And I'm supposed to be with them! Why am I here? And why are they there?' *And what am I going to do about it all?* Nimrod's brain was working feverishly, as usual, calculating angles. And wondering where his very expensive guards had got to. Guards he was going to fire if they didn't deliver the goods.

The angel sighed. 'It's like this. You've opened rather a lot of spacetime portals here. Everybody just...went. To wherever looked most attractive to them. A metaphysical scholar somewhere out there...' again the encompassing gesture...'will one day refer to it as 'jumping in the direction of your predilection.' Nobody's predilection included being in a crazy room full of staircases and no falafel stands, so nobody's here now.'

'Except you,' the being added helpfully. 'I mean, it was your idea to build this, so you're invested in it.'

'Yes, but I was invested in its having *people* in it!' spluttered Nimrod. This was really maddening. Didn't the guy get that?

The angel chuckled. 'The problem is, you can't actually control anybody else's desires but your own. Sure, *you* want them to be here. But *they* don't. So they aren't. They're wherever they chose to be. It won't be perfect there: they can't have it all their own way, any more than you can. But at least they'll be getting somewhere.'

'Don't worry, though! You can join whatever group you like.' This time the angel's smile was encouraging. Nimrod leapt to his feet. This was the best news he'd heard all day.

'Sure! I want to go with the most forward-thinking group. The ones looking for a leader to take them into the future. Let's go!' And he headed for what looked like a doorway…

…until he got there. Then, suddenly, it wasn't a doorway. It was some kind of decorative niche.

He tried another staircase. Another doorway. The same thing happened. After half a dozen futile tries, Nimrod turned and glared at the angel. 'What kind of trick is this?'

The *Annunak* shrugged. 'You must really want to be here and not somewhere else. After all, this situation was your doing in the first place.'

Nimrod cursed. 'You could have stopped me! You *wanted* this to happen!'

The angel sighed. 'I tried, remember? You wouldn't be talked out of it. Also, I'm not in charge here. I'm just the messenger.'

'Well, you tell your boss that I'm not going to take this lying down!'

With that pronouncement, Nimrod turned and ran up another staircase. This time, when he got to where the doorway should be, he tried another tack – he barreled right into it, hoping to power through.

It didn't work.

As he lay on the stone floor, rubbing a sore nose, Nimrod asked, 'What will id dake do get oud of here?'

The response was a shrug. 'I don't know, honestly. I'm not you. It could be as simple as realising what's holding you back. Or letting go of your wrong-headed desire to make the whole world pay for something that's really between you and your family.' The angel looked sober. 'On the other hand, you may have to stay here until you die and are reborn with no memory of who you were. I hope not.'

Nimrod looked around the enormous hall. Everywhere he turned, there were stairs. Stairs, and more stairs. At the top of staircases were niches with decorative statues. There were some wall sconces with lamps, and some carpet runners on the floors. The whole thing looked like a very fancy lobby, which it was.

But there was no furniture: no sofas, no beds, not even a hassock to sit on. There were no shelves of clay tablets to read. There were no braziers for cooking. Nor, for that matter, was there any food. There was no water for drinking or washing.

Nimrod had been so busy with his scheme to use sacred geometry to breach the boundaries of spacetime that he had paid no attention to the very nature of what he'd been building – which was supposed to be a place to live and work. He hadn't provided for comfort, or even the basic necessities of life. The Tower was all showy presentation on top of a structure that had one purpose: to lure anyone who entered it into working for Nimrod. It wasn't designed to reward them for it.

And now that building was all Nimrod had. His alone. Realising what this meant, the one-time dictator of Babylon threw back his head and howled.

Nimrods' wail echoed to the farthest reaches of the otherwise-silent Tower. It came back to him as the most melancholy sound in all the universe. He sobbed.

The angel stood up. 'I know what! It's awfully lonely in here, don't you think, with just you? And you might have to wait awhile until you get out…why don't we bring you some companions? Of course, they have to be in the same boat as you…'

'Oh, yes,' said Nimrod, 'that would be lovely, anybody, pleasepleaseplease, only don't leave me in here by myself.'

The *Annunak* produced a flute – and a tune. It was a haunting sound that made the hairs on the back of Nimrod's head stand on end. He'd never heard anything like it – but then, Nimrod had never been much of a music lover. The tune ended on a long, sad note.

As the last note faded in the dry air of the Tower, the niches at the tops of the staircases opened briefly. Through each doorway a figure entered: a man or woman. They were all dressed in some kind of finery – finery from other times and places. They looked like kings and queens, or war leaders. Every one of them looked as baffled as Nimrod had been, and as angry.

One had a laurel wreath and body armour. Another wore a cloth uniform and a metal helmet, with a pearl-handled pistol hanging from his belt. Another had a similar uniform, but with wider trousers. Some wore three-piece tailored suits, others ceremonial robes. One had a pointed hat, others crowns. All looked around them with disdain for anyone who wasn't them.

'What is this?'

'Where am I?'

'Who is in charge here?'

'I demand to see the manager!' This from a very imperious-looking woman whose blonde hair resembled a helmet.

Nimrod turned to the angel for an explanation. 'Who are these people?'

'Your peers, I'm afraid. All the people throughout the spacetime who did the same thing you did: took over positions of responsibility in order to get other people to try to make it up to you for what was missing in your life.'

Nimrod swallowed. 'Did any of them succeed?' The angel replied with a shake of the head – and turned to go.

A cry went up from the assembled leaders of history. 'Wait! We have questions!'

The winged being pointed to Nimrod. 'Your host will explain.' Another long sound on the flute, and a shining silver box appeared in the space above the stairs. The angel flew to the traveling exit and turned to Nimrod one last time.

This time, Nimrod caught a brief look of compassion. 'Good luck,' the angel whispered, and vanished.

Chapter 23: Misery Loves Company

Inside what Ori privately thought of as the Paternoster Annex, that angel was considering the costumes available in the dressing room and wondering which to choose.

'What exciting adventure shall I go on next?' Ori thought. 'I quite fancy this full-bottomed coat in cloth of gold. Maybe with the thigh-high boots.'

A booming laugh interrupted the sartorial musings. **'You'd look pretty funny where you're going next if you showed up in that get-up.'**

'Okay,' replied Ori, 'I'll bite. What should I wear this time?'

An outfit floated off the rack and draped itself over a chair. To Ori's complete dismay, the outfit looked extremely familiar.

'Oh, no!' sighed Ori. 'Don't tell me we're still in Sumeria! I was looking forward to more interesting times.'

'Interesting is a relative notion,' commented Prajapati. 'Besides, these people just happened to land in Sumeria. After all, the place has a really long history. Actually, before they walked into the vortex, they came from every possible place and time: high-tech, low-tech, temperate zone, tropics, desert…you name it.'

'So how did they end up in Sumeria together?' Ori wanted to know.

'They…have certain things in common,' was the reply. **'You'll see.'**

'I guess I will,' sighed Ori and put on the costume again.

'You're headed for the Tigris this time,' was all Prajapati would say.

****

Once again, the sun shone brightly down on baked mud brick. Once again, people thronged the marketplaces. Once again, Ori listened to chatter and gossip.

'Have you heard this one? A dog walked into a tavern and…'

'Mommy, what is that bird in the cage called?'

At least six old men nearby turned and with one voice yelled, 'Mushen[2]!'

Then they all laughed, except for the boy who had asked. He burst out crying. His mama gave the old men dirty looks and took the child off to find a refreshment booth.

A man walked up to a vegetable stand. 'Have you got any, er, lettuce?' He nudged the vegetable seller in the ribs. The vegetable seller rolled his eyes and handed the customer a head of lettuce.

Another passerby – of the ones who'd yelled 'Mushen!' – asked, 'Planning a big night with the missus, are you?' Others sniggered.

---

[2] A Sumerian name that also translates to 'bird'.

The vegetable seller muttered something about not carrying lettuce anymore if they wouldn't learn to behave.

Prajapati said drily, ***It isn't really an aphrodisiac, you know.*** Ori didn't know what to make of it all.

'That's what I like best about Akkad, you know?' said a voice next to Ori's ear. 'It's that wonderful, old-fashioned sense of humour.' Ori turned to see empty space – then adjusted the gaze downward to spot the speaker, a short, rotund, bald man.

'Close your mouth, young man, you'll catch flies,' said the man, jabbing his elbow into Ori's ribs. For such a round person, he had sharp elbows.

'My mouth wasn't open,' Ori started to say, but stopped, looking more closely at the man. It occurred to the messenger that the man didn't really care what Ori had or hadn't done. He was too busy enjoying his own 'joke'.

He was also too busy enjoying himself at the expense of a perfect stranger. Ori gave the man a disapproving look and decided against asking his name. As Ori continued through the marketplace, the man called out, 'No sense of humour, is your problem! Go back where you came from, foreigner!'

Ori spent a while shopping around the various corners of the marketplace. At every stand they told the same terrible jokes – and laughed with glee at the telling of them. In the centre of the marketplace, Ori saw a puppet show going on and stopped to watch it – an act Ori quickly regretted.

'Come here, Iudit! Let me beat you with my stick!' Much chasing about until just about every character fell into the Euphrates and was eaten by a crocodile, who took the last bow. Frankly, by this point, Ori was cheering for the crocodile, too. For a curtain call, the cast of puppeteers came out and sang the most earsplittingly horrible song Ori had ever heard: it was sort of like a series of terrible limericks set to a bombastic operatic aria – and, of course, accompanied by several cast members on kazoos. Ori asked a bystander what the song was.

'Why, the Akkadian anthem, of course! Hey, where do you come from?' Ori moved away quickly.

The Akkadians were also rude and abusive to customers and overcharged whenever they thought they could get away with it. Finally, having failed to find a bench anywhere, Ori sat down on the edge of a rather unattractive fountain.

'Hmpf. Tell me again, Prajapati: you say many people chose to come here based on their predilections?'

Yes, mostly. There are a few, erm, stragglers. We're here to pick them up.

With a shake of the head, Ori decided it was time for lunch and took out the morning's purchases: a reed poke of figs and raisins, some pita loaves, a grape leaf wrapped around some olives, and a jar of very weak beer.

'For some reason, I've bought too much,' commented Ori. 'I'd send you some if I could figure out how.' Prajapati chuckled.

'Hey, mister, could you spare some of that food? We're awfully hungry.'

Ori turned to see two children, both boys, in ragged tunics. Wordlessly, Ori handed out bread and fruit. With nods of thanks, the kids sat down beside Ori and began eating. Ori worried that they were a bit too young for beer, but they gladly drank water from the fountain.

'My name's Ori,' Ori offered and got in return that the boys were Agad and Habik, that they were brothers, and that they and their family had been part of a caravan that had been attacked in the desert. They'd wandered into Akkad and found themselves thoroughly unwelcome. Akkad didn't like strangers one little bit.

'Our dad and mom get odd jobs,' explained Agad, 'But half the time they don't even pay them. They just give us leftovers to eat. They say something about 'Akkad for Akkadians' and tell us to leave town if we don't like it here.'

'We don't like it here,' chimed in Habik. 'But we don't know where else to go. We don't like their terrible jokes, either,' he added. Ori agreed that the jokes were really insufferable.

After they'd all eaten, Ori wanted to go and find the parents right away, but the boys explained that they didn't know where they were. They were due to meet them by the fountain at sundown. Until then, they were on their own. Ori decided to take them under a figurative wing (no real ones in evidence while undercover), and they all set off to see what there was to do while the rest of the citizenry was taking their noon nap.

Aside from the occasional stray dog, nothing and nobody was moving as the trio wandered the narrow, unkempt streets. Ori noticed that the whole place looked neglected. They might be hostile to outsiders, Ori thought, but they don't seem to have much civic pride, either.

That's because they're too selfish to pay for improvements, replied Prajapati. **Each one is convinced that if they did anything for the city, somebody else would get the benefit. They couldn't stand that.**

So rather than see anyone else be happy, they'd rather be miserable themselves?

You're catching on. Ori shrugged and walked on behind the boys, who were leading the way.

'I guess everyone's asleep,' Ori started to say. But Agad shook his head. 'Not everyone. There are some nice people who are awake. Let us show you.' Agad and Habik found the place: a basement door, half-hidden in the ground, that was opened in response to a whispered code phrase.

Inside, the basement was pleasantly cool after the heat outside. That was the first thing Ori noticed. The second was that someone was playing the lyre – and very well, indeed. The boys had been welcomed by some older children who took them off into a corner to play, so Ori sat down gratefully on a floor cushion and listened to the music, which was being played by a young woman of obvious talent.

The music fed Ori's spirit, particularly after spending the morning being assaulted by all the mean-minded 'wit' of the Akkadians.

The lyre seemed to be opening windows in the mind: there were questions here that the universe might possibly, someday, have answers for.

When the little concert was finished, Ori joined the others in applauding the performance. 'That was very beautiful,' he told the musician, whose name turned out to be Zena.

'You're new,' said Zena. 'Hey, guys! Somebody new in town!' Unlike the rest of the Akkadians, Zena and her friends weren't at all hostile to strangers – in fact, they seemed delighted to meet someone new. Anyone, in fact. Agad's explanation that they'd picked up Ori in the marketplace, and that Ori had shared lunch, put the visitor in the group's good books.

'Is this a music club?' asked Ori.

The group laughed. 'Music, poetry, theatre, art, whatever!' said Zena. 'We're starved for anything creative. Have you seen what passes for entertainment around here?'

'I have, indeed,' said Ori, 'and I don't blame you in the least.' Ori met the others – a couple of dozen, all told, in a range of ages from young to very old. All had a similar story to tell: they were weary of the stultifying atmosphere of Akkad. Their relatives barely tolerated them. And they would all leave, if only they could figure out how, and where to go next.

'I may be able to help with that,' said Ori. Since they had to wait until sundown for Agad and Habik's parents, and since everyone was hungry, Ori and Zena headed out for more shopping while the boys went back to the meeting place to wait.

'How long have things been like this?' Ori asked the lyre player as they filled baskets with fruits, vegetables, and fresh bread and butter.

Zena shrugged. 'As long as I can remember. The old ones say that once upon a time, it used to be better. Well, not better, exactly; more like, they had a purpose. Then somehow, something changed. They'd wanted to build a big empire, you see, conquering everybody in sight. But somehow, those other people aren't there now. And there isn't any leadership anymore. Nobody to tell them what to do. The soldiers milled around, and finally disbanded because nobody was paying them. The government sort of folded. Nobody did anything. People are just sort of low-level frustrated. They don't really want to do anything. So they just buy and sell and bully each other.'

They want to do the same things they were doing before, said Prajapati. ***Only now they can't. And if they can't do that, they don't want to do anything else. That's their problem.***

Ori told Zena what Prajapati had said – without trying to explain Prajapati. 'Do you think that could be it?'

Zena nodded. 'Pretty much. It's like they keep telling the same jokes and singing the same songs. They can't do what they want to do, so they won't do anything else.'

They both sighed.

The vendors were closing up their booths for the night as Ori and Zena headed back to the club. On the way, they met up with Agad and Habik and their parents. Introductions were made and the new friends chatted happily as they walked together.

Ori noticed that the group was garnering suspicious glances. More than one whispered conversation was being held that Ori didn't like the sound of. The angel coaxed the others to hurry: apparently there was a curfew and it was fast approaching. They needed to be indoors by first starlight. They were – barely.

Dinner was a pleasant affair: Agad and Habik's parents had managed to get a dozen large duck eggs in payment for a day's work, and their mom and Zena together managed to turn out a beautiful, well-seasoned giant omelet with onions, leeks, peppers, and spices. Pita, bean paste and aubergine salad made a meal the assembled company declared 'fit for a king, at least we're sure a king would have enjoyed it if there were still any kings about.'

After they'd eaten, Zena played the lyre some more. Ori told them all the story about the Tower of Babel, with a few personal remarks about Nimrod. The story was much appreciated.

'It seems to me,' said Agad's father thoughtfully, 'That there have been more people trying to build cities here in Shinar than have a clue about how to build one.'

The others agreed. 'I think this city-building business needs more thought than it's been given,' commented Zena.

'I don't know how I'd go about it exactly,' mused one of the older members. 'But I'm fairly sure there needs to be more…er, variety of people. You know: something besides the idea that there are only so many acceptable roles for people to play in the world.'

There was a chorus of agreement. 'Or acceptable ideas, either!'

'Or ways of looking at things!' chimed in Habik. 'You know, I think the Akkadians always tell the same jokes over and over because they're afraid somebody's going to jump on them for any new jokes or stories.'

'Maybe the reason they pick on other people,' suggested another, 'is that they're afraid somebody's going to pick on them. Pointing fingers takes the pressure off, maybe.' The rest agreed.

'Would you like to go somewhere else with a little more variety?' asked Ori quietly. The others stared.

'Is that possible? How do you know where to go? Have you got any camels?' The questions came one after another. Ori gave vague answers, but generally promised that yes, it was possible to leave and yes, Ori could conduct them safely to another city, and sure, they could go at dawn if everyone was ready.

At which point there was loud banging at the door. They looked at each other in alarm. It sounded like quite a crowd out there – possibly drunk and definitely belligerent.

'Open up in there! We know you're up to no good!'

Ori walked to the door and replied calmly. 'Who's there, please? You shouldn't be out after curfew.'

'We're Akkadian Homeland Security!' was the bellowed reply. 'Let us in RIGHT NOW!'

'Don't let them in!' whispered Zena frantically. 'They do terrible things to people! I've heard about it.' The others also urged Ori not to open the door. Ori, however, had had enough and had another idea.

Throwing open the door, Ori faced the mob – and there was a mob out there, some carrying torches and most of them armed with sticks, spears, or various construction or agricultural implements. They looked ugly in the way that people do who have worked themselves up to do something they secretly know they shouldn't, like attending a cockfight. Or bullying helpless neighbours.

The mob's leaders were about to rush inside when Ori simply abandoned the 'Sumerian citizen' disguise and unfurled an impressive set of wings. This caused gasps on both sides of the doorway: gasps of delight behind Ori, and gasps of dismay in front.

Ori was sorry not to have brought a trumpet along. A blast on something in the brass-instrument line would have been a nice flourish at this point. Besides, the ringleaders of this mob were only temporarily nonplussed by the sight of an angel, it seemed.

'Rush him!' commanded the leader, and they prepared to do just that. Ori beat them off by stirring up a breeze.

Prajapati, I need help, called Ori. And help arrived.

There was a flash of bright light outside the door. Those inside couldn't see it directly. Ori closed nictating membranes against the glare.

The Akkadian mob didn't have nictating membranes.

'Ow! I can't see!'

'Get out of my way, ninny!'

'Watch where you're pointing that thing!'

An entire mob of miscreants, temporarily blinded, stumbled around, knocking things (and each other) down. Flailing about with spears and swords and shields and mattocks and other sharp, pointy things that people shouldn't be pointing at other people – particularly if none of them could see what they were doing.

Oh, and they dropped the torches. Most of them went out in the dusty street. A few flickered dimly – not that any of the crowd could see, anyway.

Ori decided that this was their opportunity. 'Grab your things and follow me!' commanded the angel. The group, astounded, did just that.

Ori might have been exposed as a supernatural being – but this supernatural being was friendly, damn it, and they needed a friend right now. So off they all went, out the back door that came out on the side street and away.

'Is everybody here?' called Ori as they reached the fountain. Ori made them stop and count everyone – then herded them out the nearest side gate and onto the main road out of town.

'Where are we going to go?' asked Zena. 'There's nothing for miles and miles in every direction except desert and bandits. I mean, if we had boats, we could try the Tigris, but it has crocodiles and really big fish.'

'Don't worry,' said Ori. 'Let's just get clear of the city. It looks like there's a storm brewing.'

And indeed there was: some distinctly odd-looking clouds were forming in the sky over Akkad. That was unusual in itself. It wasn't the rainy season. Even stranger was the fact that these clouds didn't seem to be exactly clouds: more like balls of light.

Balls that were getting closer by the minute…

'DUCK!' yelled Ori, and everyone but Ori lay flat on the ground as a ball of fire whizzed over their heads in the direction of the city gates. Ori simply rose above the fireball, which whizzed through the gate. There was an explosion as it hit a building. Then another fireball went up.

The fireballs were falling thick and fast over the city now. People inside were running back and forth, and crowds were pouring out of the gates. None of them paid Ori and friends the slightest bit of attention. 'Come with me!' shouted Ori, and they followed as Ori led the way to a small hill that seemed to be outside the range of falling meteors. Ori gave a shrill whistle, and the Paternoster appeared. Ori urged everyone inside.

Herding the small refugee group through the portal, Ori cast a last look back at the city, which was well on its way to being completely reduced to a smouldering ruin. Ori sighed and turned away.

'Careful up there! Sixth door on your right!' Ori could already hear the gasps of astonishment.

****

The next morning, the sun dawned on Akkad like any other day. Merchants opened stalls. Surreptitious requests were made for lettuce. The same jokes had the same punchlines.

'Have you heard this one? A dog walked into a tavern and…'

Nobody missed a few foreigners and malcontents. And nobody looked up at the sky. That would come later.

Ak·kad: Ancient Mesopotamian city. Location: unknown.

Chapter 24: Beachcombing

Ori could hear splashing all the way down the hall. It was a cheerful sort of noise, so Ori followed it.

Ori's guests had discovered the swimming pool.

So that's why it's there, thought Ori.

Why not? replied Prajapati. **Not everything is on a 'must-haves-only' basis, you know.**

Ori found that thought comforting.

'Hey, Ori!' called Habik. 'Come take a bird bath! Or put those wings away and swim with us!' The second suggestion sounded good, so that's what Ori did. As they sat around drying off, Zena had questions.

'Where are we, really?'

Sigh. 'I don't know that 'where' makes much sense as a question, any more than 'when' would. I think of it as the Paternoster Annex. It's sort of a traveling inn or hostelry for us while we're going between places.'

Agad nodded, a bit uncertainly. 'And where are we going?'

Ori shrugged. 'I'm not exactly sure. I need to go and consult with the, er, navigator. You all can get dressed and get some breakfast in the dining room while I find out.'

Back in the costume room, Ori had questions, too. 'What kind of clothes do we need?'

Same as usual will be fine.

'So still in Mesopotamia?'

Yes. We wouldn't want to uproot your friends too much. They'll like it where they're going, trust me.

'I always do,' said Ori cheerfully, although secretly hoping this particular section of Mesopotamia wasn't likely to go boom anytime soon.

There will be some travel involved, said Prajapati, *so pack food and sleeping rolls and something to make fire with. There's a Zippo lighter in the pocket of that zoot suit on the hanger.*

'Don't I need a map?'

I'm arranging a guide for you, chuckled Prajapati in a way that made Ori slightly suspicious. Ori went to join the others at breakfast – pancakes, naturally – and explained what they were going to do. The others were up for this: so far, this had been the best adventure of their lives.

****

The travellers stepped out of the Paternoster, rather heavily burdened with improvised backpacks and such, and looked around. As usual, the sky was blue, the air hot and dry, and the ground underneath sandy and too hot for bare feet. Ah, but here was something new: the sand filled only half of the 360° of their visual horizon: the rest was taken up by blue water.

'A lake!' said Zena in delight. 'I've heard of those!'

Ori walked over and scooped up some of the water, tasted it. 'The Mediterranean, I believe. It's...sort of a very big lake, Zena. It's called a sea. Don't worry, it won't hurt you. Just don't drink the water. It will only make you thirstier. But you can swim in it.'

To Agad, Habik, and the other children, 'swim' was the magic word. In less time than it would have taken Ori to fly to the nearest sand dunes, backpacks, equipment, and clothes were shed on the beach and kids were frolicking in the water.

Ori laughed. Agad and Habik's mother Urda said, 'You have to excuse them. They haven't had this much fun in a very long time.'

Ori gave Urda a hug. 'Or you, either, I suspect.' Ori looked at all the grownups. 'Stop being grownups, you people! That's an order! Go swim in the Mediterranean! Whatever we have to do next can wait!'

And they did. And it did. Because at least once in everyone's life, they need to swim in the Mediterranean.

****

A glorious day and a huge collection of seashells later, Ori's travelling party was building a fire as the sun set. Zena looked up from combing her hair and shouted, 'Look! There's a man swimming our way!' Ori thought this was odd because nobody had seen any boats.

Go and help him, said Prajapati. ***But take what he says with a grain of salt.***

'Who is he?' whispered Ori.

The guide I promised you.

Ori followed the others, who were busy helping the man out of the sea. As Ori watched, a rather large water mammal reared its head from the water and called out, in a language only Ori could understand, 'There! You're back on land! Stay there, please! What a terrible stomachache!'

Ori's party brought the shivering, naked man to where they were building the fire. Someone produced a towel from the luggage, and one of the men found a robe that would fit the stranger. Realising that it was going to cool down pretty fast now that the sun was setting, Ori lit the fire using the Zippo lighter. The others, used to wonders by now, paid no attention – but the stranger jumped up in agitation. He stared at Ori.

'Have I escaped from sea monsters only to be taken by sorcerers?' he exclaimed, and then fell on the sand, sobbing and elaborately bowing toward the setting sun while babbling incoherently a strange set of nonsense syllables interspersed with things like 'Oh God, forgive me!' and 'I promise I won't do it again!'

What in creation is wrong with him? asked Ori privately. *Is he that addled by being accidentally swallowed by that whale? It seems to me the whale suffered more than he did.*

It's a long story, said Prajapati. *At least, it will be when he tells it. Show him your wings, that should stop the 'sorcerer' nonsense. Feed him and let him talk. But believe about half of what he says. He's…quite a character. His name's Jonah, by the way.*

'Hey, Jonah,' said Ori, unfurling a full set of angel wings. 'We need to talk.'

The feathered display let loose another torrent of religious gibberish – this time directed at Ori. There was laughter and eyerolling from the expeditionary team. Finding out that Jonah was too nervous to let Zena (or any woman) touch him, Agad and Habik settled the traveller by the fire, gave him some fresh water to drink, and sat down on either side of him, speaking soothingly. Eventually, he calmed down enough to tell his tale while the others prepared a supper of sauce, salad, roasted vegetables, and freshly-made pita.

'You're probably the first human to travel by cetacean submarine,' commented Ori. 'Was that your intention?'

Jonah stared at Ori blankly.

'Were you trying to become famous by riding inside a whale?' Habik translated helpfully.

Jonah shook his head impatiently. 'No! It all started like this: The word of the LORD came to me, Jonah, son of Amittai, saying…'

Ori sighed. 'Were you ever, perchance, a scribe in one of the cities of Shinar?' *If so, this is going to be a VERY long tale.*

'Me, a scribe from one of those godless cities? Never! I am a prophet of the one true god.'

Ori sighed an even deeper sigh. 'I would hardly describe the cities of Shinar as 'godless'. In all fairness, they have more gods than you can shake a sistrum at.'

Jonah glared. 'But none of those gods are the true god.'

'The one who made everything?' Jonah nodded. 'And he's the one you're a prophet for?'

'Yes!' (from Jonah) and *Not really!* from Prajapati, simultaneously.

I keep trying to talk to him, Prajapati said, *but he doesn't listen very well. To be precise: he listens until he hears a word he knows. Then he goes off on a tangent of his own.*

Does this explain how he ended up giving a whale a bellyache? asked Ori.

Sort of. Let him tell it. But sit down: it's quite a story.

So Ori perched on a driftwood log, wings folded, while supper was prepared and Jonah began his tale.

> 'And the word of the LORD came to me, Jonah, son of Amittai, saying, 'Arise, go to Nineveh, that great city, and cry against it: for their wickedness is come up before me."

Not quite, glossed Prajapati. *I told him I needed to talk to them. They need to make a few adjustments after the Tower of Babel business. He put his own spin on it, as usual.*

> 'But I rose up to flee unto Tarshish from the presence of the Lord, and went down to Joppa; and I found a ship going to Tarshish: so I paid the fare thereof, and went down into it, to go with them unto Tarshish from the presence of the LORD.'

'You did *what?*' said all the kids together. 'That was really stupid,' added Habik bluntly.

Jonah shrugged. 'I didn't want to go to Nineveh,' he admitted simply.

That guy is as stubborn as a whole donkey train, said Prajapati. The only guy in Canaan who can hear me, and he turns out to be a self-referential duckweed.

Duckweed?

Yeah. He blocks the light and clogs up the surface.

Jonah continued his tale.

> 'But the LORD sent out a great wind into the sea, and there was a mighty tempest in the sea, so that the ship was like to be broken.'

That's right, blame it on me.

> 'Then the mariners were afraid, and cried every man unto his god, and cast forth the wares that were in the ship into the sea, to lighten it of them. But I was gone down into the sides of the ship; and I lay, and was fast asleep.'

'Agad sleeps like that,' said Habik. 'He slept through an earthquake once.'

'It was just a little earthquake,' protested Agad. There was a brief intermission while food was passed out. Jonah loudly thanked The LORD for the food. Everybody else thanked Ori. Ori thanked Prajapati. Prajapati said, **You're welcome, kids.**

'You were asleep during a seastorm,' prompted Ori.

> 'So the shipmaster came to me, and said unto me, What meanest thou, O sleeper? arise, call upon thy God, if so be that God will think upon us, that we perish not.
>
> 'And they said every one to his fellow, Come, and let us cast lots, that we may know for whose cause this evil is upon us. So they cast lots, and the lot fell upon me.'

'Somehow, I'm not surprised,' said Zena, 'although that wasn't exactly the scientific method in action.' Ori jumped when Prajapati let out a loud guffaw.

'Go on,' Ori said grimly.

> 'Then said they unto me, Tell us, we pray thee, for whose cause this evil is upon us; What is thine occupation? and whence comest thou? what is thy country? and of what people art thou?'

Ori groaned. This was going to take all night.

> 'And I said unto them, I am…'

'Jonah!' shouted Agad. 'You told them your name was Jonah, and you were running from the god who told you to do something, but you were too mean to go and do it – because it might possibly help somebody, anybody, who wasn't one of your tribe, or your family, or your wrestling fan club, or whatever. And yadda yadda, the god you decided to tick off happened to be the creator of the whole universe, who maybe, just maybe, likes everybody and not just the members of your fan club, and who was determined enough to get you to do the job that he SENT A WHOLE STORM and inconvenienced a whole lot of sailors just to get your attention! IS THAT WHAT YOU WERE GOIING TO SAY?'

There was a collective holding of breaths. Everybody looked at Jonah. Ori almost dropped a piece of pita with tzatziki. That would have been a shame. It was really very good tzatziki.

'Yes,' said Jonah in a very, very tiny voice.

Everyone breathed again.

'Xenophobia is a phenomenon with which everyone here is only too well acquainted,' said Zena archly. 'Now you will tell us that the sailors threw you overboard.'

'Er, yes, they did,' said Jonah, surprised. 'How did you guess?'

Habik and several other children laughed.

'Because that's what I would have done if I'd been captain of the ship,' Zena replied. 'To save the others. And then…'

'I know!' guessed a small boy whose name really was Mushen. 'And then you were about to drown…and…'

'…and?' encouraged Ori, who was glad the little ones were getting over the trauma of Akkad.

'…and then the whale showed up and SWALLOWED YOU!' crowed Mushen.

'Gave him a ride, you mean!' corrected Agad.

'That was nice of the whale,' said a small girl named Erish. Everyone laughed.

'You owe that whale about a ton of sardines and an antacid tablet, a big one,' added Habik.

When they'd all settled down, Jonah finally admitted what the group had guessed: yes, the whale had brought the reluctant prophet back almost to his starting point. No, he still didn't want to go to Nineveh, but yes, he'd go because he was afraid that if he didn't, something even worse would happen to him.

Good, said Prajapati. ***I really didn't want to resurrect that terror bird.***

Ori stepped in because the kids needed their shuteye. 'So you know how to get to Nineveh, is what you're saying?'

Jonah nodded.

'Good,' said Ori. 'Because that's where we're going. You can lead the way. Tomorrow. But tonight, we're going to have a very nice sleep here under the stars.'

And they did. Zena played and sang them all to sleep with a lullaby, while Ori went on a postprandial patrol flight.

No terror birds. Just an owl hooting in the darkness. And bright stars above. Soon even the overwrought Jonah was fast asleep.

Chapter 25: Halab

'Now Nineveh was an exceeding great city of three days' journey.'

'What does that mean?' asked Habik.

'What do you mean, what does it mean?' retorted Jonah. 'It means what it means, kid.'

Agad sighed. They hadn't gotten Jonah to shut up since sunrise, and here it was the middle of the day and he was still talking. Agad had about decided that 'prophet' was another word for 'endless talker.' *Just please don't get him started again about that poem he composed inside the whale*, he thought. That one took all morning.

'Folks, here's an oasis!' called Ori. 'Let's stop to water the animals and rest until the sun is lower.' Everyone agreed happily, including the donkeys and their drivers. Ori had hired them that morning: it turned out they were headed east anyway and didn't mind taking some paying customers along. Their remark that 'something told' the lead muleteer to 'swing by the beach on his way' hadn't surprised Ori but had filled Jonah with inexpressible smugness as proving that the one true god was looking out for him, Jonah, in particular.

'Inexpressible smugness' is, of course, merely a turn of phrase. Jonah spent a good hour that morning expressing his smugness before the group threatened to bury him in the sand if he didn't change the subject. After that, they got a couple of hours of 'my prayer from inside the whale, a particularly fine set of verses,' which he proceeded to recite until the company wished he'd talk about something else again but nobody dared suggest it because they knew it would just be about him again, and were afraid of getting blamed when the new topic turned out to be worse than the one before it. It had been a long morning, filled with high-minded (and boring) poetry like this:

> *For thou hadst cast me into the deep,*
> *In the midst of the seas;*
> *And the floods compassed me about:*
> *All thy billows and thy waves passed over me.*

'Do you always do that?' Agad wanted to know.

'Do what?' asked Jonah, irritated at being kibitzed by kids and ignored by grownups.

'Say something, and then repeat it in different words.'

'That is our national poetic form! Of course you wouldn't understand it. It's called 'parallelism.' And it's very classy.'

'It's kind of boring,' said Habik.

Jonah pretended not to hear this and proceeded to recite more examples of parallelism.

> *The waters compassed me about,*
> *Even to the soul:*
> *The depth closed me round about,*
> *The weeds were wrapped about my head.*

'I'd like to wrap some weeds around your head,' muttered Agad. Ori caught the boy's attention and gave him a warning look – and a reassuring wink.

What the boys noticed about this poem was its conspicuous lack of remorse: at no time did the prophet/poet/professional religious loudmouth express any acknowledgement of the fact that his predicament (being inside a whale) was entirely due to his own stubbornness (refusing to go on an important mission). Instead, Jonah praised himself for being so 'faithful' in loving his hometown and its famous temple.

Agad and Habik exchanged winks and made faces behind Jonah's back. They thought he was kind of an idiot.

Ori lightened the mood by producing a different version of the Jonah story.

> *The LORD said to Jonah, here's a job for you,*
> *Go up to Nineveh is what you'll do.*
> *I've got a message for the people there,*
> *Without your help they haven't a prayer.*
>
> *CHORUS:*
> *Here I sit in the belly of a whale,*
> *Oh, my friends, it's a sorry tale.*
> *I cried to The LORD, please set me free:*
> *I know now it's not all about me.*
>
> *Nineveh didn't sound like fun,*
> *So Jonah turned and ran with the sun,*
> *He got into a boat, yelled, don't spare the sail!*
> *But wouldn't you know? 'God prepared' a whale.*
> *CHORUS*
>
> *Jonah hated that whale. He wished he was dead.*

He cursed and he swore. He bargained and pled.
He finally cried, LORD, I get it, okay?
Just let me out and we'll do it your way!
CHORUS

The tune Ori chose was catchy, and the kids soon caught on. They sang it the rest of the way to the oasis. Even the donkeys seemed to like it.

The only one who didn't like it was Jonah. The prophet grumbled to himself but didn't dare start an outright argument with an angel. He looked really relieved to be getting off the road for a bit. Like everyone, he was looking forward to a rest and some food.

Of course, that didn't stop him from talking.

'Well, which is it?' demanded Habik. 'Is Nineveh, that great city, three days' journey from here, or three day's journey across?'

'I don't know!' snapped Jonah. 'That's just what the man I talked to told me. 'A city of three days' journey,' he said.'

Ori pulled a small scroll out of a pocket – robes with pockets were a perk of the Costume Room and, judging by their popularity, were about to set a trend in Sumeria – and consulted its text.

'Well, according to the donkeymen, Nineveh is a three days' journey by donkey train from the coast, so three days for us. As for the city being that big? I kind of doubt it, although it's the biggest any of us has ever seen, I think. It has a population of 120,000.'

'Wow!' said the kids.

Ori nodded. 'Yes, wow, indeed. However, I think the 'three days' journey' might refer to how big around the wall is. Apparently, it's over two farsangs in circumference – which could take you three days to stroll around, I guess, if you weren't trying to win any races.'

'Wow!' repeated Agad. 'That's…er…' (quick calculation) '20,000 cubits. That's a big wall!'

'I'll bet I could run it in a day!' said Habik. Then he thought, 'But why would I want to?' He shrugged and went off to find his mother and see what was for lunch.

Jonah wanted to see Ori's map-scroll, so Ori showed it to him. For once, Jonah appeared to exhibit some curiosity about an object that did not directly concern himself. But then he got started on the inferiority of the script, which he could not read, to the script of his own language, which he insisted was 'more elegant' than cuneiform.

Zena arrived with food. Ori shoved the end of a pita wrap in Jonah's mouth, stopping him in midsentence.

'Less talking, more eating,' advised the angel.

****

Food and a nap later, the travellers continued northeastward in the general direction of Halab. Ori did a quick flyover and determined that the city looked reasonably safe to approach.

At least it isn't under siege, Ori thought. And I'm not getting any seismic or meteoric vibes.

The sun was just setting as they approached the city gates. The guards there seemed listless and uninterested. They poked desultorily among the baggage but didn't steal anything or even ask for a bribe, much to the surprise of every single person in the caravan including Ori, who was by now an experienced Mesopotamian. The party were waved on through without a single question as to their political allegiances, what god(s) they bowed down to, or even what wrestling team they liked best. The guards didn't seem friendly or unfriendly, merely bored.

Everybody (except Jonah, who hated all cities that weren't Yerushalayim) was looking forward to a break from the road, some restaurant food, a bed in an inn, and a bit of shopping. Ori doled out pocket money to the travel party, paid the donkeymen their per diem, and agreed to meet everyone later at the Sign of the Two Lions.

In the meantime, Ori and Zena decided to go shopping. Agad and Habik had their parents' permission to accompany them. A bit reluctantly, Ori decided to bring Jonah along, just to keep an eye on him. Ori didn't feel right saddling anyone else with the responsibility and was afraid of what mischief the prophet might get up to alone – even if his command of the local language was sketchy. So the five of them set off through winding streets toward the market area.

'Oh, look!' said Zena. 'They have some really nice fabrics in that shop!' Ori looked: indeed, the textiles on display were finely-made, with bright colours. The boys thought so, too – Sumerians all had a good eye for cloth – so they turned in, dragging a protesting Jonah along. (He muttered something about 'vanity of vanities', but Ori shushed him.)

'How much is this, please?' asked Zena. But the two women in the shop barely glanced at her before they went on talking.

How rude, thought Ori, and said aloud, 'Ladies? Could we talk a little business here, please?'

The first woman sighed and rolled her eyes. 'Don't you customers realise that it's a privilege just to be in our shop? Isn't that right, Jamilla?'

Jamilla nodded. 'You're right, Jira. Why, they should pay us for letting them look at our goods.'

Jira sniffed. 'After all, we didn't get into this business to do any work! Work is for other people!'

Zena, Agad, and Habik stared at the two women open-mouthed. They'd never heard anything like this before, even from the rudest Akkadian. Jonah, who hadn't understood a word, was busy gazing with disapproval at a wall painting depicting somebody doing something obscure with a herd of goats. He only turned and frowned when he heard Ori laughing.

Oh, dear. Is this what I think it is? It can't be! thought Ori, trying to stop laughing, but not succeeding, as everybody looked at him, his friends with astonishment and the two shop women with surprise and displeasure.

Oh, yes, it is, chuckled Prajapati in Ori's head. ***When what I like to think of as the Babel Effect hit out here, it took out the main driving circuits of this civilisation. Which, frankly, was commerce and acquisitiveness.***

The movers and shakers are gone, of course: they're in their own personal loop of misery – one where each tries to impress the others, and fails, because of course they all want to be the leader. Unfortunately for them, this is a really old city. That means there are oligarchs, flim-flam artists, crooked used-carpet salesmen, and assorted feather merchants from a couple of thousand years all vying for the top spot. It's…er, highly entertaining watching them try to con each other. But that's in a parallel universe.

Here, they're left wondering what to do with themselves. Oh, and they can't stop telling the unvarnished truth about everything. Sorry, but the truth filter was necessary. It was the only way to get rid of the con artists.

This explanation didn't help Ori's composure one little bit. An attempt to turn the laughing fit into a coughing spell didn't work, either.

'I don't know what they've said that's made you laugh so,' complained Jonah. 'I mean, those women are obviously vulgar, cheap hussies from an idolatrous, inferior people, but they are really attractive – especially the one with the extra-large breasts. Of course I'm terrified of talking to them. I just became a prophet hoping to impress women, and it has never worked.'

Jira and Jamilla may not have understood Jonah, but Zena and the boys did, and now they were staring at the prophet. That individual turned beet red and ran out of the shop. Ori checked quickly to see where he'd gone. As it turned out, he'd ducked around a nearby column and was hiding. Good.

'Don't worry,' Ori explained in Sumerian. 'There's some kind of, er, spell on this place that makes everyone tell the truth. We'll just have to roll with it. Don't take Jonah too seriously. He can't keep his thoughts to himself.'

Agad and Habik looked at each other. They went outside to talk to Jonah. Ori watched as Agad put his arm around the distraught prophet. They took him to a nearby bench and ordered him a beer from the sidewalk tavern keeper. Good boys, thought Ori.

Zena was still trying to get some service. 'Listen, ladies, I'll tell you what I'll do. I'll give you two silver drachms for three cubits of this cloth. It's really very nice. And since I can see you are both very lazy, I'm willing to do the measuring and cutting for you. Do you agree?'

Jira nodded, afraid to say another word. Jamilla said, 'Good. I'll watch to see that you do what you said. Two silver drachms is more than we've earned all week – now that we can't lie and pretend we care about our customers, it's hard to earn a living.' Both of them looked very sorry for themselves, but they perked up when Zena expertly measured and cut the cloth, put the bolt away, folded her own purchases and gave each woman one silver drachm. They waved bye-bye at the pair as they left the shop and looked at them wonderingly.

'They must be from Warka,' said Jira. 'They're well-dressed and well-spoken.'

'Yeah,' said Jamilla. 'I've always been envious of Warkans. It must be nice to be so cosmopolitan. Anyway, now we've got money, let's close up shop and go home. I want to yell at my lazy husband for about an hour.'

'And I want to have an argument with my sister-in-law,' said Jira, 'about whose turn it is to cook. I'll bet the lazy cow didn't remember. Good thing I left the bean casserole at the baker's this morning!'

Overhearing this exchange set both Zena and Ori into a laughing fit that was still going on when they joined the others for beer.

Halab is an interesting place, thought Ori.

Wait until you get to Nineveh, replied Prajapati drily.

Chapter 26: The Cats of Halab

Ori and the others took a stroll around Halab. The streets weren't crowded. What people they saw seemed to be listless. It was as if everyone had lost the will to do much of anything: their motivation was missing. The kids, however, were enjoying themselves. Everywhere they went, they saw cats. The cats seemed happy and well-fed.

Cats sunning themselves. Cats washing themselves. Cats grooming each other. Cats purring. *Halab is cat heaven,* thought Ori. Ori also noticed that no matter how uninvolved the locals were in their surroundings, they still found enough energy to feed and pet the cats.

Zena whispered to Ori, 'Look! I think I've found the Chief Cat Carer.' Ori looked. There was an older man sitting in the archway between two houses. He had a cat on his shoulder, a lapful of kittens, and cats milling around him, brushing against his ankles and purring loudly. Ori smiled at him, and he smiled back.

Introductions were made. The cat man, whose name was Lusua, explained that cats were almost universally beloved in Halab. They kept mice and rats out of the grain and away from the houses. Besides, what was not to like about cats? They were beautiful and friendly. As they talked, a few people came by with gifts of food for the cats. Some children stopped to play with the cats – some brought homemade cat toys. Others stayed to help tidy up Lusua's courtyard and fill water dishes.

'Sometimes people around here don't like each other very much,' said one boy truthfully. 'But everybody likes cats.' Everyone seemed to like Lusua the cat man, too. Oddly, these people who wouldn't give their neighbour the time of day – and couldn't be motivated to carry on business if they weren't allowed to cheat – would voluntarily contribute to the welfare of kitties.

That gives me an idea...' said Ori. 'Come close, let's have a huddle.' Zena, Habik, and Agad joined Ori for a confab. So did some of the local kids.

Jonah kept his distance, saying something about cats not being in Scripture, and besides, being worshipped idolatrously in Egypt, which was even worse than Mesopotamia. The kids ignored him: they were used to him by now.

****

The sudden lack of ambition on the part of the grownups of Halab had puzzled the kids. No adult had the urge to make breakfast, although most of them woke up hungry. Kids all over town made the family breakfast. New taste sensations were discovered. A few fires broke out but were easily put out in such a dusty city. After the kids had made breakfast, milked the complaining goats, tidied the kitchen and fetched the water, they were, frankly, at loose ends.

Nobody made them go to school and learn to read and write on clay.

Nobody made them open the shop and sweep the floors.

Nobody sent them for water or dung for fuel or told them to fetch anything from the market or go check on Aunt Mupallidat. In fact, nobody seemed to care what they did. Deprived of the impetus of avarice, drive for power, or simple malice, the grownups of Halab couldn't figure out what to do with themselves. Most of them were just sitting around their courtyards watching the shadows migrate across the walls.

So the kids entertained themselves. They also gravitated to the only adults in the city who seemed to be doing anything interesting – Lusua the cat man and whoever happened along to help him.

And then there were the visitors. There was a strange man who kept babbling on about something in a foreign language. The kids found him extremely entertaining at first. After a while, not being able to understand him got frustrating. The bigger kids hit upon the idea of trying to teach him the local language. As it turned out, the strange man (whose name was Jonah) was so frustrated himself that he was ready to learn. Sumerian lessons commenced.

Sign language was employed. And drawing in the sand. And acting-things-out, which led to much hilarity. And whole groups of kids saying things like 'The fox, having peed into the sea, said, The whole sea is my pee,' clearly, distinctly, and in chorus, with exaggerated mouth movements.

For such a closed-minded individual, Jonah was a fast learner and a surprisingly good mimic. The kids were enjoying themselves – finally, an adult with some motivation left.

Ori and Zena sent Habik and Agad to go and find the others from their party. This was not as hard to do as it might have seemed because the Akkadians were actually moving rather than staring into space. Ori introduced the adult Akkadians to Lusua the cat man and put them all to work.

The kids had a different task, one which made them giggle.

The cats followed whichever group they found most interesting.

All in all, it was a busy day in Halab — at least, for those whose get-up-and-go hadn't got-up-and-gone.

****

By evening, things were ready. Kids had been sent out to announce that an entertainment would be held in the open square near Lusua the cat man's place. And that there would be food.

People stirred from their torpor at the words 'entertainment'. When they heard 'food', they actually got up and followed the kids. Some of the more active actually thought to comb their hair first.

The square was lit by torches and the fading glow of the setting sun. A stage had been erected in the open space. As people sat down in groups, the Akkadians, their new local friends, and groups of kids went around passing out rounds of fresh-baked leek-and-onion bread stuffed with grilled vegetables and fresh garlic sauce made from the milk of all those goats the kids had been tending.

'Oh. Dear. Enlil,' said one woman, who hadn't eaten since breakfast. 'This food is fit for the gods!' Others murmured agreement, but their mouths were too full to say anything.

'Thanks, Mama,' said her son, who had been handing out the bread. 'I followed Grandma's recipe.' His mother looked at him with new eyes.

People were perking up. People were getting full. After the meal the kids passed out beer and snacks, such as sunflower seeds. People munched and chatted. Cats picked their way through the crowds, generously allowing themselves to be petted, and head-bumping those who failed to pay attention.

It had gone dark by this time. The kids picked up the torches and set them in stands around the stage, making an illuminated space. From behind a colourful backdrop (painted that afternoon) came exquisite sounds – Zena had organised the band. Ori came out and bowed.

'Friends of Halab! Tonight, the children of Halab…and the cats of Halab are here to entertain you. We have songs, dances, stories…and…what is it?' Ori stopped because a girl was tugging at the angel's robe. Ori bent down, the girl whispered. Ori nodded and walked away with a smile and the universal hand-gesture signal that said, 'The stage is yours.'

'Ahem,' said the girl, whose name was Semiramis. 'Before we get to the main event this evening, we want to welcome a special guest. His name is Jonah, and he's come a very long way to be with us. We've spent all day helping him learn the language so that he can tell you his story – and we're going to help him do it. So please give him a warm welcome.'

With that introduction, two teams of children came out on stage. One team, the singers, hummed a happy tune. The other team, the visual-aid chorus, did gestures. In between them walked

Jonah, wearing a brand-new tunic the kids had given him. He took a rather stiff bow, and the crowd applauded politely. Jonah looked nervously at Semiramis, who nodded encouragement.

'Now the word of The LORD came to me, Jonah son of Amittai, saying, arise, go to Nineveh, that great city, and cry against it; for their wickedness is come up before me. But I, Jonah, rose up to flee unto Tarshish from the presence of the LORD…'

As the now-familiar story (to the Akkadians) unfolded, the Halabian children supplied appropriate music and gestures. When Jonah hesitated for a Sumerian word, Semiramis whispered suggestions, and Jonah soon got back on track. Ori was impressed with Jonah's learning curve.

The entire audience was impressed with the story – you could have heard a pin drop in that square. At the appearance of the whale, there was a collective gasp of surprise, largely because some kids linked arms behind one with a whale mask, imitating the animal, while others waved a blue cloth in front, rhythmically, to indicate the waves of the sea.

When the story was finished, there was more applause and not a little muttering among the audience. Apparently some people accepted the whale story, while others insisted that 'things like that don't happen.' At the same time, there were those who were ready to believe that Nineveh was such a den of iniquity that a god might send the city missionaries, while others were more skeptical.

'A god sends an emissary who can't even speak the language? That sounds like poor planning to me,' grumbled someone in the front row.

After Jonah's performance came a brief intermission for more snacks (and bathroom breaks). Then the children sang and danced to old favourites that had the adults singing and clapping along. They also sang Ori's new song about Jonah, much to Jonah's chagrin and everybody else's delight.

Lusua took the stage now and demonstrated some tricks the cats had learned. They walked on rolling barrels. They ran races. They climbed walls and knocked things off ledges to general amusement. One even played a lyre! Some even sang on cue. Judging from the applause, the performing cats were a hit.

The final performance of the evening saw the return of the sound-effects and motions chorus, this time as backup to Zena, who told a story about the goddess Ninsun, 'Lady of the Wild Cows', and her husband, the human king Lugalbanda.

> *Once upon a time, King Lugalbanda and his wife, the goddess Ninsun, went on a journey. They didn't take anybody with them: no courtiers, no attendants, no servants, not even a coachman or chariot driver. Lugalbanda drove the chariot himself. They traveled into the desert, seeking peace and quiet – and they found it.*
>
> *Evening came, and Lugalbanda built a fire. Ninsun prepared a meal. After they had eaten, Lugalbanda sighed with contentment as he sat beside the fire and gazed up at the starry night.*
>
> *'Oh, my wife,' said the king, 'I want for nothing in this moment. I wish I could preserve it for all time – the sweet softness of the smoke that rises, the bright twinkling of the stars in the sky, and the quiet flickering of the fire.'*

'You shall have it,' replied the queen.

Ninsun took the smoke in her hand. She reached up and plucked a bright star from the night sky. She passed her palm over the flickering flames.

Ninsun held out her cupped hands to the king. She opened them. Sitting in her palms was a tiny creature – it was soft, with grey fur. It gave a tiny meow.

'Look at this!' exclaimed King Lugalbanda. 'Its fur is grey and soft, like the smoke of the best fire. Its eyes sparkle with the light of the stars. And its tiny tongue darts like the flames of the fire. What a beautiful creature! What is it, my love?'

'It is a cat,' said the goddess queen. 'And I have made it out of love and contentment.'

The audience applauded loudly – which was a good thing because it drowned out the protests of Jonah, who was trying to give everyone a lecture on theology. He was placated with more food and told to sit down.

After the show, the children took the torches, found their families, and led them home, singing softly.

At the last minute, somebody remembered to get Ori and the other guests to the Sign of the Two Lions, where they were given beds for the night.

Chapter 27: Wassukanni

The next morning, the travelling party – Ori, the Akkadian refugees, a chattering prophet, the donkeymen, their donkeys, and an impressive number of cats (Halab was generous with them) – assembled to continue their journey.

'I regret leaving Halab without holding a few meetings,' Jonah was saying to Agad and Habik. 'I mean, they are completely in error about so many things.'

'Like what?' mumbled Habik through a mouthful of breakfast roll.

'Like cats,' said Jonah, as the one on Agad's shoulder swished its tail in his face. He batted it away and continued, 'That pageant last night! They attributed the creation of cats to some heathen goddess! When of course The LORD made everything, including cats…'

'And then completely forgot to mention them in His Book,' put in Zena, who had overheard. 'Ori told me, and besides being an angel, Ori is a scribe.'

'I'm sure it was the merest oversight,' countered Jonah, 'based on the fact that the Chief Priest at home is ailurophobic. Anyway, there are lots of lions in there. I'm sure the lions make up for it.'

'Meow!' replied Agad's new kitty, a grey-striped tabby. The others laughed.

Jonah ignored them and the cat. 'The more I think of it, the more I realise I ought to stay in Halab and organise religious instruction here. After all, this is a worthy endeavour requiring my services. And it's a nice tow-, er, I mean an environment conducive to spreading the word...I'd almost be willing to forego the trip to Nineveh if...'

'...if you didn't vividly remember what it was like to be inside a whale,' Ori finished for him. Ori came up behind Jonah and patted his shoulders, leaning in and whispering in his ear, 'You're not safe on land, either. I've heard about plans with a very large bird. Would you like to explore the possibilities of involuntary air travel?'

Jonah gulped. 'No, no...of course I'm going to Nineveh with you! I was just, er...thinking aloud.' To the astonishment of anybody who hadn't heard the discussion, the usually work-shy prophet ran over to help the donkeymen load supplies provided by the generous people of Halab.

Everything was loaded, goodbyes were said. Agad even got a surprise kiss on the cheek from one of the girls in the previous night's tableaux. Habik was still teasing his big brother about it a league-and-a-half later.

The donkeymen knew where to go. More importantly, the donkeys knew where to go, so the caravan was in safe...er, hooves, so to speak. Ori took advantage of this to make brief reconnaissance flights over the area, spotting desert plants, interesting rock formations, oases that sheltered wildlife...

...but no giant birds. Ori was relieved.

****

They stopped for lunch. The cats had been snacking on voles all morning but appreciated drinks of water. Everybody else was happy to get off their feet for a bit.

'Ori,' said Zena thoughtfully. 'Will we get to Nineveh tonight?'

A shake of the head from Ori. 'The donkeymen say no. The next stop is Wassukanni.'

Zena made big eyes. 'I've heard of Wassukanni! Everybody has. But nobody knows where it is.'

Ori shrugged. 'The donkeymen do. They say they have a couple of deliveries to make there.'

Zena sighed. 'I suppose it would be too good to be true.'

'What would?'

'If the legends were true. They say,' she stared wistfully across the desert, 'that those who have no home can find one there.'

It was Ori's turn to stare.

****

Plodding across deserts takes time, and a summer day is still only 13 hours long, and an hour is still only 60 minutes. At least, that's how the Sumerians counted them. Ori knew that on Penthouse time, a day could be as long as a thousand years or long enough to sound a hemidemisemiquaver and didn't sweat it. In fact, Ori didn't sweat, although the donkeymen were making up for it.

Anyway, it was midafternoon before they reached the gates of Wassukanni. There was a carved inscription over the portal. Habik gave a shout. 'Hey, Agad! What's the sign say?'

Agad read it for them. 'All are welcome. Except gods.'

Ori laughed – then, looking a bit guilty, went to 'wings on stealth' mode. The kids saw this and giggled.

'Somebody corral Jonah,' whispered Zena, and Agad kept a close eye on the prophet (who couldn't read the sign, anyway) as they passed in the city.

The very welcoming city.

The newcomers were soon the centre of attention from a friendly crowd.

'Hello! Have you come far today? Are you hungry? We'll have to find rooms for all of you. Marani has plenty of space. Let Habib help you with those donkeys. Oh, great, kids! Do you want to meet some more kids? We've got several nice playgrounds. Does anybody play music? There's a concert next week. Can anybody read Hebrew? We've got a scroll we can't make head or tail of. You can? Oh, good, you can give us a reading…welcome, welcome, friends.'

No 'What are you doing here? Why are you in our space? Which wrestler do you support?' Ori found Wassukanni refreshing and decided to go with the flow.

Pretty soon the kids, along with Agad and Habik's parents Urda and Omer, were being shown to a large house where they were surrounded by laughing, chattering children. Zena and the other instrumentalists were met by members of a group calling themselves the Musicians' Guild, who spirited them away in the direction of their hall. The donkeymen were greeted by Habib, whom they seemed to know well, and headed off to the stables. The donkeys went willingly – they seemed to have nice memories of treats and ear rubs. As they rounded a corner, Ori heard Habib laugh loudly at something one of the donkeymen said.

Probably talking about Jonah, thought Ori. There was a chuckle no one else could hear.

Speaking of Jonah, that individual was staring around him in wonder, trying to take it all in.

'Stop gawking.' Ori poked the prophet in the ribs. 'You look like a country bumpkin in town on market day. Close your mouth and try to act…human.' Jonah shook his head to clear it and tried to follow instructions.

Ori had another thought. 'And if you find anybody who can talk to you? Don't tell them I'm an angel. They seem to have a ban on supernatural beings around here. So ixnay on the opagandapray. No talk of gods or whales or me having wings, okay? Keep this on the down-low.'

Jonah nodded warily and Ori suddenly wondered, *Why am I talking like this? Is it another field like the truth filter in Halab?*

'Why actually, yes, it is.' The voice – a pleasant basso profundo, was startling. It wasn't coming from inside Ori's head. It was, however, reading his thoughts. And it was definitely here, in Wassukanni. Ori turned around.

The speaker turned out to be standing between Ori and the sun. Ori didn't mind. The man's face was kind and wise, and he was as welcoming as everyone else in Wassukanni.

The man smiled back. 'I'm Gudea, the Ensi here.'

Ori smiled. 'I'm Ori. Jonah and I…er, came with the caravan and our friends, who are seeking a new home. You're the governor? We're pleased to meet you. You serve the king, then?'

Gudea chuckled. 'There is no king here. No need for one. Only for a shepherd.'

'I've brought you some lost sheep.'

'Sheep are my specialty.' And indeed, Ori suddenly noticed that Gudea was being followed by a lamb, which obviously adored him. Gudea indicated that Ori and Jonah should come with him and the lamb. Ori was glad to let someone else lead for awhile, and Jonah's mouth was hanging open again, so they followed Gudea to an imposing building on what appeared to be the main square. The fired-mud bricks were beautifully dressed and painted in gorgeous colours with elegant motifs.

Of course he lives here, thought Ori. *He's the leader, even if he only calls himself a governor or shepherd.*

Ori had forgotten that Gudea could read thoughts.

Gudea chuckled, not offended. 'No, I don't live here. This is a public building. I live nearer my sheep.' He added, 'My sheep-sheep, not my human sheep.' He made a dismissive gesture. 'I'll take you home with me later…that one' indicating Jonah 'shouldn't be running around loose, and you and I have lots to discuss. But first, I thought you'd like to see the Treasure Room.'

Ori was fascinated and delighted by Gudea, who was by far the most interesting human Ori had ever met. If Gudea had suggested going to see the camel-chip gatherers at work, Ori would have been just as eager to follow as when the Ensi said, 'Treasure Room.'

For his part, Jonah appeared to be in a state approaching a hypnotic trance. He seriously did not know whether he was coming or going and let himself be led along.

The lamb bleated at Jonah encouragingly as the group mounted the steps and entered the official building. Oddly (thought Ori), there were no guards of state or officious scribes or, indeed, any people in the building at all. Ori counted three cats, a small dog, and a crow sitting on a pillar.

'Here.' Gudea stopped in front of a door, which opened easily. 'This is the Treasure Room. I'd like to show it to you.'

Ori looked around the room and let out a small gasp of surprise. Jonah just gawked.

'Let's find a seat,' invited Gudea. 'I'd like to tell you a story.'

Chapter 28: An Exchange of Information

The two guests followed Gudea into the Treasure Room: Ori willingly and eager to hear the tale, Jonah automatically, as if he'd lost all independent volition. A little worried, Ori steered the speechless prophet to a chair and pushed him gently into it.

Ori looked around. The room was sumptuously appointed, like everything else in the Wassukanni palace. Fixtures gleamed in polished gold and silver. Well-appointed shelves were stacked with clay tablets or small, carved boxes. Case upon case in the room held musical instruments and craft tools. It looked like the well-appointed supply room of a temple school.

In answer to Ori's questioning look, Gudea smiled gently. 'Our friend will be all right. I expect that's his usual trance state. He's a prophet, isn't he?' Ori nodded. 'They go into altered states. This room induces a similar state in order to perform its function for the people of Wassukanni. You didn't notice because you are, after all, one of the gods.'

It was Ori's turn to stare. 'Er, well, yes, I suppose by your definition, that's what I am. I didn't mean to...er, invade your space. It's only that I promised the Akkadians I'd help them find a new home, and I have to make sure they're safe...'

Ori stopped babbling apologies because Gudea was laughing. The Shepherd held up his hand. 'Oh, don't worry! I can read minds, remember? Even yours. If you weren't totally harmless to these people, I wouldn't have let you in. Please take a seat.' He gestured to one of two chairs. Ori sat down: it was a nice chair and well-made.

'Before you tell me about the Treasure Room,' Ori said, 'Would you mind explaining why you felt it necessary to ban gods from your city? I mean, yes, if beings like Marduk and Tiamat were real, I'd see why you wouldn't want them around. But…'

A thought struck Ori: a sudden image of one of the thousand-eyed singing creatures from the Penthouse. Ori winced: nobody in Sumeria needed to see that.

Gudea laughed again. 'That would definitely be an undesirable sight in our streets. But that's not the reason. Perhaps it would be better if I told you the story from the beginning.'

Ori nodded, ready to hear the tale from this unusual human. Talking to Gudea was almost like talking to Prajapati.

At that thought, Ori heard the more familiar voice.

Gudea's a good man. Listen to him. Ori nodded again.

'In the beginning,' began Gudea…

> …the gods made humans, but they didn't make them very well. The reason they made the humans was that Prajapati told them to stop messing about and do what he'd made them for: to figure out what the world needed to be a Whole Thing. But the gods were lazy and only wanted to dance and sing and eat…'

'I know,' said Ori. 'Pancakes.' Ori had heard that part before. Gudea nodded.

> 'The gods, of course, made nothing out of nothing, so they took an animal that stood on its two legs and had hands, and turned it into a human. It wasn't very happy about it.'

Ori thought about Ardi and almost cried in front of this stranger. Gudea gave Ori a sharp look but continued.

> 'The gods wanted the humans to do the work Prajapati had assigned them, so they gave the humans skills – like the ability to make clothing and build houses and farm. By figuring out things like this, the humans were supposed to figure out what the world needed to be a Whole Thing. The humans grumbled about all this work – they didn't like it any better than the gods had. But they didn't have a choice: they didn't have the same powers as the gods. But that gave them an idea.
>
> The humans built cities for protection: from predatory animals, from the weather, from other humans. They thought out problems. Whenever they had a problem that required new technology, they called on the gods. The gods didn't want to answer them, of course: they were too busy…'

'…singing and dancing and eating pancakes,' said Ori with a weary eyeroll. Except for the pancake part, it was true.

> 'The humans came up with a clever way to make the gods pay attention.'

'Tell me it didn't involve cooking,' begged Ori.

Gudea's eyes twinkled as he shook his head. 'No. Statues.'

'Statues?'

'Statues. And flattery.'

> 'Whenever the humans built a city, they dedicated it to one of the gods. They built statues of the gods – very beautiful ones, of course, in gold and silver and precious jewels – and put them in prominent places, like gates, where the gods could watch out for the people, and temples, where people could go to ask them important questions like 'how do we store information for the future?' Each city boasted that its god was better than the other gods. That created a healthy sense of competition, which led to progress. And they told each other many, many stories about the gods and their adventures.'

'Just wait a sixty-second minute!' exclaimed Ori. 'None of those gods are real! There isn't anybody up there named Marduk. Or Tiamat. They don't have husbands and wives and weird pets and magic weapons. Nobody ever elected a king. Humans made all that up!'

Gudea laughed heartily. 'Of course they did! That's the beauty of it – and the horror. You see, those statues are like…like…' He stopped, stumped for a way to describe the action of a statue on spacetime.

Tell him they're like telephone kiosks, suggested Prajapati.

Ori didn't have a clue what a 'telephone kiosk' was, but shared the phrase with Gudea, who clapped his hands.

'Yes! Exactly like that! They're like communication devices!' he said. 'And the stories are ways to focus on the kind of message that is needed. In this way, humans bend space and time to gather the information they need. The information those lazy gods refused to use in the first place.'

'I see,' said Ori – and did. 'So in theory, once humans have gathered all the knowledge that is needed to make the world a Whole Thing, and put that knowledge into practice, then everything will be perfect? There will be no sickness, or sadness, or death, and we'll all be able to learn and grow and do, the way we should?'

Gudea sighed. 'It would work like that, if humans were doing a job they were meant to do. But they aren't. They're trying to do the job the *gods* were supposed to be doing.' He squinted at Ori in sudden surmise. 'The job you're probably trying to do, since you're here of your own free will.'

Ori blushed and shrugged. 'I just asked a question,' Ori said simply. 'Then there was an elevator.' Gudea laughed, and Prajapati laughed, inside Ori's head. Finally, Ori laughed, a little.

'Humans are hopelessly out-tasked,' Gudea went on. 'We're here inside a matrix of space and time that we're constantly influencing without having the slightest idea what effect our next action will have. We can't even ask the questions without changing the answers. It's a dilemma.'

Suddenly, Ori could see it: like fish in one of the ornamental palace ponds of Warka trying to figure out where they were, how they got there, and what their purpose in life was. 'No wonder most of them choose to spend their time looking for food and a friend,' Ori muttered, not sure whether 'most of them' referred to humans or fish.

Gudea smiled gently. 'Now you see why we need extra-dimensional help. You came down in the…er, elevator…and I learned to go up, just for moments at a time, by working on my thought patterns. That's also what mystics do, and prophets…'

There was a sudden sharp noise: a cross between a small explosion and the snarl of angry boar. They both turned involuntarily to look at Jonah, whom they'd totally forgotten during the intense discussion. Jonah wasn't taking part in the metaphysical discourse, but not because he was in a trance. The tired prophet had fallen asleep and was now snoring.

Ori and Gudea laughed. (So did Prajapati.)

'Okay, some prophets better than others,' said Gudea between chuckles.

Ori thought. 'This is beginning to make some sense now. Trying to figure out how to make the world a Whole Thing is far too hard for humans alone. Especially if they're only looking at one level of The Building.'

'The Building?' Gudea lifted an eyebrow.

Ori explained about The Building, briefly.

Gudea nodded. 'We each experience reality in our own way. It's when we have to talk to each other that the compromise sets in. To each his own metaphor.'

Ori got about half of that, but nodded. 'The bipedal animals that became humans? They were really nice. A few floors up.' Ori didn't say anything else, but Gudea seemed to have caught a hint of Ori's feelings. He reached over and squeezed Ori's hand gently.

Ori had another question. 'How long has this city been here?'

Gudea shrugged. 'None of us can tell. Not long, I'm guessing. I was in the desert out there' he gestured vaguely, 'when one day, I looked up and there it was, on the horizon. It seemed to be calling to me, so I gathered my sheep and went.' Gudea stroked the little lamb that was sharing his chair. Like Jonah, the lamb was sleeping, but unlike Jonah, it wasn't snoring.

Ori had a thought. 'I'll bet I know when this city came into being: right about the time the Tower of Babel collapsed in on itself.'

'Tell me,' said Gudea – and Ori did. It was Gudea's turn to beg for details, and Ori's turn to tell the story, and Gudea's chance to be surprised and enlightened.

Jonah continued to snore through the entire performance, and thus was neither surprised nor enlightened. The lamb slept on in innocence and did not care.

'That makes sense,' commented Gudea when all had been told. 'After all, Wassukanni is the City of the Source.'

Now Ori lifted an eyebrow.

Gudea said, 'It means 'source' or 'well' in the local dialect. People come here to replenish their spirits. Whatever they were missing where they were before, is supplied to them here. Those who lacked friends will find them here in abundance. Those who were unable to practise a skill…' he spread out his hand to indicate the tablets, the instruments, and the tools, 'will find plenty of opportunity to learn and make and do. Here, they can explore to their hearts' content. And perhaps, who knows? They may play a role in finding the way to make the world a Whole Thing.'

Ori smiled. 'From your mouth to Prajapati's ear.' And Prajapati murmured assent.

Gudea stood. 'Let us go and meet the others. Our friends will have prepared a meal by now. There is surely more to learn, but for now, you need rest and refreshment, and to see that your friends are happy.'

'Come on, Jonah,' said Ori, and shook the prophet gently. With a final snort, Jonah's head sprang up.

'According to the number of thy cities are thy gods, o Judah!' he shouted, confused. Ori and Gudea laughed and bundled him and the lamb out of the Treasure Room, down the steps, and in the direction of a beautiful garden, from which good food smells were coming, as well as the welcome sound of Zena and her lyre.

Chapter 29: A Place of Their Own

Ori and Jonah stayed in Wassukanni for a week. Ori had a great time. Jonah, not so much.

Agad discovered a previously unsuspected talent for weaving.

'The patterns make me. . . happy,' Agad told Ori. 'I like the rhythm of the work, as well.' He hummed as he worked. Ori hummed along. Pretty soon, it turned into a song.

'Why didn't you take this up before?' asked Ori.

Agad shrugged. 'In Akkad, they wouldn't let me in the guild. It was only for the members' kids. Here, if you want to try something, you can. If you turn out to be good at it you can keep doing it. This,' he pointed to his loom, 'turned out to be what I was good at. Thank you for bringing me here.' Ori patted his shoulder.

Habik also found a subject he was interested in: writing. Where boys all over Mesopotamia dreaded their schools, with the rote learning and angry teachers and endless poking at clay, the instructors of Wassukanni took a different approach.

They assumed their pupils wanted to know something.

They started with the question all learners everywhere always have about everything: *Where does this stuff come from and why do I want to know it?*

And miraculously, they answered the question: not with technobabble, or stories about gods, or 'because I said so!' With a bit of history.

'Of course, they prettied it up in poetry,' explained Habik with a knowing air. After all, the boy had been with Ori. He had seen some things. He didn't fall off the parsnip cart yesterday, as they say.

'It all goes back to King Enmerkar,' Habik told Ori. 'He was a king in Warka. He had a long-running feud with another king in a city called Aratta. Enmerkar had got a bee in his bonnet about the language business, you see, and. . .'

'Wait!' said Ori. 'You mean Enmerkar knew about the languages breaking up? Before there was writing?' Ori was puzzled. This made no sense. But then, when did human explanations ever add up? 'Go on,' Ori told Habik.

Habik nodded. 'Enmerkar got into a feud with the king of a city called Aratta. You see, there was a carp flood, and. . .'

'A carp flood?'

'Yeah, a carp flood! A big flood of all the rivers that brought lots and lots of carp. They taste good.'

'That is a matter of opinion,' replied Ori drily.

'Do you want to hear this or not?' asked Habik. Ori waved a hand, and Habik cleared his throat. 'There's a lot of poetry involved. . .'

Ori groaned.

'But I will sum things up in prose.'

'Thank you,' replied Ori fervently.

'King Enmerkar was worried about the language problem. He thought it was a barrier to trade and the. . .er. . .the economic growth of the region, that's it. Now, after the carp flood and a bumper crop of grain, everybody in Mesopotamia was feeling pretty flush, so Enmerkar decided it was a good time to collect money for his big project: a think tank to work on the language problem.

'Of course, the think tank would have sumptuous headquarters. And it needed a temple. Because, also of course, Enmerkar's idea for solving the language problem involved massive whining. . .er, supplication to the gods to pretty-please-with-honey-on-top put the world's language back together so we only had one, preferably Sumerian because it's the best language. . .'

'I get the idea.'

'They needed money also to pay for mobs. . .er, organised choirs of special chanters to invoke the god Nudimmud...'

'Nudimmud?'

'Nudimmud. Honestly, Ori, if you keep interrupting I'll never finish this.'

With a supernatural effort, Ori kept a straight face and nodded – because saying anything at this point would have been impossible, even for an angel. *Nudimmud,* was all Ori could think.

'The invocation of Nudimmud begins:

> "The land of Dilmun is a pure place, the land of Dilmun is a clean place,
> The land of Dilmun is a clean place, the land of Dilmun is a bright place. . ."

'STOP!' Ori pleaded, wiping tears from angelic eyes. 'Just. . .go on with the story. But leave. . ..' choking 'Nudimmud out of this. I can't take it. Just. . .' more choking, 'what did Enmerkar do next?'

'He sent a messenger,' replied Habik with a sniff, 'Messengers are all right, aren't they? Nothing funny about messengers. . . Okay, the messenger had to repeat what Enmerkar told him, word for word. He was like. . .'

'A herald,' supplied Ori, who had recovered enough to talk as long as nobody mentioned Nudimmud. Habik nodded. 'That's it, a herald.'

'So the herald told the King of Aratta (we don't know his name because Warka won this one) that King Enmerkar needed convertible currency in the form of precious stones so that he could build the think tank to. . .er. . .' with a quick glance at Ori, 'solve the language issue, so cough up the gems tout-de-suite. The king said he'd think about it.

'He sent the herald back to Warka with a list of counterdemands. Of course, they weren't like one, two, three. That isn't how kings talk.'

'Don't I know it,' muttered Ori.

'Oh, no, there were 'whereases' and 'heretofores' and a lot of 'lo and beholds' and poetry. You know, like

> *I want a dog that is not black,*
> *A dog that is not white,*
> *A dog that is not brown,*
> *A dog that is not red,*
> *A dog that is not pied,*
> *To come and fight with my dog,*
> *To see who's boss.*

'And then the herald ran back and forth between Aratta and Warka, over and over, and repeated all this mishmash, and then had to memorise whatever super-clever retort came from Enmerkar (remember, this is Warka's version of the story), and finally, finally, the poor guy. . .'

'Had a nervous breakdown,' said Ori.

'How did you guess?'

'I've dealt with these people,' the angel replied. 'So what did Enmerkar do? I'm assuming, because it's Warka's story, that he gets to do the clever thing.'

Habik nodded vigorously. 'Of course! When the herald got completely tongue-tied, Enmerkar had an idea. He took some damp clay and made marks on it. Then he taught the herald how to read the marks. The herald was very grateful for the memory aid.'

Ori laughed, clapping. 'Excellently told! So that's how writing got started?'

Habik beamed at the praise, which he hadn't had enough of in his short life. 'Yes! Well,' he said thoughtfully, 'I imagine most of it is made up. But you know what? It's a good story. It tells us that the reason we write things down is to remember them – but also to communicate. If we write things down correctly, other people who aren't there can read them, and then they will know what we know.'

He looked at Ori earnestly as if imparting a confidence. 'You know, I think writing things down helps keep business honest.'

'How so?'

'Well, if Merchant A is supposed to send Merchant B 60 bushels of barley, and they count them out at the beginning of the journey, and the donkey-man signs that he got 60 bushels of barley, and they get to Merchant B's house and only count 59 bushels, then it's a pretty good guess that somewhere along the way, the donkey-man lost a bushel.'

'Or his donkeys got hungry,' suggested Ori.

Habik nodded. 'Either way, it's clear who needs to make good on the transaction. I guess that's one of the reasons we do writing, even if we don't want to invoke...'

'Don't say it!'

'Nudimmud!' shouted Habik, running out the door. Ori ran after him, laughing.

****

'Look at this,' Urda held out the round object for Ori's inspection.

'Very nice,' commented Ori, looking at Urda's cuneiform hormework – and meant it. They were in the family's new apartment, part of a small complex with its own water source and gardens which they shared with a dozen or so other families. The group voted on all decisions involving care and maintenance and paid a small fee to the city government for such services as waste removal and pest control.

Of course, the neighbourhood got a discount on the pest control fee now because they now owned cats. This had made Urda and Omer very popular with their new neighbours. When it was discovered that Omer possessed skills in irrigation design and Urda knew how to make linen lace, the couple were plied with baked goods and dinner invitations.

Now Omer sat happily near a window, playing with a cat that had followed him companionably into the dwelling, while Urda prepared their supper. Ori joined Omer at the window. The two of them sat watching the kids playing below. From a nearby building came the sound of Zena's lyre. She and some friends were rehearsing their new number for an upcoming festival. It was a somewhat satirical song.

There's a place you go
When the water's getting low,
And you dance for the god
Like the people in Akkad.
And you really shake your booty
As you call to Nudimmudi,
If you sing real good
You might get a big carp flood!

Habik appeared in the doorway. 'Ori! You wrote that, didn't you?'

'Guilty as charged!'

****

After dinner, Ori told his friends regretfully that he'd have to be leaving Wassukanni soon. 'But I'll try to visit when I can.' It was more a hope than a promise.

All would be sorry to see their friend go. 'But you've got to get Jonah to his destination,' Habik remembered. Ori assented.

'He can't stay here much longer,' Ori said. 'The place…isn't agreeing with him. I've left him with Gudea for the most part, and everyone has treated him kindly. But he's hardly said two words together since we got here, and that's not like him at all.'

Agad laughed. 'Whenever you say anything to him, he starts to disagree. "But…" and then nothing. He gets that frustrated look on his face and then subsides.'

'I think it's Wassukanni itself,' said Ori. 'The very field that makes it possible for so many who come here to find the opportunity to fulfill their purposes in life seems to be keeping Jonah from expressing himself freely.'

'It's the *me*,' said Habik. 'Our scribe instructor explained it to me. Do you know what a *me* is?'

The others shook their heads.

'The *mes*,' Habik traced the character on the table with his finger, 'are a set of rules – sort of operating instructions – that make civilisation work.'

'Oh, like work rules,' said Agad.

Zena was thoughtful. 'You know what? I'll bet in most places, like Akkad, people say the gods made those me rules.'

Habik snapped his fingers. 'That's it! But most of the time, they're lying. They're making up the rules as they go along.'

'And probably cheating to take advantage of the poor and less powerful,' commented Omer.

'Does anybody want another honey cake?' asked Urda. 'There's a gracious plenty here.' Cakes were passed around. Date wine was poured.

Ori reflected. 'But somehow, Wassukanni has a better *me*. One where nobody takes advantage and people work together, not against each other. And it works.'

'Do you think this is all the doing of humans?' ventured Omer. 'Maybe it's because they decided they could do without the divine and rely on common sense. . .'

Before Ori could reply, Habik spoke up. 'Then why can't Jonah speak? I get the feeling he wants to contradict everyone. But when he tries, he fails.'

'That's a good sign that somebody, somewhere, is looking out for us,' said Zena. 'I'd like to tell them thank you.'

Somewhere in Ori's mind, there was a soft chuckle and the faintest murmur. It sounded like **aww, thank you, sweetheart.**

'Just do the Nudimmudi dance!' suggested Agad with a grin. Their laughter filled the neighbourhood.

Chapter 30: Stairway to Heaven

It was getting late, and the air had a distinct chill to it. The sun had set about a half-hour ago: it would soon be too dark for humans to see where they were going. Ori and the donkeymen decided to make camp for the night near a small creek which they assumed flowed eventually into the Tigris (which was where they were headed). The donkeys appreciated the water and the cook appreciated some brush and dry wood that he found to build a fire with. Soon meal preparations were underway, sleeping places were being staked out for the night, and lots were being cast for the order of guard duty. They were getting close enough to the world's largest city that, even though they hadn't seen a living soul all day, they thought it prudent to take precautions against bandits.

Ori planned to augment the donkeymen's night watch with a bit of aerial reconnaissance. For now, the angel helped water donkeys. This activity was somewhat hindered by Jonah, who was more of an encumbrance than an assistant. The spell-struck prophet had seemed to come alive about an hour out of Wassukanni. Acting for all the world as if the last week hadn't happened, he'd started talking and hadn't shut up since. Just now, Ori had overheard one of the donkeymen lamenting the fact that the creek was too small for whales.

Jonah was oblivious to other people's input. He had a new theological theory and he was on a roll with it. Nor did the fact that he was explaining the Divine Purpose to an actual practising angel deter him in the slightest.

'I've finally figured out why The LORD wants me to go to Nineveh,' he told Ori.

'Oh?' said Ori, lifting a filled bucket from the creek and handing it to Jonah. Ori turned to fill another bucket.

'See, it's like this,' said Jonah, setting the bucket down so that he could gesticulate properly, and promptly forgetting its existence. 'Someday, The LORD will send his *Meshiach*, his Messenger-King, to rule over my people. When that happens, everybody else will be judged.'

'Judged?' Ori turned around to hand Jonah another full bucket. Ori saw the situation, shrugged, and placed it next to the first bucket. Picking up a third bucket, Ori asked, 'Judged according to what standard?'

'Whether they have helped my people,' said Jonah, as if it were the most obvious thing on Earth, as, indeed, it was – to Jonah.

Ori sighed. 'So by going to Nineveh and propagandising for your sociopolitical theories, you're helping the Ninevites because…?'

'They will earn favour…' said Jonah.

'…they will rack up brownie points…' said Ori at the same time.

'…with The LORD,' continued Jonah undeterred, 'so that when the *Meshiach* comes, they will get particularly nice places in the new society. They'll probably have jobs near the Palace, and such. Not like those nasty people to the south who think they're as good as we are and won't let our tradesmen cross their territory without paying tolls. They're going to end up as hewers of wood and drawers of wat-...er, what's this?'

Ori thrust two buckets at Jonah. 'Two buckets of water. Which you will carry because I also have two buckets. Between us, we have four hands and four buckets. And it is the least you can do, you insufferable snob, because these nice people didn't have to take us with them.'

Seeing the look on Jonah's face and knowing what he was about to say, Ori added, 'And yes, I paid them for their trouble, and because we shared their supplies. That is not an excuse for behaving like a Nimrod. So pick. Up. The buckets.'

With a shrug, Jonah reluctantly picked up the buckets. He even managed to get them the short distance to the campfire without spilling more than half of the contents.

****

While all were asleep except for the donkeyman on watch, and Jonah was snoring unmusical snores, Ori went for a flyover to see that all was well. All was, indeed, well in the vicinity of the little camp: there was a conspicuous lack of humans with weapons. To be sure, there were furtive rabbits and hungry foxes and wolves, and even the occasional sand cat, that deceptively fluffy-and-cute-but-absolutely-deadly night predator. They wouldn't bother the humans (being quite tiny), so Ori didn't bother them. Ori was enjoying the cool night breezes, the peaceful twinkling of the stars above, and the occasional thermal updraft to glide upon.

Coming down from one of these glides, Ori was brought up short by an alarming sight: a solitary human. Standing on a medium-sized, loaf-shaped rock. Staring up in wonder at an open staircase.

A staircase that appeared to reach into space.

A staircase with dismayed, fluttering angels at the top.

'Oh, unresolved dissonance!' muttered Ori. 'How did THAT get there?' And flew to inspect.

It was definitely there, that staircase. Rather majestic-looking, apparently made of stone or marble, and rising in a sweeping way up to the farthest heavens. Or possibly the Penthouse. The décor sort of matched: also the sort of oozy light that hazed its way around the top of the top flight. I suppose if The Building has a paternoster, there must also be stairs. I mean, in case the paternoster is being used.

Or in case of astral fire emergency, chuckled Prajapati. Ori was startled by the thought but reassured by the chuckle.

'Oh, look, it's Ori!' called a voice from above. The voice was loud and liquid and somewhat distorted in the night atmosphere. Ori looked down at the human, who was staring at the staircase. His mouth was open farther than Ori had thought a human mouth could open.

He probably didn't understand that, said Prajapati. **Don't worry about him, he'll call it 'the voice of many waters.' I know them. Settle the Heavenly Choir down for me, will you, please?**

'Hey, Ophaniel!' called Ori. 'What's going on?'

'That human tried to use that rock for a pillow! Who uses a ROCK for a pillow?'

'A human with a dire need to ease his neck muscles?' ventured Ori, talking and soaring at the same time.

'Well, that rock happens to be sitting on a doorbell!' complained Ophaniel. 'The porter thought it was one of us and opened the door, and now the staircase is there for just anybody to see, and it's *stuck*!'

At least, that's what Ophaniel said, and what Ori heard. What the human heard was probably more like a sustained roar. Ori looked down at the human, who was visibly shaken but seemed determined not to move.

'How do we get it unstuck?' asked Ori.

'Get him to move!' Ophaniel shouted (roared) back.
'Once he gets off that rock, we might be able to close the door. Before the High Priest of Whatever sees this, please!'

Or Jonah, thought Ori desperately. *This is how religions get started.* Ori waved assent to Ophaniel and flew down to talk to the human, not bothering to conceal the wings because, obviously, that cat was out of the bag.

The human was still frozen to the spot. The spot the entire heavenly host wanted him off of. And his mouth was still open.

Ori suggested, politely, that he close it. Somewhat to Ori's surprise, he did.

'Hi,' ventured the angel. 'I'm Ori.' Ori gave the man the right-hand-over-heart gesture, as that seemed to reassure them.

The man returned the gesture. 'Greetings, O Exalted Messenger. Just the feathered being I wanted to see.'

Ori cocked an eyebrow. 'You…wanted to see one of us?'

The man nodded. 'I am Ya'akov ben Yitzak. And I need some heavenly help. Just listen to what I have to say and…' he looked a bit shifty. '…I'll leave your portal alone. I assume that's what all the yelling is about.'

Ori turned to look up just as the whole blessed chorus showed up, glaring down the staircase and yelling. Unfortunately, since it was the Heavenly Choir, the yelling sounded like a rather complicated number involving a lot of vocal runs in four-part harmony. Ori waved to them in the universal conductor signal for 'stop, stop, stop!' They subsided, not gladly, and continued to glare in the general direction of Mesopotamia.

Ori turned to the man, confused. Ori, who could understand all human languages but sometimes wasn't sure which one was being spoken, had understood him to say, 'I am He Who Supplants, son of Laughter.'

'You are…oh, wait! You're Ya'akov, and your father is Yitzak. Got it. Pleased to meet you.'

Watch out for that guy, said Prajapati. He's well-named. **Don't turn your back on him. And count your fingers when you're done talking.**

Got it, thought Ori, but said aloud, 'Would you mind stepping off the stone while we talk?'

Ya'akov shook his head stubbornly and folded his arms. 'Not on your heavenly existence! If I do that you'll shut off the portal and go away without listening to my supplications.'

Ori thought – about humans, about the way they think, about how much this guy reminded the angel of someone… 'Okay,' said Ori simply, and sat down on one edge of the stone. This, too, reminded Ori of something in a vague way. 'Okay,' Ori said again. 'I'm listening.'

Ya'akov sat down on the stone and turned to face Ori. 'You see, I'm in need of some divine assistance,' he began. 'I'm in a bit of a spot – and it's partly to do with my family's religion.'

'I'm listening,' said Ori, who was.

> 'My grandfather used to live in Ur. He herded sheep for a living, and the place was kind of marshy, so he went further and further out into the countryside to graze them. Sheep have a terrible habit of getting stuck in marshes. Shepherds – well, you know shepherds, they sit around and think a lot. Commune with nature, stuff like that. Some of them are birders. They fill lots of tablets with records of the sparrows, larks, blackbirds, thrushes and such that they see. My grandfather's had a lot of marsh birds like herons. But he also liked to get philosophical and mystical, and he started to wonder about…gods.

'To hear Granddad tell it, one day this god spoke to him, just out of the blue, as it were. 'Leave Ur,' this god said. 'I don't like Ur. It's noisy and full of Sin.'

Ori started to point out that Sin was the other name of the moon god Nannar, then thought better of it. This language business could get tricky. Besides, Ori was trying not to think of Nudimmud and failing. So Ori decided not to interrupt.

'So Granddad packed everybody up and became a nomad herder. That was his story, and he was sticking to it.

'Dad was a late baby. He showed up after Grandma was sure she couldn't have any babies. She laughed so hard when she turned out to be pregnant that she decided to name the baby Laughter. It takes all kinds, and Granddad and Grandma were *sui generis*, let me tell you.

'Granddad was serious about this god of his – the one with no name – and he made everybody swear an oath to this god by standing in the middle of a bunch of slaughtered animals. Half of a cow on one side, half on the other, same with a goat, a ram, a dove, and a pigeon.

It was a mess, and the birds didn't make much of a barbecue after all that, let me tell you. Anyway, they did whatever Granddad said, but if they'd been back in Ur, I suspect somebody would have called for an exorcist.'

Ori was astonished at all of this. All Prajapati would say was, **Hm,** in an ambiguous tone of voice.

'Anyway, it's called a Covenant, and it gets passed down from one generation to the next. Somebody has to be the Patriarch, the decision-maker: where to take the flocks, which group of nomads to be friends with, how much we're willing to pay for water privileges, who gets to marry what girl from what tribe, that kind of thing. Also, the Patriarch has to promise to worship the god with no name. No biggie, that's fine.

'The catch is: this Covenant thing is *attached*. Whoever gets to be Patriarch also owns the whole shebang: all the sheep. All the goats. All the poultry. Every tent and tent peg, every donkey. And that Patriarch has to be the First-Born Son.'

Ya'akov's expression was grim and deeply offended.

'So the fact that I was born about three minutes after my pain-in-the-ass brother is a Big Deal, see? And it's completely unfair!'

Ori gasped in sudden comprehension. 'So your brother got everything, and you got nothing?'

'THAT was the plan,' said Ya'akov grimly. 'And it was a stupid plan! Esaf is really athletic, see? He's a mighty hunter, like legendary Nimrod, and…'

No! interjected Prajapati. **Don't say anything about Nimrod! If you get him sidetracked, we'll be here all night.** So Ori was silent on the subject of his least-favourite Sumerian architectural visionary.

'…and he's Dad's favourite. But Esaf is thick as two planks! If you ask him where we should go next, he says, 'Duh, gee, I dunno. What month is this? Is it Nissan yet?' And as you may have noticed, I'm pretty bright. I would obviously make a better Patriarch.

'I've been mad about this my whole life. Once, when we were teenagers, Esaf went out hunting. I stayed home to help Mom with the cooking. I made this lentil stew…it is the bomb, I tell you, killer recipe, best lentil soup in the whole watershed if I do say so myself. So when Esaf comes home, all sweaty and bloody from shooting innocent creatures, he takes one sniff and says, 'Hey! Lentil stew! Gimme some now! Dish it up, bro!'

'But the lentils weren't the only things that had been stewing. I'd been brooding all day about how Esaf was the Heir and I was the Spare. And I'd had it.

'You want stew?' I said. 'I'll trade you for it.'

'Okay,' says the Nitwit. 'What do you want for it?'

'The Birthright.' That's what they call it: The Birthright. Like that.

And the fool says, 'Sure.' Just like that. Sure, why not? Seems fair. The whole leadership role and all that goes with it, in exchange for whatever-it-is I want right now. What a doofus!'

Ori had witnessed a lot of dodgy human doings, but this family saga set records, even for Mesopotamia. The angel didn't say anything – what was there to say? Ori merely waved for Ya'akov to continue. Hopefully he'd get to his 'supplication' before breakfast-time.

'I told Mom and Dad about the bargain we made but they ignored it completely. Dad only pays attention when it suits him. And Esaf is his favourite, so...

'Things all came to head the other day. Dad decided he was old enough and sick enough that he'd better hand down The Birthright while he still could. So he told Esaf to go hunting.

Hunting! And get some venison, and make him 'that stew' that he liked so much...

'Don't you get it? 'That stew' was my stew! Esaf can't cook! And venison's tough! Not good for old people's teeth. But off he went, the nincompoop, with his little bow and arrows. Mom told me. Mom is on my side. I'm her favourite.

'While the great hunter went a-hunting, I went to work. I killed a nice, plump goat kid. I cooked up the best stew anybody ever tasted, with my special blend of herbs and spices. Now to take it to the old fool.

'Did I mention he's blind now?

'The biggest difference between me and my not-so-twin brother, besides smell, is hair. Esaf's a hairy beast. So I made myself some long gloves – out of goatskin. Hairy enough for Dad. It also helped with the smell. Eau de Esaf.

'I took it in. My voice confused him, but he was convinced by the goat hair. My brother, the hairy goat. I got the expected 'blessing'. May the god give thee of the dew of heaven, yadda yadda, may everyone bow before thee, yadda yadda, But the main thing was, *I* inherited. Not him. *Me*.

'When they found out, they were furious. Of course. Dad moaned about it but said there wasn't anything he could do. A Blessing was a Blessing. It was official. The same as if it had been sealed with one of those rolling seals they have. Mom was secretly happy: she's never trusted Esaf to take care of her when Dad's gone, and she hates his wives. I don't have any: who would marry me with no property? And subject to a more powerful family member?

'When Esaf found out, he roared. 'I'll kill him! Let me at the little weasel!' Et cetera. Mom packed my bag. That's it, over there. She said, go to her brother's. He'll take me in. He's got his own herds. Wait until the coast is clear.

'Mom gave me one piece of advice before I ran. 'Don't take the god lightly,' she warned. 'This god business is serious stuff. If you get a chance, get the people in Pancake Heaven on your side. It never hurts to have allies.'

Ori stared at him. Ori blinked.

Prajapati said…nothing.

'So, you see,' finished Ya'akov smugly. 'I lucked up. I found the Stone. When I opened that staircase, I knew what I'd got: a get-out-of-jail-free card. So I'll make a deal with you guys. You bless me and promise that I'll be okay. And in return, I'll worship you. Heck, I'll even *tithe* to you. Can't say fairer than that, right?' And the shameless vagabond spat in his palm and held out his hand for Ori to shake.

Prajapati? What do I do? We don't want any sheep or goats or donkeys or ducks. We certainly don't want to get mixed up in this fellow's schemes. But if I don't 'bless' him he's going to sit on this stone until Ophaniel blows up a tornado.

Prajapati said quietly, **Give him what he wants – a 'blessing'. He'll do the rest, he and his mother and their shifty clan.**

Aloud, Ori said, 'Ahem. Okay, you've got it.' Unable to repress a grimace of distaste, Ori took the proffered hand and intoned, as solemnly as possible:

> 'The land of Ya'akov is a pure place, the land of Ya'akov is a clean place,
> 'The land of Ya'akov is a clean place, the land of Ya'akov is a bright place…'

…and more Nudimmud nonsense, until Ya'akov seemed satisfied that the spell was sufficiently binding on all parties.

Now tell him to save our tithes until you come to collect them – and let's get out of here. This has gone on long enough.

Ori told him. Ya'akov beamed. Ya'akov ceremoniously stepped off the stone.

The staircase unceremoniously disappeared. Like an owl's beak snapping shut.

What a scam artist, was Ori's thought flying back to camp.

Chapter 31: That Great City

As the donkey caravan got closer to Nineveh, Jonah seemed to cheer up.

'You know,' he confided to Ori as they rode along, 'I'm glad you insisted I complete this journey. I think it's what I was born to do. After all, it's a prophet's destiny to make a journey like this once in his life.'

Thinking inwardly that this might be something to regret asking, Ori asked anyway, 'How did you get started being a prophet, Jonah?'

Jonah sighed in a satisfied sort of way and glanced up at the sky as if for confirmation (or checking to see that there were no terror birds around). 'It happened to me when I was a teenager,' he said. 'I wasn't always such a spiritual person, you see.'

'Oh, really?' said Ori, carefully keeping a straight face.

Don't look him in the eye, warned Prajapati. ***You'll it, trust me.*** Ori suppressed a laugh and watched the road while Jonah unfolded his tale.

'When I was young,' Jonah began, 'I was a hellraiser.'

Ori raised one eyebrow but said nothing.

'I was!' protested Jonah. 'I talked to *girls*! Even ones I wasn't related to!'

'I am shocked,' said Ori. One of the donkeymen sniggered, but the others shushed him. They wanted to hear this (the road was very boring).

'This got me into fights with their brothers and uncles,' Jonah went on. 'I also drank wine, even when it wasn't Shabbat. And I smoked hemp, out behind the bathhouse, with some other dissolute types. I really did it all before I saw the light, brother.'

In Ori's head, Prajapati sighed. **Sorry, but this tale is as old as time. Pardon me while I take a break and go play with my cats. Talk to you later.**

'You have cats?' Ori said out loud without thinking.

Jonah looked at the angel sharply. 'No, I never sank so low as to keep *pets*. But I did everything else that was wrong. I even ate a beef-and-goat-cheese-filled pita wrap once. I was incorrigible. And I thought I was pretty tough.'

Ori patted the donkey and carefully avoided looking at everyone else.

'My parents were really unhappy with me, but I didn't listen to them,' Jonah went on. 'My mother, rest her soul, prayed for me morning, noon, and night. As King David wrote, Evening, morning, and at noon will I pray…'

One of the donkeymen started whistling something that sounded like the Nudimmud song. Another threw a dried-up pomegranate at the whistler, and he shut up.

Jonah was oblivious, anyway. 'So one night, I was out behind the bathhouse, drunk, stoned, and sexually frustrated. I shouted to the heavens, 'If you're up there, give me a sign!' And lo and behold…'

Here it comes, thought Ori with dread.

'…I saw a bright light in the heavens! It glowed as it made an arc in the sky. It streaked over the bathhouse and disappeared with a thunk! just the other side of a scrubby hill. I followed. It took me a while,' Jonah explained, 'because like I said, I was drunk and stoned and not walking too steadily.'

Ori managed to nod without saying anything.

'I climbed over the hill and saw where the falling star had come to rest. There was no mistaking it: when it landed, it made a big hole in the ground. I went to the edge of the hole and looked down. There was a small, glowing piece of rock in the centre of the hole. I picked it up – and it burned me! See!'

He held up his right palm – there was a round burn scar.

'Well, if you will pick up glowing rocks…' said one of the donkeymen.

Jonah reached into his tunic and held out the stone, which he wore tied to a leather thong around his neck. The stone *did* look a bit unusual, mainly because it had a hole bored through it. Apparently there was no rule against wearing meteorites – as long as they didn't look like anything animal, human, or celestial.

'I knew right then that I had proof that The LORD was looking out for me,' said Jonah. 'Moreover, I was chosen to do great things. I immediately turned my life around – stopped drinking, smoking, and chasing girls…'

'The girls were probably relieved,' Ori heard one of the donkeymen mutter.

'…and started studying the Law and the Writings. And going to the Temple as much as possible to drink in its atmosphere of holiness and listen to the teachers. Which is why,' he continued, 'I was so upset when The LORD started telling me in no uncertain terms that I was supposed to go to Nineveh. I mean, what could I find there that I couldn't find better in my own country?' He shrugged.

'I think you might find out when we get there,' said Ori and rode on ahead to talk to the lead driver. One thing was clear to Ori: his big 'conversion' notwithstanding, Jonah was as bossy and self-referential after his alleged supernatural encounter as before. Ori doubted that Prajapati had much of anything to do with Jonah's prophetic career other than telling him to go to Nineveh – but was pretty sure the Creator had plans for the self-styled seer in the near future.

Ori thought of asking Prajapati about it, once he got back from playing with cats.

****

There it was: the biggest city in the world. Nineveh, that great city. You could hear it before you saw it: from a couple of miles away, on the other side of the hills, the chattering of 120,000 people, the braying, lowing, baaing, and quacking of their livestock, mixed in with the sounds of brass, woodwind, and percussion, all in competition with each other, almost made Ori want to turn away. Or at least find some ear protection.

By now, Jonah had psyched himself up for this, his 'destiny'. He actually urged his donkey forward. The donkey turned his head and gave Jonah's calf a small but sharp bite, which curbed the prophet's enthusiasm. The donkeymen went on in their workmanlike way, although it was clear they were glad to be near the end of their run. For them, Nineveh meant getting paid and taking a week off the road – baths, good meals, and catching up with acquaintances. Ori was glad for them: they had been good and generous travel companions.

At the gate, the donkeymen were passed through with a nod. They and Ori waved goodbye to each other. By the time Ori had turned around, Jonah had marched up to the guard with a self-important air and announced, 'Behold, I, the prophet Jonah, have arrived…'

The guard cut him off with an imperious wave of a beefy hand. As the beefy hand was attached to a beefy arm, Jonah actually backed up. 'Get back in line, pipsqueak,' growled the guard. 'We don't want no prophets here.'

Ori went into Sumerian courtier mode.

Approaching the guard with just the right mixture of assumed privilege and condescending affability, Ori gave the guard the slightest bow. 'Good day, my good sir. I am Orion, a scribe of Warka, here on a mission to your leaders. My credentials.' And Ori produced from a robe pocket a handy little tablet that Bidi had conferred upon his apprentice scribe what seemed like several worlds ago. It did announce that Ori was a member of the scribal college. It also entitled him to subsidised dinners at the Two Lions Facing restaurant on Fountain Street. Ori was willing to bet the guard couldn't read, at least, not well, and wouldn't be willing to admit it.

Ori was right. The tablet did the trick, along with the fact that Ori always managed to look well-dressed and well-groomed in any locale and weather (even when fighting terror birds). Ori passed the disheveled and somewhat ornery Jonah off as an assistant of some sort, and the two of them soon found themselves inside the gates and looking around.

That is, Ori looked around. Jonah mostly gaped.

Gaped at the imposing buildings.

Gaped at the crowds.

Gaped with disapproval at the ziggurat and its obligatory five-legged lamassu.

Gaped at the beautiful, well-dressed women walking the streets. Jonah gaped too long at one of them: the lady's escort picked the gaping foreigner up by the neck of his tunic and threw him against a mud-brick wall.

He was still gaping when Ori picked him up and dusted him off. 'Be politer,' advised Ori. 'We need to go and find a hotel. You need a bath and a haircut before we can meet with anyone in authority.'

Ori looked around the marketplace. A boy of about twelve was sitting on the edge of a well, petting a cat.

Ori thought: it was late afternoon and the boy's face was unbloodied and relatively clean. He was playing nicely with the cat and not threatening to throw it into the well.

Ori asked the boy for directions to a hotel. The boy gave directions and Ori gave a coin, then watched the boy skip off, holding his cat and the coin, to tell his mother about his good fortune. Ori, pleased, fetched the still-gaping Jonah and took him to the Inn of the Two Friendly Donkeys.

'Welcome!' said the landlady, a cheerful widow named Nisaba. She lifted an eyebrow at Jonah, but liked the looks of Ori well enough (most people did), and soon had the scruffy prophet in a tub of steaming water.

'Here!' Ori handed him a light-green cube with a pleasant smell. Jonah sniffed it suspiciously, of course.

'What is it? And what do I do with it?'

'Dunk it in the water and rub it on yourself. It's called soap and it's made of olive oil and spices and such. It will help get rid of the dirt.'

'It's foreign.'

'This is Nineveh. *You're* foreign. Use the soap, or I won't introduce you to anybody.'

While Jonah was disinfecting himself, Ori got to know Nisaba and her two friendly donkeys, which she treated like children. Also her staff, whom she treated like children, as well. Nisaba didn't have any kids of her own, so she was busy passing along her considerable cooking expertise to deserving young people, who managed to make her proud and Ori and a scrubbed-up Jonah very full and happy.

The sensation of being this clean and this full made Jonah so sleepy that it was all Ori could do to keep his head out of the soup. Settling the gently snoring prophet into a corner chair, Ori briefly explained Jonah's mission to Nisaba and her family – even the donkeys, because they stuck their heads in through the windows and listened in to the conversation. People fed them chestnuts and gave them pats on the heads, which probably more than made up for the lack of donkey-related discussion going on.

'He's got a message for everybody from the Creator,' said Ori. 'I think it might be of interest to the city, but I want to make sure he stays out of trouble, if possible. Who should he talk to?'

Nisaba cocked her head. 'Well, there are two possibilities. One, he could try talking to the City Council – they're elected by the merchant patricians, we don't have a king. If they'll give him a hearing, it will be official. If they're not interested, he can always go to the open platform night at the Fish-in-House over on Riverside Street. People practise their standup and singing there in front of audiences. Just one thing, though,' she grinned. 'If the audience doesn't like you, they throw fruit.'

'At least he'll have something to eat!' replied Ori. They laughed so hard they made the donkeys laugh, too, and that woke Jonah up, and then they had to put him to bed.

Chapter 32: Hassling the Bureaucracy, Old-Style

The Nineveh Town Council building wasn't tall, but it was impressive. Not because of its architecture: Ori had seen better-designed tool sheds in Warka. This structure had loose bricks and decayed bas-reliefs. On one wall, some wags with chisels had defaced the bas-reliefs with Egyptian graffiti. Ori found the effect curiously artistic. At least, the building couldn't get any worse-looking.

Ori hustled a newly-spruced-up Jonah up the stairs before he could demonstrate a facility for reading rude bas-reliefs. Nisaba had summoned her friend Fredi the barber to give the ragged prophet a trim and brush and Jonah looked 100% better than he had on arrival in the Big Pomegranate, which Ori found out was the locals' name for their bustling metropolis.

Privately, Ori thought the hype was a bit over-the-top: once you'd got used to the sheer size of the place, it all seemed a bit shabby and run-down. Even here in front of the Town Council building the trash seemed not have been picked up in ages. Stray dogs picked among the discarded grape-leaf wrappers of old lunches, and lizards slithered in and out of crevices. The two went in.

There was no security at the door, and there were hardly any people inside. Nobody seemed to care that the City Council was meeting today. There was a wooden bench in the lobby outside the Council chamber door: Ori and Jonah joined a couple of petitioners who were waiting their turn.

The first petitioner was a bald, rotund, well-dressed man of about forty. He sniffed when Ori and Jonah sat down and then ostentatiously looked straight ahead in a self-important way. Whoever he was, he was obviously too exalted a personage to talk to anyone else. Besides, he was next in line and eager to get his chance to present his petition before the Council. He clutched his clay tablet in a sweaty hand – this must be important to him.

The second petitioner was an older woman dressed in the fashion of widows. A young man, her son apparently, was with her. They, too, had a clay tablet to present. Somewhat to Ori's surprise, Jonah seemed interested in this pair and began a quiet conversation with them.

Ori was trying to listen in to find out what interested Jonah about the widow and her son, but a distraction arrived in the form of someone sitting down on Ori's other side.

'Hey, buddy, move over a bit. Share the bench.' Startled, Ori sidled over about a foot, but didn't look at the newcomer in case it wasn't polite. Didn't look, that is, until the stranger started singing softly.

> *...old Jonah said no*
> *I'm a true hard-shell Baptist, and so I won't go*
> *The Nineveh people are nothing to me*
> *And then I'm against foreign missions, you see...*

Ori stared. 'Haniel.'

Ori got a laugh in reply. The stranger threw back the hood of his cloak to reveal a mischievous face and a shock of unruly, curly black hair. 'Your favourite trumpet player,' Haniel winked. Haniel played second trumpet in the Celestial Orchestra. Haniel also perpetrated more practical jokes of a musical nature than anybody else, and had been twice placed in Time-Out (which is just what it sounds like) for blowing raspberries during solemn choral numbers.

In other words, Haniel was a trickster. What was worse, Haniel played jazz and had been known to pick up a trombone.

Ori chuckled involuntarily: humour was catching. 'Hani. How did you get here? Did you ride on the Paternoster?'

A headshake from Hani. 'Naw. I'm a-scairt of that thing. I come down the stairs when that feller with the rock fetish held it open. Thought it looked innerestin'.'

'And then you followed me to Nineveh?' Ori arched an eyebrow. If Haniel thought this looked 'inneresting', they'd better watch out. Hani's jokes could get kind of rough-and-tumble. Also, when no one else was around, Hani played the banjo.

Haniel laughed: his good nature was infectious. 'Twarnt like I had annathin' better to do with my eternal time. So is our boy gonna address the bosses?'

Ori nodded. 'When it's our turn.'

Since they would obviously be waiting a while, Hani pulled out what looked at first sight to be a clay tablet, and began reading it, occasionally poking at it with a finger and frequently chuckling. When Ori asked about it all Hani would say was, 'Cats are the best thing Prajapati ever invented.'

The rotund businessman was called for. The rest waited on. After about an hour, there was a smattering of applause from inside the chamber. The rotund businessman came out looking pleased. Ori saw that as he exited the main door, the businessman slipped something to the official who held the door for him. Both smiled knowingly. Ori sighed as the widow and her son were summoned and went inside.

'I hope her petition is granted,' Jonah whispered to Ori. 'She reminds me a lot of my Aunt Simcha. All she needs is an extension for her late husband's lease on a garden plot. They need it to grow vegetables, also herbs for the local market.' Jonah didn't seem to notice Haniel: once he had spoken to Ori, the prophet retreated into his own inner world.

> *What a funny sight, bud, that ever was seen*
> *When Jonah rode off in his new submarine…*

Ori poked Haniel, but it did no good. All that resulted was giggling and an offer to show Ori a moving picture of cats knocking things off of shelves.

****

Jonah's thoughts must have bored him to sleep because he was snoring gently when the widow and her son came out of the Council chamber. The woman was sobbing gently on her son's arm. Ori shook Jonah's shoulder and he woke with a start as their names were called. Following Jonah into the chamber, Ori just had time to notice Haniel walking the pair out of the building, whispering something to the son while patting the mother's back comfortingly. Ori was both reassured and troubled by the sight.

Now it's time to go into bureaucrat mode, thought Ori and bowed a carefully-calculated bow in the direction of the Council, who looked to the angel like a right bunch of knaves as they sat around rickety occasional tables in the grungiest room Ori had ever been in. The place looked like it hadn't been dusted in half a century at least. There were sunflower seed husks all over the floor.

These guys would get along with Nimrod if they weren't too cheap to hire a cleaning crew, Ori reflected sourly, while at the same time giving them the standard speech about 'greetings from afar' and introducing 'a travelling prophet who has visited many of the major cities of the north, including lively Halab and far-famed Wassukanni.'

'Cat-ridden Halab and backwater Wassukanni, you mean,' retorted one of the Council members drily. As he said it, he looked around for the approval of the others, who chuckled appreciatively. The Councillor smirked with pleasure.

'Yes, yes,' the Chief Councillor gave Ori a sharp look and waved his hand imperiously. 'Never mind all that. Let the prophet speak. What can he do for *us*?'

Somewhat to Ori's surprise, Jonah stepped forward and answered boldly. 'What can I do for you, oh councillors? Why, absolutely nothing!'

There was a sharp intake of Council breath at this seeming effrontery.

Jonah continued, 'But The LORD can work wonders for you! The LORD can change your lives, reform your city's morals, and alter your eternal destiny!'

'Quite an ambitious agenda,' murmured the 'witty' Councillor. Another spoke up. 'Can you tell us who this 'LORD' might be, pray?'

Jonah fixed them all with what Ori could only think of as a Sunday-School-pageant stare. Pointing straight up, presumably to the heavens, Jonah thundered, 'The LORD is the Maker of Heaven and Earth! And he commandeth you all to repent! Your sins are manifold and your doom certain – unless you pay heed to my words!'

There was silence in the chamber for a moment. Ori was thinking this might not have been exactly the most diplomatic way to begin when a thought broke into Ori's thoughts, accompanied by a groan.

Oh, you nincompoop!

Prajapati! Ori thought back. *I didn't know if you were…er, back from petting cats. I haven't heard from you for a while.*

I'm here, came the reply. **I'm just laying low because I don't want that joker Haniel to know I'm around. I want to leave that one under the illusion of having got the drop on me. But Jonah is doing a terrible job here. Why do reluctant emissaries always render the most twisted messages?**

Ori didn't have anything to say to that.

'Go on,' said the lead Councillor through tight lips – and Jonah did, because Jonah was too self-absorbed to catch, as Ori had, the ominous undertone of the invitation.

'Men of Nineveh!' Jonah declaimed. He was actually declaiming, too, Ori thought, arms spread out like a prize orator...

A prize nincompoop, corrected Prajapati.

...as the prophet continued to sermonise in the direction of the Council. He enumerated Nineveh's sins, which according to Jonah involved drinking excessively, allowing 'lascivious performances' in the places where the excessive drinking was taking place, including ones in which men dressed like women. For some reason Jonah was sure this offended The LORD.

Prajapati, did you ever...?

I did not ever, was the grim reply.

After enumerating a list of 'sins' that were mostly things Jonah didn't like, including mixing meat and milk at dinner (Huh? from angel and spirit simultaneously) and the appalling sartorial crime of weaving linen and wool together, as well as marrying Egyptians, or one's great-grandfather's widow (Where does he GET these things?). The list went on.

At first, the bizarre turn the discourse had taken had kept Ori's attention riveted on Jonah and away from the Council. But then Ori heard it: low at first, then louder, growing into a rolling thunder.

Ori looked over at the Council. They were holding their sides and laughing. Laughing until the tears came.

Jonah droned on, oblivious. 'In addition, it is necessary to sacrifice, on occasion, cows, sheep, pigeons...then there is the wave offering, where you wave the grain in front of the altar in the prescribed manner…'

'Stop, stop!' chortled the 'witty' Councillor. 'You belong on the stage.'

'No, seriously,' commanded the Chief Councillor. 'This is too much! How dare this madman come before this chamber? Out, before we have you committed to the Home for the Hopelessly Bewildered! Sergeant-at-Arms, remove these people!'

As the Sergeant-at-Arms and his men hustled them out of the chamber, across the lobby, and out the front door, Ori exercised admirable restraint by not suddenly displaying a pair of angel wings, instead leaving meekly like an ordinary mortal along with Jonah, who, incredibly, was still talking. When Jonah got wound up it was best to let him stop on his own, Ori had found, and so didn't say anything, merely picked him up where the guards had rather ceremoniously dumped him at the bottom of the steps, dusted him off, and looked around for Haniel.

'Didn't go so well, I reckon?' Haniel was leaning casually against a pillar that had seen better days, probably the Assurbanipal Administration. It, too, was covered with Egyptian graffiti. Haniel was adding to it by etching funny birds into the dried brick.

Ori shrugged, and the two angels sat down on a dilapidated park bench, completely ignoring Jonah. For his part, the prophet was a bit disoriented: he seemed to have lost his audience but not his will to keep talking. In desperation, he addressed his further remarks to the bas-relief figures, whom he appeared to mistake for particularly shabby Ninevites.

Ori sighed. 'That didn't go well at all. Jonah's talk was calculated to turn off the most sympathetic audience, and those men…well…'

'I have to ask. Did they laugh?'

Ori nodded glumly. They sat in silence for a while – or as much silence as was possible with someone babbling, 'and lo, an angel came upon them, and…' in the background.

Haniel spoke first. 'I've had a jaw with the locals, and that Council is about as useless as a flock of ducks in a sandstorm. They never fix annathin'.' He gestured at the general desolation around them. 'They never lift a finger unless they can turn a shekel with it. They'll steal your underwear if they get half a chance. I suspect that's why the place is in serious danger of being nuked from orbit…er, destroyed by heavenly fire.'

'Smite them, O LORD!' shouted Jonah suddenly. 'Obliterate them utterly with heavenly vengeance!'

'Prajapati doesn't do that,' admonished Ori. 'He's not into 'smiting'.'

'What about Akkad?' asked Haniel. 'I understood that place got smitten all to smithereens.'

'That's not Prajapati's fault. The Akkadians did it to themselves. They kept doing the same rotten things, over and over and over, until it wore a groove in their world and caused the spacetime locus around them to collapse.' Ori turned to Haniel. 'I suspect that's why we're here. If something doesn't happen, and soon,

Nineveh will collapse, too. And take a lot of innocent people with it.'

The two angels sat quietly for a long, sober moment, contemplating the imminent destruction of 120,000 people, plus livestock and pets.

Slowly, something dawned on them.

The square around them had grown quieter. They looked around: no, there were still street vendors hawking wares, and passersby chatting. Lawyers were still milling about at the top of the steps, trying to enlist clients with matters before the Council. But it was…quieter.

Then they realised what it was.

Jonah had stopped talking. They found him asleep on a nearby park bench. A friendly bird was trying to stuff a worm into his ear.

They woke him up, and then the three of them headed to Nisaba's for lunch and a planning session. On the way, Haniel entertained Ori (but not Jonah) by singing the whole song about Jonah.

Chapter 33: A Night Out

Over lunch at Nisaba's, Ori introduced Hani as a 'friend from home' and summarised their lack of success with the City Council.

'Typical,' was the consensus of the lunchtime round table.

'I guess Jonah needs to go to the open platform night at the Fish-in-House, then,' said Nisaba. 'Everyone's welcome. It's pretty informal.'

'It would be a bigger hit if he could bring the whale along,' commented the cook. 'But I guess that's out of the question. Maybe the donkeys? Animal acts are usually well-received.' Nisaba's donkeys, listening in as always, seemed to agree.

'Not on your life!' protested Jonah. 'A practising prophet from home always told me: never work with kids or animals. Stick to visual aids, like cow horns[3] and iron griddles[4].'

'Leave the horns, kitchen utensils, and livestock at home,' advised Ori.
'Yep,' agreed Hani. 'Just be your own sweet self. You'll have 'em rollin' in the aisles.'

Jonah shot Hani an offended look but went off into a corner to practise while the others relaxed by playing the Royal Game of Ur. It passed the time until the dinner rush. Hani and Ori pitched in when the place got crowded and turned out to be surprisingly

---

[3] 1 Kings 22:11.
[4] Ezekiel 4:3.

good waiters – especially Hani, who had a knack for pushing appetisers.

****

'Ladies, gentlemen, and worshippers of Inanna[5]! Welcome to the Fish-in-House! Tonight we have for your delectation and enjoyment singers, dancers (yes, we've got the one with the veils!), the very best joke-tellers in Mesopotamia…' Groans from audience, 'No, seriously, they're not bad at all, once you get used to them, and later, a special feature guest appearance that you won't want to miss! To start us off, please welcome Santana the Juggler!'

Santana juggled well while the house band played the latest hits. He juggled balls. He juggled scarves. He juggled rings and fruit. He juggled eggs – until one of them 'hatched' and a small duck flew away. There was laughter and applause, and people tossed the performer coins.

'Oh, look!' Haniel nudged Ori. 'If he does good, Jonah might make a right smart of money.' Ori favoured Hani with an eyeroll.

The next act was Sher – an extremely tall, slender woman with enormous dark eyes. She was obviously an audience favourite: the crowd sang along on the choruses of what seemed to be her greatest hits. Ori and Hani particularly appreciated this one:

> *Ninkasi, Ninkasi, she makes beer,*
> *Up in heaven like we make it here,*

---

[5] **=gender-fluid.**

Oh, Ninkasi, make mine good,
Make it the talk of the neighbourhood.

Ninkasi, beer-lady, handles dough,
Into the pit the bappir *goes.*
Piles up high the well-hulled grain,
Waters the malt like the winter rain.

The song went on for several verses, step by step, as Ninkasi, the beer goddess, made everybody's favourite drink. Her heavenly dogs guarded the precious brew even from kings… The audience happily sang along, stamping their feet and clapping their hands, on the rousing chorus.

Ninkasi, Ninkasi, she makes beer,
Up in heaven like we make it here,
Oh, Ninkasi, make mine good,
Make it the talk of the neighbourhood.

'They sure like beer,' said Haniel in Ori's ear. 'Makes me wish Ninkasi was real. I'll bet she wouldn't wish that-air date wine upon us.' Ori almost choked laughing.

Next came the Dancing Grandpas, about a dozen extremely wiry elderly men who danced in a line, bounced up and down, did handsprings, jumped through hoops, and made everybody laugh. Again there was much clapping along and singing of choruses. More money was thrown: the audience was well aware that the Grandpas lived in a nearby old folks' home and danced for beer money.

The next person to take the stage was completely different. He was outrageously dressed by Sumerian standards, with glittering, shiny beads all over his tight-fitting vest and baggy trousers, and he had beautiful, elaborately coiffed hair that glistened with fragrant oils. He was behung with what Ori felt to be an excessive amount of jewelry – the pinky ring was particularly ostentatious. He obviously thought of himself as a charmer. His name, he announced, was Elvipres.

'I'm proud to be back here in the Big Pomegranate,' Elvipres announced in a deep voice with a bit of a Lower-Euphrates accent. 'Are you ready to ROCK, Nineveh?'

There was a smattering of applause. Apparently Elvipres wasn't too popular at the Fish-in-House. Several people decided now was a good time to hit the privy or go outside for a quick pipe.

The house band started up with a familiar tune.

'Oh, no!' groaned Ori and looked at Haniel accusingly. 'You didn't put them up to that, did you?' Hani replied with a vigorous shake of the head and a laugh.

'I didn't have nothin' to do with it! That song sure gets around, though.'

Elvipres opened his mouth and sang – if you could call it that, which Ori doubted.

> *My girl on a dare took me to the public square,*
> *A player entertained us with his music there.*
> *We danced, he sang, we filled our cup,*

> *My girl and I got all shook up*
> *We let down our hair in the moonlit public square.*

He really crooned on the higher notes. Ori and Hani winced: Elvipres was about a half-tone off on most of the notes. Worse, when he danced, he *shimmied*, rocking to and fro and shaking all over so that the glittery beads on his costume shone in the lamplight. He was having a great time.

Unfortunately, the audience wasn't. Suddenly something round hurtled toward the stage. Elvipres dodged the missile expertly and kept 'singing', while the soft, squishy fruit splattered against the painted wooden backdrop. The first fruit hurled seemed to be the signal for the rest of the disgruntled customers at the Fish-in-House: soon the air was thick with flying figs, plums, peaches, even slices of watermelon, all overripe and messy. Elvipres' routine became even more elaborate, involving a combination of gyrations and avoidance manoeuvres.

'I call that first-rate evasive dancing,' was Hani's comment.

After the second chorus the stage started getting too slick to walk on safely, let alone do the dances which Elvipres assured the audience 'were a big hit in Warka.' Ori, who had been there, merely laughed.

Finally the management had had enough. They brought out The Hook – an oversized shepherd's crook designed to snag, not woolly lambs, but woolly-headed performers who didn't know when to get offstage. In the case of Elvipres it was safer to use The Hook than to allow stagehands out onto the stage, which was now dangerously slippery. Elvipres was dragged off to much laughter and applause.

The emcee stuck his head out from the wings and made a couple of announcements.

'Elvipres has left the building. There will be a brief intermission while we clean up the stage. In the meantime, your wait staff will come around and take your orders.'

While the cleanup was going on, Hani ordered drinks and snacks for everyone, and Ori slipped backstage to see how Jonah was doing.

****

Ori sidestepped a team of cleaners busy using sand and brooms to soak up the fruit juice on- and backstage. 'Sorry, man,' said one of them. 'That stuff gets everywhere. Watch where you step.' Ori's queries as to the whereabouts of Jonah resulted in shrugs and a lot of 'Who?'

Finally, one of Sher's backup dancers said, 'Oh, him! Try Gili's dressing room. He's busy crying on her shoulder.'

Gili turned out to be the dancer with the seven veils – and, indeed, there was Jonah, sitting in a corner surrounded by veils and feather boas. He looked deeply unhappy. Gili was plying him with tea and cakes and talking to him in a soothing voice.

'I'm afraid to go out there!' the prophet wailed.

'There, there,' she was saying. 'They're not that bad. They won't throw things at *you*. They just hate that Elvipres and his smug attitude.'

'Not to mention all the wrong notes,' said Ori. 'Look, Jonah: man up. Look what you've been through already. You've survived three days and nights inside a whale. You've adventured across half of Mesopotamia. You're finally here. You can't let a few fruit-throwing drunks intimidate you!'

'You've got to learn to deal with hecklers,' said Gili. 'It comes with the gig.' She shrugged elegantly, which caused several dozen yards of shiny material to swish.

Ori patted Jonah on the shoulder. 'Just tell them your story. Don't editorialise so much on the message. And remember: we'll be out there, too.'

It took most of the interval, but by the time Ori left to join the others, Jonah had brightened up and was more cheerful. It helped that he was surrounded by sympathetic chorus dancers.

****

'Ladies, gentlemen, and worshippers of Inanna! Welcome back to the second half of our entertainment! Are you ready for some jokes?'

There were cheers. There were also groans. Ori and Hani exchanged looks of resignation.

'Please put your hands together for Allan the Funnyman!' There was a smattering of applause from a particular group near the stage. These were obviously Allan's friends. Allan came out, a very large man with long, very curly hair wearing a multicoloured robe and hat. He greeted the audience like old friends, calling out a few names, who shouted back. Ori thought this might be a good way to stave off criticism and ingratiate himself with the crowd.

I hope it works, Ori thought. *Otherwise the stage will get slippery again and Jonah will fall coming out.*

'Hello, Fish-in-House People, I'm Allan. As you know, my name indicates a very noble tree[6]. But my mama called me that because the day I was born she looked at me and said, 'That kid is squirrelly.'

Much to Hani's amusement, this 'punchline' was punctuated by a beat from the house band drummer.

'They're letting us know when to laugh,' Hani told Ori.

'Good thing, too,' replied Ori. But the audience didn't seem to mind.

Allan went on. 'A dog walks into a bar, but he doesn't see anything. And so he asks: shall I open one?' *Ba-DUM-pum!* from the drummer.

To the angels' surprise, the audience laughed on cue.

'What the heck does that *mean*?' demanded Hani.

Nisaba shrugged. 'You kind of had to be there,' she said. Hani and Ori gave up and braced themselves for more Sumerian humour.

---

[6] ='Oak'.

'You like my new haircut?' *Cheers, boos, and catcalls.* 'I got it over at Adibi's, you know, near the fish market. I suspect he uses fish oil as an aftershave. Anyhow, Adibi says to me, How do you want your haircut? And I says to him, In silence.' *Ba-DUM-pum!*

More laughter, especially from Adibi's customers. Hani commented, 'That's a two-eyeroll joke, feller.'

'While I was at the barber's, guy comes in and says, Is anybody here educated? I say yeah, I've been to the School of Hard Knocks. He seems impressed. So he holds out this clay tablet, see? And he says...' *Pause for effect.* 'And he says, What does it say? And I say...' *Bigger pause.*

The whole audience yelled, 'IT DOESN'T SAY ANYTHING! YOU GOTTA READ IT!'

There was a scuffle in one section of tables: apparently some audience members were brandishing rotten fruit but were suppressed by Allan's fans.

'Aha!' said Hani. 'That's the trick! Bring your own claque.' Nisaba nodded knowingly.

'I tell him the tablet says, Don't buy from Ea-Nasir.' *Laughter.* 'He says, This tablet's full of old news, what's it good for? I say, you can use it to shore up that hole in your garden wall.' *Ba-DUM-pum!*

'Those guys at Adibi's are big gossips, the biggest. One of them's going on about this one, that one, who's taking bribes, whose wife is, you know, what they got up to over at the Temple of

Inanna (no disrespect intended), and such. He dishes all the latest dirt. Finally he says, Did you hear the story about the butter?' *Pause.* 'What? What about the butter? He says, well, I'm not gonna spread that one.' *Ba-DUM-pum!*

Groans, howls of laughter, and a couple of angelic eyerolls. A lone apple went *plop!* on the stage.

In the sudden silence that followed the 'joke', Allan stared at the apple as if he'd never seen one before. Everyone waited.

The rotund comedian approached the apple as if it were Ori in the Garden of Eden. He prodded it with a sandaled toe as if to see if it would move. He squatted down, picked it up, sniffed it. There were titters in the audience. Allan inspected the apple: it wasn't *that* overripe, just a few spots. Allan stood up and walked back to the centre of the stage, all the while polishing the apple on his sleeve.

When he reached his spot again, he calmly took a bite out of the apple. 'Um, dinner,' he said.

The crowd roared with laughter.

'And that's how you handle hecklers,' said Nisaba.

Ori and Hani laughed and resigned themselves to another twenty minutes of horrible Mesopotamian jokes.

Chapter 34: Something Happens

'Immigrants from Hellas, gotta love 'em. One of them runs a tailor shop. The other day, a landsman of his walks into the shop with a pair of torn trousers. 'Euripides?' 'Yeah. Eumenides?' Sure, have 'em ready tomorrow.' *Ba-DUM-pum!* Have a good evening folks! Remember to tip your server!'

And Allan the Funnyman ambled offstage to loud applause, leaving Ori and Hani utterly confused by that last joke, since they were angels and multilingual and didn't understand how hilarious it was to mispronounce other people's languages.

'At least the audience is in a good mood now,' Hani whispered to Ori.

If they weren't in a good mood before, the audience was about to be, because the insinuating music began (you can guess the tune) accompanied by rhythmic drumming. Gili came out. She was wearing all seven of her veils, but not for long.

In addition to being a warm and sympathetic human being, Gili was an expert practitioner of what was an ancient art even in Mesopotamia – to wit, Gili was an accomplished ecdysiast. There was nothing indecent or even indecorous about Gili's dance: even when all seven veils had been shed Gili was still quite well-dressed. Nor could the movements themselves be called lewd – at least not to a well-ordered mind. Even Jonah, whose mind could hardly have been called well-ordered, found nothing objectionable as he watched from the wings. Gili danced beautifully, as she always did, and the audience hummed and clapped along with the band. Lots of customers tossed coins into the basket Gili's assistant passed around.

'You know what I like best about this dance?' said Hani, only he pronounced it 'daynce'. 'It doesn't have any bad puns in it.' Ori agreed, and slipped over to the counter to order some sunflower seeds.

For her closing number, Gili sang.

> *There's a place you go*
> *When the water's getting low,*
> *And you dance for the god*
> *Like the people in Akkad.*
> *And you really shake your booty*
> *As you call to Nudimmudi,*
> *If you sing real good*
> *You might get a big carp flood!*

The audience applauded enthusiastically when Gili was finished. The graceful dancer went off with a smile and the emcee announced, 'And now for our special guest! Jonah and his whale of a tale!'

Applause was polite – the audience was still in a good mood – but tentative. Jonah was obviously going to have to win them over. Ori, who had never known Jonah to be particularly winning with people, was a bit worried as Jonah walked out. The prophet-on-a-mission didn't so much 'take' the stage as venture onto it as onto unknown territory. He stood there hesitantly.

'Er, er, er…' Jonah started. He stopped, cleared his throat. Then he looked with desperation and panic in his eyes. He turned as if to leave the stage – but an urgent whisper from the wings made him reconsider.

Ori groaned. Hani said, 'Well, what do you know? A prophet with stage fright. Now I've seen it all.' Again that offstage whisper. *Who is coaching him now?* wondered Ori.

'The word of The LORD came to me, Jonah, son of Amittai, saying, arise, go…to…' He trailed off and stopped, staring straight ahead. 'Go…to… you know what? I have absolutely no idea what I'm doing here.'

There was murmuring in the audience. Then applause as Gili walked out of the wings. With her were a couple of stagehands bearing stools. They set the stools down and left the stage. Gili perched gracefully on one and patted the other, invitingly.

'Sit,' she said to Jonah. Jonah sat. The dumbfounded prophet looked at the dancer, mesmerised. The audience grew quiet again.

'Tell us what your god told you,' Gili said. Ori and Hani held their breaths. 'Don't mess this up now,' whispered Hani. 'She's handed it to you on a plate.'

Jonah looked at Gili. He looked out into the hall. He sighed. 'I used to think I knew what The LORD was saying,' he confessed. 'But now, I'm not so sure. '

Gili patted his knee. 'That happens to us all now and again. The trick is to keep asking questions until it comes clear. What is the first thing He told you?'

Jonah took a deep breath. 'Well, you see, it all started when I was a teenager...'

Gili and the audience paid perfect attention while Jonah unfolded the tale of his mental journey – from wild teenager to awestruck ufologist to self-righteous (he now admitted) theology student to panic-stricken fugitive from supernatural command to unwilling submariner.

'...and if the Mediterranean were any deeper, I'd be dead by now,' concluded Jonah. 'Fortunately, the whale got a bellyache and, er, barfed me up on shore...'

Ori clapped a hand over Hani's mouth to stop the inevitable guffaw.

'...and some wonderful and patient people took me with them on their journey, and here I am.' Jonah looked around in mute appeal as the audience let out a collective sigh and then burst into spontaneous applause. Gili patted Jonah's knee.

Ori called out. 'That's a great story, Jonah!' More applause.

'The book will be a best-seller,' chuckled Hani. Ori made shushing gestures.

'But what do we need to DO?' yelled somebody from the crowd. 'You said Nineveh was in danger of destruction!'

'It *is!* said Jonah. 'Look around you! Can't you see it? Your infrastructure is crumbling! Everything is falling apart because nothing is ever repaired. Your officials take bribes and dispense favours to the highest bidder. The rich get richer, the poor get poorer. People with public jobs are completely incompetent. Education is practically nonexistent. People are suffering.' Agitated, the prophet paced up and down on the stage. 'I think I've finally understood what The LORD's been trying to tell me all this time!'

Oh, blessed melodic development, thought Ori. *I think he actually has.*

'We need to fix things up and help each other!' Jonah said. There were murmurs of agreement. 'The problem is that everybody's been sitting around waiting for someone else to start. So far, nothing's happened.'

'You see,' said Jonah, 'it's like this everywhere. Selfish people are enthusiastic – about their big plans. About what they want to do for themselves. Everybody can see the harm they do. And everybody knows they ought to do better. But when it comes to actually doing it, they just…'

'…sit on their hands!' yelled somebody in the audience. There were murmurs of agreement.

Nisaba stood up. 'You're right there. We've gotta start somewhere. Let's start with Iaba's allotment. The City Council took away her husband's garden plot because some rich guy wanted it.'

Ori remembered the widow who had left the Council chamber crying.

'I have an idea,' Nisaba said. 'Whoever can help, come to my place tomorrow morning. Bring tools. You know that old vacant lot at the end of my street? We're going to turn it into a neighbourhood garden.'

'Won't the government object?' somebody asked. Nisaba shrugged. 'Let 'em try!' There were more affirmative noises from the crowd.

'This is promising,' Ori started to say to Hani, but when Ori turned around, Hani wasn't there. Ori finally spotted the jocular angel on the other side of the room, in conversation with some Ninevites Ori had never seen before. Whatever Hani was saying, they seemed to like it: there were nods of approval and the occasional grin.

Something Jonah and Nisaba had said seemed to have inspired the crowd. Suddenly, nobody was looking at the stage anymore. Instead, people were breaking up into separate groups engaged in animated conversation. Passing among them on the way to the stage, Ori overheard snatches of talk.

'There are lots of vacant places around town where we could plant vegetables…'

'My cousin's an irrigation expert. He's been out of work since he had that accident. He could help us…'

'I know at least three scribes in this section of town we could get to start a school…'

'Look, I know the aldermen's elections are rigged, but here's what we could do…'

Onstage, Gili and Jonah sat in earnest conversation, heads together, as oblivious to the crowd as the crowd was to them. *What in the world has happened here?* thought Ori.

'There's more than one way to reorient a human,' said Hani in Ori's ear. Ori jumped – Hani had a way of sneaking up on you – and then laughed.

'Hey, Jonah and Gili!' Hani said. 'Y'all want to come back to Nisaba's with us? We've got some more planning to do.'

Jonah blushed. 'Er, you two go on ahead. Gili has, er, promised to show me the Tigris by moonlight. It's a very special sight.'

Hani laughed. 'I can imagine it is. You two kids have a good time.'

The crowd at the Fish-in-House broke up into smaller groups and headed out into the night. Some were headed, like Ori and Hani, to Nisaba's hotel to continue the discussion. Others were headed home. A few, like Gili and Jonah, perambulated to more romantic spots. As knots of folk with torches wound their way through the crooked streets of Nineveh, somebody started a song, and the others took it up.

> *There's a place you go*
> *When the water's getting low,*
> *And you dance for the god*
> *Like the people in Akkad.*
> *And you really shake your booty*
> *As you call to Nudimmudi,*
> *If you sing real good*
> *You might get a big carp flood!*

Ori made a sound between a sigh and a chuckle. 'Hani, I think there's a renaissance starting tonight.'

Hani laughed. 'Maybe it's an 'Enlightenment'. You never know.'

Ori looked up at the stars. 'Did we do this? I don't remember doing anything in particular. Or was it Prajapati? Or Jonah? Or Gili?'

Hani shrugged. 'Maybe it took all of us together. Who knows? Let's see what develops.' On a sudden impulse, Hani sprouted wings. 'Tell you what: once around the town before we turn in? I'll race you!'

'As long as it doesn't take us three days!' laughed Ori. The two of them flew off in the general direction of the river.

Jonah and Gili were right: the Tigris was really nice by moonlight.

Chapter 35: Anatomy of a Minor (?) Miracle

It was a beautiful morning in Nineveh, that great city. Ori looked out the window of the top floor of Nisaba's hotel on the splendour six short weeks had wrought. Everywhere the eye could see – and that was pretty far, considering the flatness of the landscape and the dearth of tall buildings (nobody wanted another Babel, word had got around) – the maze of houses, squares, and marketplaces was dotted with green. Assiduous group gardening coupled with expert irrigation engineering had done wonders for the city. There were places to sit. There was fresher air. There were even ponds, shaded by awnings and fast-growing vines in order to minimize evaporation. There was even birdsong.

The Big Pomegranate looked and sounded like a different city.

It hadn't been easy at first. The City Council, puppets of the moneyed merchant classes, had reacted sharply to the public's takeover of public land.

'Not allowed!' they'd shouted. 'Improper permits! Lack of eminent domain! Etc, etc.' They'd sent armed guards to tear out the plants and trees and destroy the irrigation canals.

The guards had been disarmed and beaten by teenage gangs. Cooler-headed adults had taken the guards aside and persuaded them that they really ought to be on the side of their fellow citizens rather than those ungrateful oligarchs, who were forever firing them at no notice just to prove how powerful they were. Who withheld their wages on a whim or fired their colleagues and expected them to take up the slack with no benefit to themselves.

Besides, their fellow citizens knew where the guards lived. Soon the City Council was faced with a severe henchmen shortage.

'Hire more!' screamed the Chief Councillor.

'From where?' retorted the Sergeant-at-Arms. 'Warka's a long way off. We've tried Halab. They just laughed at us and offered to sell us some cats.'

When he heard this, Jonah laughed. The teenage gangs had been Jonah's idea, drawing on his misspent youth. The prophet was a founding member of the Nineveh Redemption Society, which was basically a coordinating committee for the urban renewal projects. He wasn't the leader, though: most people went to Nisaba, who was older and wiser, for good advice. Jonah was content to help out where he could, but he and Gili were still basking in the glow and tended not to be available 24/7.

The City Council was also short of cash with which to attract new henchmen...er, peace officers. This was because its patrons, the city's merchants and import/export tycoons, were experiencing a severe cash flow problem.

This had nothing to do with prophets, or angels.

The merchants' problems were due to the dispute they'd got into with the donkeymen.

It seemed that the donkeymen who had brought Ori and Jonah to Nineveh had been talking to the other caravan operators in town. These donkeymen had been with Ori and Jonah since they left the Mediterranean coast, and they had seen some things. They'd been impressed with the situations in Halab and

Wassukanni. They thoroughly approved of the civic improvements now going on all around Nineveh.

They had put their heads together and concluded that public participation in the regulation of city affairs was a good thing – not only for the citizens, but most particularly for the caravan men and their donkeys.

Smaller-scale merchants didn't make unreasonable demands. Small-scale operations didn't change schedules on no notice or alter the terms of payment with an airy 'take it or leave it.' Smaller-scale merchants were a lot easier to deal with.

Also, like the guards, some of these caravan men lived in Nineveh. They liked having parks and gardens and pools to splash in. They liked having better food at better prices. They appreciated not being cheated when they bought donkey feed. They were hopeful about the educations their kids were getting at the new community schools.

In short, this new combination of republicanism and civic pride was sitting very well with just about everyone except the previous ruling class. The previous ruling class wasn't ruling anything right now because they couldn't get anybody to do the enforcing for them. In the last few weeks, big-shot merchants and city officials had scarcely been seen. Nobody was quite sure where they'd got to – some said they'd gone to visit their richer relatives somewhere, but nobody was sure and frankly, nobody cared enough to inquire.

In fact, only one of the old oligarchs was still around. His name was Manishtushu. For years, his firm had been the biggest dealer in cloth and notions on this stretch of the Tigris. His wife and daughters were carried about the city on stately litters, decked in the best of his finery. They held court at elaborate banquets.

Manishtushu was an aged widower now. His daughters had married Assyrian nobles and moved away: their trousseaus had been truly awe-inspiring. Manishtushu was left alone with his factories and his boardroom. When the Nineveh Redemption Society started its activities, Manishtushu's workers had simply walked off the job. A lot of them had taken their tools with them. All of them had taken their expertise. With the other oligarchs doing midnight flits to avoid creditors, strikers, or mobs of aggrieved employees, Manishtushu had nobody to answer to – or to demand answers from – other than a housekeeper, a chariot driver, and a factory foreman. They were all as old as he was and stayed with him out of habit.

Thus it was that Ori and Hani, out on a stroll through the now-bustling Nineveh garment district, came upon an unusual sight under one of the awnings: an old man in a rather nice robe weaving on a loom while an equally old woman operated a spinning wheel. They were singing, one after the other, alternate verses to a song that was so old nobody knew where it had come from.

> *I will bring you, I will bring you plucked flax,*
> *I will bring you plucked flax, sister mine.*
>
> *Who will comb it, who will comb the plucked flax?*
> *Who will comb the plucked flax, brother mine?*
>
> *I will bring you, I will bring you combed flax, etc.*

And thus the song went on, until the flax had been spun and braided and woven and dyed. And then a god and a goddess went to bed together – a development that startled Ori and made Hani laugh.

Ori thought to have perceived a chuckle from Prajapati as well, only quietly, because Prajapati was still not letting on to Hani that he knew about the new addition to the team. Ori had the sneaking suspicion that Hani might be on probation, as it were, until Prajapati could be sure this wasn't another elaborate practical joke on Hani's part.

As Ori and Hani stood by and watched, two other old men arrived at the booth with a handcart full of more flax. They, too, were singing.

> *The gakkul vat, the gakkul vat!*
> *Which makes us happy, just like that!*
> *I'm spinning in a lake of beer,*
> *My mood is blissful, full of cheer,*
> *My heart is joyful, my liver is happy,*
> *More beer, more beer, and make it snappy!*

The song made the angels laugh out loud, which in turn made the flax workers look up in surprise, since they hadn't been aware that anyone was paying attention to them.

'We're sorry to interrupt,' Ori apologised. 'We enjoyed your singing.'

The old people bowed ironically, but Ori could tell that they were pleased by the compliment.

'Aren't you Manishtushu?' Ori asked the man at the loom.

Manishtushu looked around to make sure nobody else was around and made shushing motions with his hands. 'Less of that, please, good sir. I tell people my name is Mani these days. And these are my friends, Utu and Nabu – ' he gestured to the two men, 'and Degi is at the spinning wheel.' The old folks grinned their greetings, displaying gap-toothed smiles.

Ori and Hani bowed in turn, not ironically. Ori asked, 'Are you sorry that you lost your mercantile empire?'

The four looked at each other – and laughed. 'Not a bit of it!' said Manishtushu...er, Mani. 'Life had got pretty dreary once the girls moved away. We only did all that society stuff to please them, anyway. Once they'd snagged their dream husbands, there didn't seem to be much point to it. And then when the wife died...'

He looked pensive. 'I was just going through the motions, you know? Showing up at the polo matches out of habit, going to the baths...but all the gossip was just boring me to death, I'd heard it all before, many times. When the bottom fell out of the fashion industry – good thing, too, these young folk have some really good ideas, they ought to get their turn at it – I'll admit I was worried for a bit.'

Mani's face took on a puzzled expression. 'I mean, what if everybody was so mad about how bad things had got that they just threw us all to the wolves? I wondered if I'd die of loneliness or be abandoned and starve to death. But...' he gestured to the other three, 'it turned out I had friends.'

'Oh, pish and tosh, old man,' grumbled Degi. 'We were just used to you. Besides, I like you a lot better now that you aren't anybody's boss.'

Ori and Hani hung around a bit longer, admiring their cloth, making a purchase, and learning the spinning and drinking songs. On their way back to the hotel, they stopped at the Nineveh Redemption Society to tell the people there about Mani and his group and recommending that someone keep an eye on them to make sure they had everything they needed.

'Will do,' said the young man on duty, making notes on his tablet. 'We'll add them to the list for the Committee on Seniors to check up on.'

****

'I wonder,' mused an airborne Ori that midnight while flying about over the city. Hani wasn't along, being preoccupied with singing the beer song to some appreciative waterfowl while taking a late-night dip in the Tigris.

What do you wonder? asked Prajapati.

'Is it really that simple? Get rid of greed and people get better?'

Well, not exactly. But it helps once they figure out that there are a lot of things more important to them than acquiring goods and status. Things like friendship. Love. Something rewarding to do with their time. Greed makes messes, yes. Letting the greedy people set the agenda is a recipe for disaster. Nothing gets better, because everybody's too busy figuring, 'What's in it for me?' Sooner or later, everything runs down. Greed and competition will lead to the heat death of the universe if you let it. I'm not going to let it.*

Ori sighed. 'Me, neither. Not if there's anything I can do about it.'

You're a good kid.

Ori shrugged, a gesture that startled several bats out looking for mosquitoes. 'Are we done here in Nineveh? It doesn't seem like I did much.'

You did more than you think, and no, you're not done. But let's let the humans do some work for a change. I've got an errand for you and Hani, but I'll tell you about it tomorrow.

And so Ori continued to make lazy circles above the surprising city of Nineveh, while below, a lot of revolutionaries who didn't know they were revolutionaries slept the sleep of the tired and happy.

Chapter 36: Ramble On

'Tell me again,' said Hani, 'Why you had an irresistible urge to go roaming around on foot in this desert at night?'

'It's where I do my best thinking,' said Ori honestly. It was true: Ori did get a lot of good thinking done walking (or flying) around at night. Sleeping humans left Ori with more free mental space. It wasn't the whole truth, though: Ori didn't want to tell Hani that Prajapati had suggested the after-dark perambulation. And had warned of an upcoming bit of weirdness. Ah, there it was...

The air around them shimmered. The landscape and skyscape before them fractionated into thin, translucent layers, like shards of crystal. For a moment, the two angels could see the planet shaved into slivers of spacetime: tiny moments in the continuum. The effect lasted only a split second: only an angel could have perceived it. And Prajapati, probably, thought Ori, who suspected the source of the disturbance.

The two hikers stayed put until the timeslip had completed itself. One slice of crystal glowed brighter and the others disappeared. A new spacetime had asserted itself. Hani and Ori looked at one another and shrugged. They walked on.

'Now, what was that all about?' wondered Hani. Ori just laughed.

****

'Me-eh-eh! Me-eh-eh!'

'What in the world…?' said Hani. 'Somebody must really not be impressed by this landscape.'

'Oh, don't be silly,' said Ori and pointed. Coming over the horizon was a curious sight: a fair-sized herd of goats – nannies, billies, and leaping kids. The meh-ing might have been a complaint about the lack of interesting edibles along the road – but was more likely caused by the humans chivvying them along. After dark, no less. Obviously, the goats felt it was past both their dinnertime and their bedtime, and were telling the men about it.

'Stay incognito,' whispered Ori. 'We don't want to start any more cults.' Hani nodded as they approached the goat herders with a peaceful greeting and stretched-out arms. After dark, it was advisable to let people know you weren't packing while you were still out of reach.

'Peace be upon you!' called Ori. 'Whither go ye so late, brothers?' I've really been hanging around Mesopotamians too long, Ori thought. I've caught the rhetoric bug. Hani suppressed a giggle, but the greeting appeared to reassure the lead herdsman.

'And peace to you,' replied the herdsman. 'Come ye from Esaf? We are emissaries from his brother.'

Without thinking, Ori exclaimed in surprise, 'You're with Ya'akov? He's done well for himself.'

'Indeed,' replied the herdsman. 'In the twenty years since he left the land of his fathers, Ya'akov has truly prospered in the house of his father-in-law. He has four wives.'

'That's three too many,' muttered Hani. Ori poked Hani in the ribs while looking attentive and respectful.

'Don't criticise!' Ori hissed. 'And never interrupt an emissary when he's speaking. We'll be here all night.'

Fortunately for them, the emissary was nervous and didn't notice the whispering. Goat herders weren't often chosen as messengers and this long speech was doing his head in. He cleared his throat and started again, 'Lo, Ya'akov sends greetings to his brother Esaf. He has heard that his brother cometh out with four hundred horsemen. This doeth...er, doth Ya'akov great honour, indeed.'

And scareth the living daylights out of him, thought Ori.

Hani, overhearing, suppressed a chuckle. *So that's the way the wind a-bloweth, is it?*

Aloud, and to speed things along, Hani said, 'Nice herd of goats you got there, friend.'

'They're for Esaf!' said the herder, totally forgetting all the highfalutin' speech he'd memorised. 'It's part of the present. So Esaf won't attack.'

Ori thought. 'I'm pretty sure Esaf's intentions are peaceable, in spite of the entourage. Tell you what: I'm more worried about you folks wandering about in the dark. The moon's rising...' as, indeed, it was, conveniently, 'but even still, a man or a goat might stumble into a hamster hole.'

The herder nodded solemnly. 'You've got a point. Hamsters are a menace.'

'Why don't y'all pitch camp for the night?' suggested Hani. 'Looks like some decent fodder for goats around here, you can set up a campfire and rest, and y'all can see anything comin' from miles away in this moonlight. I certainly wouldn't want to be stumblin' around at night with about...' he guesstimated, 'two hunnerd goats to keep track of.'

'220,' replied the herdsman. 'I have the pebble bag here.' He patted his pouch, which contained 220 pebbles – goats, for the counting of. 'Thank you, gentlemen. 'You're right, it's a good idea for us and the goats to rest. Thank you for giving us permission.'

Ori and Hani didn't bother telling the herdsman that they had no authority to give them permission to park goats – they also figured nobody would care. The herdsmen and the goats would be more comfortable encamped for the night – and Ori had taken a quick look at the book and knew the goat herders need not fear Esaf's home cavalry. They bade the herders and the goats a pleasant night and went on their way.

The yellow moon, nearly full, shed a bright light across the landscape. This early in the evening, shadows were tall: shrubs looked like trees. Hani was briefly spooked by a hare. That made Hani laugh and sing.

> *Oh, John the Rabbit, yes, ma'am*
> *Got a mighty habit, yes, ma'am*
> *Jumpin' in my garden, yes, ma'am*
> *Cuttin' down my cabbage, yes, ma'am*
> *My peas and greens, yes, ma'am*

My lentils and beans, yes, ma'am
And if I live, yes, ma'am
To see next fall, yes, ma'am
I ain't gonna have, yes, ma'am
No garden at all, no, ma'am!

'No potatoes or tomatoes?' asked Ori drily.

'Not unless you're expectin' a ship from Peru to sail over the horizon there?' replied Hani.

Ori looked at the horizon and realised with a start that Hani's song had covered another sound. It sounded something like 'Baa, baa, baa...'

'That's either a shrivel of music critics or a flock of sheep,' remarked Hani.

It wasn't music critics. The sheep flowed over the hill, pouring down the sandy road like a really long flokati. The moonlight, more silver than gold now that the orb had risen, made the sheep look cleaner than they probably were. Ori called to the lead shepherd, alerting him to their presence and expressing good will — also suggesting that his colleagues the goatherds had found a good camping place a couple of miles down the road and would probably welcome the company. The shepherds thought this was a fine idea, 'And besides, these sheep are a gift from Ya'akov to his brother Esaf, like the goats. Maybe we should bring them all together.'

'Sure,' said Hani. 'What's another couple of hunmert ruminants, more or less?'

'220,' corrected the shepherd, and patted his heavy sack of pebbles. Ori and Hani nodded understanding, and wished sheep and herdsmen a good night.

'Is this some kind of family feud we're walking into the middle of?' Hani asked Ori.

'Oh!' said Ori. 'I forgot: you didn't hear all that when you came down the Staircase. You remember that guy with his foot in the door?'

'Do I ever!' laughed Hani. 'I thought Ophaniel was going to sweat a comet. What was that all about?'

And Ori told the story as they walked the now-deserted road. It made a pleasant tale, there in the silver moonlight, Ori explaining, Hani laughing and exclaiming in surprise. It occurred to Ori how nice it was to have a friend who actually got all your jokes. In fact, if the Penthouse had contained this much companionship and fewer vocal exercises Ori might not have left.

As the two crested another low hill, their ears were assaulted by an outrageous amount of noise.

'That,' said Hani, 'Completes my sonic education. I've always wondered what the opposite of music sounded like.' To call what greeted their ears 'bellowing' didn't quite do it justice.

It sounded like a herd of beasts with very bad, very vociferous stomach aches.

It was, in fact, a herd of camels. Thirty of them, all with calves.

'These are milk camels,' explained the chief herdsman. Ori could feel Hani beside him, shaking with silent, uncontrollable laughter. Ori poked Hani in the side, hard, causing Hani to let out a sound not entirely unlike that of the camels.

The lead camel herdsman looked at Hani quizzically. 'Are you all right, sir?' he asked.

'Must've been something I et,' said Hani with a straight face.

The camels and babies were already bedded down for the night. The camel herders didn't want to catch up with the shepherds and goatherds. ('They fight,' they said, meaning the livestock and not the herdsmen.) They invited the strangers to stop with them for the rest of the night, but Ori demurred, saying that they were travelling by night in order to avoid the heat of the day. Privately, Ori was afraid Hani would get into a bellowing contest with the camels – or worse, one of the camels would fall in love with Hani. A lovesick camel would be a serious complication. So they bade farewell to the camels and their humans and rambled on.

Ori had just finished telling Hani the story of the Birthright business when they met up with an encampment of 40 cows and a lesser number of humans. A 'hill and a holler' later (according to Hani), they found 20 bulls and their keepers. The bulls were sleepy, and so were the humans. Ori and Hani called out, 'For Esaf?' The herdsmen waved assent, and they went on.

Hani laughed. 'Ya'akov is really afeared of that brother of his. Amazing that he did what he did all those years ago.'

'His fear has probably grown over time. Also, twenty years ago, Ya'akov was just a kid with nothing to lose. Now look at him: if these herds are a gift he's doing really well in material terms. He must also have something he's willing to pay to protect.'

'Humans and property,' mused Hani. 'They do worry about it. And fight over it.' Ori nodded.

Finally, they rounded a hill and came upon a brook, quietly burbling through a greener landscape. There were even some trees, under which a group of people were settling down for the night. They had a few donkeys, but no livestock. Some children were snuggled into blankets by a banked campfire while a woman sang softly to them. It was a peaceful sight – but not for long.

Two armed men jumped up and stood between the strangers and the families. 'What do you want?' they demanded.

Ori and Hani held up placating hands. 'We are only travellers, passing through,' said Ori. 'We wanted to tell you that we'd met your herdsmen as we journeyed, and all is well with them.'

The men relaxed, slightly. 'You're not from Esaf?' the leader asked. Headshakes from Ori and Hani reassured him.

'We'd like to speak to Ya'akov, though,' said Ori. 'Where may we find him?'

The other guard pointed across the brook. 'Back there,' he said. 'He's spending the night alone. In meditation, he said. He'll join us in the morning.' Ori and Hani nodded and left, bowing in the direction of the family groups.

As they followed the road toward the little bridge that crossed the brook, Hani asked, 'What do you think he's 'meditating' about?'

'What he's going to say to Esaf after twenty years,' replied Ori.

'He'd better make it good,' said Hani.

On the other side of the brook, the road rose sharply again. As they neared the top, Hani took a deep breath of the night air and looked around at the landscape, so bright in the moonlight. A look back reassured them that the encampment by the brook was hidden from view by the trees.

'I'm tired of walking,' Hani announced. 'The brook's too small for swimming. I'm going to have a flyover, get a better view.' And the angel spread wings. Ori followed suit and they flew over the crest of the hill. The vista was impressive...

...and so was the bright light streaming down from the sky. From the open portal that shone onto the large, flat rock.

The large, flat rock on which a lone figure was sitting. Ya'akov, they assumed.

'Oh, lord, he's gone and opened the portal again,' said Hani. 'Ophaniel's going to have a cow.'

Ori didn't know whether to laugh or curse. 'I should have guessed it! The offkey buzzard wants insurance!'

Chapter 37: In This Corner...

'We'll give him insurance!' fumed Hani. 'Ever' time that Staircase opens it makes a tunnel in spacetime. It nudges random planetoids out of the way. That scheming polecat has just inconvenienced a thousand solar systems in formation!' With a majestic flap of wings, Hani flew into the shaft of light streaming down the staircase.

Ori blinked. I never knew Hani paid such close attention to sidereal engineering.

Oh, Hani isn't all fun and games. That angel is a big geek. Collects statistics, which is a very bad habit.

The voice in Ori's head was startling. 'Oh, hi, Prajapati! I'm glad you're still around. We could use some perspective here.' Ori didn't ask what 'statistics' were. (Ori didn't want to know.)

Chuckle. *I've been here all along. I just didn't want to get into a discussion with Hani. That angel could talk an ophan into wearing sunglasses. Follow Hani into the lightstream, honey. I don't want that Ya'akov to see you yet, and this way, he can't tell one angel from another.*

This was true, because as Ori approached it was evident that the entire soprano section was dancing, enraged, at the top of the Staircase. 'Not again! You're interrupted cantata practice again! That's twice in one century!' The others weren't far behind.

Ya'akov probably couldn't understand them (Ori hoped) because what they sounded like was a very fierce (but totally harmonious) rendition of 'Gloria in excelsis Deo'. This frustrated and amused Ori in equal measure, partly because Latin hadn't been invented yet.

Ori glanced at Ophaniel and confirmed Hani's assessment: indeed, that angel looked about to have, if not a cow, at least a lesser form of livestock. Angelic fits weren't a good idea in the skies over Mesopotamia/Canaan. They tended to start urban legends. Urban legends turned into fireside tales, then myths, and finally ended up in somebody's sacred scriptures and had to be explained in some way. Ori did not want future generations to have to make up a moral to account for spontaneous unseasonable meteor showers. Theologians tended to have overactive imaginations and were too liberal with the footnotes.

Ori was about to suggest opening a negotiating session akin to the one that had got the portal closed last time, twenty years previously.

Twenty years? How time flies, thought Ori. For some reason Prajapati found this hilarious.

Before Ori could say anything to calm down the Choir, or make a move toward the 'supplicating' human with his foot on the doorbell, Hani had flown down the light beam and landed right in front of Ya'akov.

Hani glared at the human in a way that was unmistakably confrontational.

'Just what do you want this time, feller?' Hani demanded in a voice that was commanding and an accent that was, well, not.

How does Hani do that? wondered Ori. *Manage to have a hick accent, no matter what language we're speaking?*

When you figure it out, let me know, replied Prajapati. **Some of the emergent properties of this universe puzzle even me.**

Ori decided to ignore the unsettling implications of that remark, including the business about 'this universe', and concentrate on the problem at hand, which was getting Ya'akov off the portal stone. (Again.) Ori was about to fly down and help negotiate, when Prajapati said **No. Let Hani do it. This is going to be interesting.**

So Ori hung back with the rest of the angels, and watched while Hani dealt with Ya'akov.

'What in the key of G-flat major do you want, you whiny nincompoop?' roared Hani, glaring at the man on the stone. Ori was impressed, having never heard Hani get that loud before. If you didn't know better (and humans didn't), you might be intimidated. The angels watched, curious: even the heavenly choir practice was stilled as they waited to hear what Ya'akov would say.

None of the host, however, were prepared for what came next. Instead of answering, Ya'akov let out a roar of his own. Okay, it was a puny sort of a roar. If the Choir hadn't been playing a rest nobody would have heard it. It didn't exactly set the wilderness to echoing. Nevertheless, it was unexpected. The angels all blinked.

Then Ya'akov charged. Seizing Hani around the waist, the human attempted a tackle. Surprised, Hani took a step backward – but Ya'akov clung to his feathered opponent like a limpet.

The Choir blinked twice.

'Let go of me!' yelped Hani. But instead of letting go, Ya'akov held on tighter, attempting another wrestling hold. Having seen Sumerian wrestling, Ori recognised the technique.

'Hani! Don't let him throw you!' yelled Ori. *Why is he doing this?* Ori wondered.

The wrestling match commenced in earnest – Ya'akov seeming determined and Hani too surprised by the whole thing to put up much of a defence at first, merely fending off the holds of his ridiculous opponent.

The angelic host, fascinated, sat down on the steps to watch. Somebody ran upstairs for snacks.

Well, punch holes in me and call me a flute, thought Ori. *They're fighting back now.*

I guess it was just a matter of time, said Prajapati. **Awe only lasts for so long. And Hani did provoke him. He's been through a lot in the last twenty years, you know.**

'Really?' said Ori aloud, since nobody could hear him in the crowd noise, anyway. Ori sat down on a step and accepted a bowl of what looked like buttered popcorn. Tasted like it, too. Far up the Staircase, some angels had formed a doowop quartet and were singing something about the eye of a tiger.

While Hani and Ya'akov wrestled, Prajapati explained.

You remember when you met Ya'akov last time, he was on his way to his uncle's place?

Ori nodded. Prajapati continued. *His uncle lives in Paddan Aram. Back then Ya'akov was younger. And single. The first thing he did was fall in love with his cousin, a pretty girl by the name of Rakhel.*

'Darfdatdat?' mumbled Ori in the wrong language and with a mouthful of tasty popcorn.

Prajapati laughed. *Yes, they're allowed by the local ordinances. Rules about inbreeding can be exaggerated, although they probably need to tone it down after this. Their parents and grandparents were related, too. Anyway, the problem isn't Rakhel. The problem is her dad. Let us say that when it comes to character, there is a strong family resemblance between Ya'akov and his uncle Laban.*

Do tell, thought Ori. *It looks like we've got time*. Indeed, it seemed as if the wrestling match wasn't going to end any time soon: what with Hani trying to get away and Ya'akov determined not to let that happen, the contest seemed to be set to go on all night. The angels started placing bets.

'What are you guys betting?' yelped Ori in alarm, and heard Prajapati chuckle.

Who's going to dust the music stands, sort the scores for a week, stuff like that. Don't worry, they're mostly harmless. Oh, yeah, Ya'akov and Laban. Ori settled in to learn the tale while angels passed out chocolate-covered raisins. The quartet came up with a new number called 'In the Still of the Night":

In the still of the night
I held you
Held you tight...

If Hani hears that... thought Ori, but waved the thought away and listened to Prajapati tell the tale of Ya'akov:

> **Laban promised Ya'akov he could marry Rakhel if he would work for him for seven years as an assistant supervising herdsman. Sort of indentured servitude in exchange for matrimony. Humans come up with the oddest commercial arrangements. Anyway, they agreed to the bargain, and there was a wedding. The bride hid her blushes beneath a veil, and the partying went on all night. It was dead dark by the time the couple got to bed.**

'We care about human weddings, why?' wondered Ori.

'What did you say?' A burly basso profundo punched Ori in the side, then bellowed, 'Get him in a half-nelson, Hani! This is the most fun I've had since the Milky Way got started!' Ori sighed.

> **Now, back to what I was saying before I was so rudely interrupted... oh, yes. We care about human weddings, this one in particular, because these two are the biggest con artists in Mesopotamia. Worse than Nimrod. When Ya'akov woke up in the morning, he found out that he wasn't married to Rakhel after all. The wedding had been for her older sister Leah.**

> *Ya'akov was furious. Nobody asked Leah what she thought about it. Or Rakhel, either, for that matter. At breakfast, Laban was in full oil-on-troubled-waters mode. Can't marry the younger daughter before the older one, it's against local laws, etc. Tell you what I'll do, he says, like the used camel salesmen he started out as: give me another seven years and I'll throw in Rakhel, too. You'll be a patriarch before you know it.*

Ori choked on a kernel of popcorn and was rescued by an angel passing out fizzy drinks. 'They allow polygamy?'

Of course they do, was the reply. *If it's a bad idea, these people are all for it.*

> *Ya'akov accepted the offer. He now had two wives. But he didn't stop at two. Leah and Rakhel are also...a bit competitive. In their case, it was the baby-making department. At first, Leah was having all the babies and poor Rakhel was having none. She blamed this on me, naturally – or rather, the 'God with no name', who got constantly petitioned.*
>
> *Before you ask, yes, I can interfere sometimes. But there's a price. And who do these women think they are, expecting me to put half the planet in disarray just so they can one-up their sister with another infant? That is NOT a good reason to be having babies. And it's not like they ever offer to do anything helpful in return, oh, no. It's, 'Let me have a boy baby (boys are better, for some reason) and I'll put up another standing-stone monument for you,'*

> or 'Let me have the most kids and I'll name one after you.' They are as bad as the men.
>
> **The worst thing the sisters did was to rope their MAIDS into the whole business. Once Leah stopped having babies, she 'gave' Ya'akov her maid Zilpah. To marry. Because then Zilpah's babies were part of Team Leah. Not to be outdone, Rakhel 'gave' him HER maid, Bilhah. The maids had nothing to say about it. Last I paid any attention, they were up to 11 boys among them and an unspecified number of girls. They give me a pain, these people.**

Ori listened in fascination but kept one eye on the wrestling match. Once, Hani seemed about to become airborne – only to be slammed back to the mat by Ya'akov. Since the 'mat' was a flat piece of limestone, Ori winced, worried that his friend might be hurt. Ori made a move to go and help Hani, but Prajapati demurred, saying they needed to 'play fair' and mumbling something Ori didn't catch about 'history'. So Ori sat back down and listened to Prajapati complain about Ya'akov some more.

> *Once Ya'akov and Laban were related by marriage, they settled down to cheating each other at business. You've seen some of what Ya'akov's accumulated over the years. That's just the tip of the – ...a small corner of the ziggurat. Those two were in the livestock trade, big-time. Cows, sheep, goats, camels, donkeys, horses: anything on four feet. And the by-products, of course: milk, wool, leather, things like that. They don't mind trading in people, why would they care about animals? Only most of*

the time, they're very careful with the livestock. Otherwise it brings down the prices.

Laban never played fair with Ya'akov. He's a slippery character, is Laban: worse than Ea Nasir. Laban changed the terms of their agreement seven times. Ya'akov got tired of it – after all, these were Laban's daughters and grandchildren the man was cheating. Ya'akov decided to get even as only Ya'akov could. He studied animal husbandry by bribing the oldest and wisest herdsmen in the area. Then he made a deal with Laban: he, Ya'akov, would take all the spotted, speckled, and dark lambs and kids in the flock as his wages.

Laban was really pleased about this – and tried to keep his spotted and speckled ewes and she-goats away from Ya'akov's.

Ya'akov had studied enough animal reproduction to write a book about it. But he didn't write a book, oh, no. He kept this information to himself. It would be tedious to explain how he did it, but he made his flocks grow and Laban's shrink, and Laban couldn't figure out how he did it. It basically requires a sophisticated understanding of genetics and the reproductive habits of sheep and goats. Really odd when you realise that the human who could explain

> all this won't be born for several thousand more years⁷.

'That family sounds hard to deal with,' commented Ori. Down in the arena – that is, on the flat portal stone – Ya'akov was taking a pounding as Hani buffeted him with beating wings. The stubborn human refused to let go.

> *Finally* [said Prajapati] ***Ya'akov had enough capital to set out on his own. He packed the whole family and started back in this direction. He didn't tell Laban he was going because Laban would have tried to stop him. In fact, once Laban found out about it, he DID try to stop him, coming out with an armed force. That's this trip, by the way. You've already seen the reception committee on this end. When he set out from Paddan Aram, his father-in-law was ready to fight him.***

'Ya'akov seems to have that effect on people,' commented Ori, waving a cup for a refill. One of the catering angels obliged.

> ***He does, indeed. This time it was because somebody stole Laban's household gods. Now, Ya'akov may be very scientifically-minded and all, but he and his whole clan have a superstitious streak a yard wide. As it happened, Rakhel stole those household gods – she's particularly fond of the Inanna statue, which she used to play dress-up with as a kid...***

---

[7] If you are interested in exactly how Ya'akov did it, please consult Dr Scott B Noegel, 'Sex, Sticks, and the Trickster in Gen. 30:31-43: A New Look at an Old Crux,' *Journal of Ancient Near Eastern Society* 25 (1997), 7-17.

'Wait a minute!' interrupted Ori. 'I thought these people worshipped *you*. Or at least, the 'God with no name'. What's all this polytheism about?'

> *From humans you want logic? How long have you been here, anyway? They like to hedge their bets. Besides, what's a Mesopotamian fashion doll among friends? Anyway, Rakhel's still got those gods because she's as devious as the rest of them.*
>
> *When her father's men showed up to search her wagon, she hid the gods in the sofa cushions and claimed she couldn't get up because she was having her period. They have a taboo about it.*

'They obviously fail to fear retribution from those gods when they take their names in vain.'

Or they think I'll protect them, laughed Prajapati. *The bottom line is: these people do what they please and then make up what they consider to be good excuses for their behaviour. And no, I'm as interested as you are to see what reason Ya'akov has for angel-wrestling. Other than to release twenty years of pent-up frustration about his relatives.*

They were about to find out.

As the first rays of dawn were peeking over the horizon, Hani decided to throw the match. The tired angel simply sat down on the stone.

'All right, Bubba,' said Hani, panting, 'you win. Thou hast wrassled with Heaven and hast prevailed. Boy, hast thou prevailed. Thou shalt henceforth be known as the Divine Wrassling Champeen of Mesopotamia. Happy? What else do you want? Spit it out!'

Still hanging onto Hani, Ya'akov studied the angel and then, in fact, practically spat it out: 'I. Want. A. Blessing.'

'A blessin'? Son, ain't I done blessed you seven ways to breakfast? I've declared you the champion. What else do you want?'

'A. Real. Blessing. Like the one Esaf got.' Ya'akov's eyes glistened with hope: hope balanced against the memory of every slight and disappointment of his life. Every angel watching saw this at the same time, and every angel suddenly understood that Ya'akov was a human who hoarded hurt as if it were money in the bank. Ugly money, sure. But something that accrued to him as personal capital.

Hani got it, too. Placing a hand gently on the man's shoulder, Hani pronounced solemnly, 'You shall have it. Because thou hast wrassled with Heaven and hast prevailed, I hereby give thee a new name. Instead of Ya'akov, thou shalt be...' Hani faltered for a moment, unable to come up with an impressive-sounding name.

For a moment, all was silence – the noisy Staircase-full of angels held their breath, the birds of dawn temporarily forgot to tweet, and even the nearby brook flowed more quietly. Then, out of a pale sky, from behind the fading stars, came a deep Voice.

Everybody heard it.

'Israel,' it said.

Chapter 38: Make Yourself at Home

Ya'akov he said.

Only it came out sound like, **'IS-RA-EL!'** Big, booming. Portentous.

Basically, utterly unlike Prajapati as Ori knew him. *No wonder he doesn't want to talk to these people,* thought Ori.

The sound echoed across the sky. It was heard in The Penthouse, of course. It was heard by the hyperactive soprano section on The Staircase. It seemed to galvanise the heavenly host. Who did a curious thing.

They burst into song. Like most Penthouse numbers, it was very beautiful and in perfect harmony. Also like most Penthouse numbers, it went on for quite a while. Ophaniel got into the spirit of things, revolving and spinning wheels and flickering and giving off coloured lights. It was quite a show.

Ori, Hani, and Ya'akov were surprised, but for different reasons. Hani was surprised because the music seemed to be spontaneous and in Hani's experience, Samya and the choir didn't do spontaneous. Ori was surprised because the choir sounded particularly fine, possibly due to the acoustics over Mesopotamia, possibly augmented by the configuration of the hills, the ambient temperature, and the dryness of the climate. Anyway, it seemed as if the ensemble had really found its sound tonight.

Ya'akov was surprised because, frankly, he didn't realise anybody cared enough about him to offer him a serenade – let alone a whole angelic chorus. He began reevaluating his life choices.

Most surprised of all were the heavenly choir members themselves. Immortals that they were, all of them remembered, if they tried hard, that once upon a time there had been this Creator. You know, the One who made all of this. Nice fellow, never put on airs or anything. Pleasant to talk to, unassuming. They couldn't remember when it had happened, but He seemed to have gone away. He just wasn't there anymore. It hadn't made much difference to the heavenly host: they'd gone about their singing as usual. Over time they began to think of themselves as an autonomous collective.

Samya always chose the music, just as Ophaniel guarded the portals (and scared the living daylights out of anything that wasn't part of The Penthouse). Sami was the choir director, after all. But this time they'd all begun singing, spontaneously as it were, something the eight-winged conductor had not announced: an Amen, in fact. A grand signal of sidereal agreement that imported…what? That this puny, whining, manipulative, annoying human was somehow important enough to merit a whole choir number just for *him*?

What ruffled the most angelic feathers was the realisation that wherever or whenever Prajapati was in spacetime, He was still very much in charge. If He wanted an Amen he got an Amen. They were still coming to terms with this information as the last 'A-a-a-men' resounded from the hills of Canaan. Then all was still.

You could have heard a mouse squeak.

Hani let go of Ya'akov (Israel).

Ya'akov (Israel) let go of Hani – and stepped off the rock.

Without so much as a whoosh, a sigh, or a feeble 'Amen', the portal snapped shut. There was a tiny beat as all of reality adjusted to alterations.

Hani looked at Ya'akov (Israel) with a grin of admiration. 'Well, son, you got your miracle. Now go in peace. And try to stay out of trouble, will you, please?' And Hani offered Ya'akov a hand to stand up. Realising that he had been kneeling, Ya'akov accepted the hand. And groaned a bit as he tried to walk: he seemed to have developed a limp.

'Looks like you pulled a muscle there, friend,' said Hani. 'When you get to camp, heat a bag of salt and slap it on there. It'll help with the swelling.'

'How do you figure these things out?' asked Ori as the two angels flew away in the direction of the rising sun.

Hani combined a shrug with an Immelmann turn. 'I'm not sure. Probably comes from the same place the choir got that Amen. Which reminds me, old son: when were you gonna tell me He's been listenin' in the whole time?'

The answer was a laugh that echoed in both their heads. ***You're as bad as Ya'akov. Now he thinks he's important because he 'wrestled with God'. He thinks I pay more attention to him than to his neighbours. And you're worried I'm eavesdropping.***

'Why don't you just talk to people?' asked Hani, flying upside down for the fun of it.

Because when I do, they hear bellowing like that, said Prajapati grumpily. *We have to take things slowly. But tonight was a start, kids: thanks for your help.* Hani seemed to be satisfied with that. The two angels flew on, enjoying the chance to stretch their wings and catch a cool breeze. They flew until they were out of sight of the scene on the ground. Ori was beginning to wonder how they were going to get back to their version of Mesopotamia and check up on the Ninevites, when they spotted a sight familiar to Ori.

'Oh, good, here's The Paternoster.'

'Wow. After you, bro,' said Hani. They took turns landing and by folding their wings both of them managed to stand inside the car.

Hani looked around. 'Kinda small.'

For answer, Ori took Hani by the shoulders, turning the other angel around. 'Ah,' Hani said, seeing the door. Ori opened it and they both stepped inside.

'Far out,' was Hani's only comment.

Ori gave Hani the grand tour: bedrooms with angel perches, the pool, the dining room ('for company'), the kitchen, the library, the music room with instruments of all kinds. They ended up in the large dressing room. Hani gave a whoop of glee and started trying things on.

'Holy fashion design! This is amazing! You mean humans all wear these getups?'

Ori shrugged. 'Somewhere, sometime, I guess. So far it's all been robes and such.'

'Do I want to know somebody who would wear this?' Hani mused aloud, holding up a feather boa as if it might bite. 'Looks like a birdsnake.'

Ori groaned and collapsed onto an overstuffed sofa. 'Don't mention snakes! Did I tell you about the time I got turned into a cobra?'

'No, you didn't,' replied Hani, holding up an ornate coat of embroidered finery. 'Do tell.'

And Ori related the whole saga in the mythical Garden, complete with voice impersonations of Kava and Idim. The impersonations were satirical and not very flattering.

'I can tell you're still sore about it,' commented Hani, still pulling out outfits and throwing them all over the place.

'Hey!' protested Ori. 'Less of that! Do you think we have maid service in here?'

Actually, you do, Prajapati broke in.

'There are other people here?' asked Hani.

A chuckle. ***No, not people. But I put in an AI for housekeeping.***

'What's an AI when it's at home?'

Artificial Intelligence. The humans will think they invented it in a couple of millennia. It's just a sub-sentient form that performs certain automatic tasks, like dusting, pool maintenance, and putting clothes back on hangers, since you seem to be unable to do it.

Ori laughed. 'Haniel, agent of chaos.'

In reply Haniel threw a pile of clothes at Ori. The pile of clothes had been a neat stack of well-folded garments before Hani got to them. Ori examined them.

'Hey, these are nice! Look, Hani: these shirts are soft and comfortable. They sort of move with you. Not stiff like wool. Or scratchy. And not as wrinkly as linen. What is this stuff?'

Cotton, said Prajapati. *The humans in Sumeria will figure it out soon. It's good stuff, you're right – as long as people do their own work and don't force others to do it.*

'Always the way,' agreed Ori, who'd seen enough bad human behaviour to guess at Prajapati's meaning. Ori slipped on a shirt – easier than it sounds because angel wings, being dimensionally transcendental, are not stopped by things like mere cloth and simply permeate the material and settle themselves nicely on the outside. Ori's did. Ori took a look in the mirror and was satisfied. 'I like it. Try it, Hani.'

'I will, soon's I can get into these bottom parts,' said Hani. The trousers, made out of a heavier, blue cotton, were even more intriguing to the two angels. Hani managed to get one leg into the thing, which Prajapati explained was called 'jeans', but was having trouble with the other leg, and hopped around precariously, threatening to fall over at any moment.

'That jeans appears to be winning,' commented Ori, fiddling with the strange brass thing on what they assumed was the back. Ori slid the little square up and down, watching as it opened and closed by bringing the teeth together.

'Them jeans is tricky,' agreed Hani.

That's a zipper, explained Prajapati. *It goes in front.*

'Now he tells me,' said Hani, trying to turn them around – and promptly falling down.

It took a lot of wrangling – and considerable laughter – but eventually both angels were attired in t-shirts and jeans. Which Hani declared were the 'best clothes I've ever worn and I don't wanna take 'em off, ever. Besides, I've done forgot how that-there zipper thing works.'

Humans will often wear those shirts with writing on the front and/or back, Prajapati said.

Hani liked this idea. 'What will they say? Things like 'All Praise to Nudimmud'?'

Sometimes religious stuff. But mostly they will advertise their wares or praise their favourite musicians…

'Good,' said Ori. 'Musicians deserve praise.'

'Oh, no!' groaned Ori.

'I'm going to get the AI to help me print t-shirts!' announced Hani. 'I want the one about the dog.' Ori groaned again and threw a sofa pillow at Hani. This resulted in a pillow fight.

More jokes, a short nap, and a hot dinner later, the two angels discovered something else they liked about The Paternoster: it had a bowling alley. Prajapati explained the rules, Hani modified them to 'make them more fun,' and Ori figured out both how a bowling approach was supposed to work (by looking it up in the library), and, which was harder, how to keep score.

Ori and Hani enjoyed this new game. It was fun to watch the balls roll down the lane. It was satisfying when the pins fell with a loud crash. It was delightful to clown and pretend to compete and occasionally roll a gutter ball, accidentally on purpose, and generally act like a couple of human children. Best of all, it was a joy to relax, just be, and forget about the fate of the universe for an hour or two.

Chapter 39: New Nineveh, and Where the Old One Got To

When Ori and Hani returned to Nineveh they found a completely different city than the one they had left.

The streets were clean.

People and animals appeared to be well-fed and content.

There was greenery everywhere, thanks to expert gardening and irrigation.

Everyone looked busy but happy. Kids went to school in the mornings, came home for the midday meal followed by the early-afternoon siesta, then helped their parents in homes, stalls, and workshops, combining family time with learning. Grandmothers tended stewpots and babies. Grandfathers hung around street corners playing board games, drinking beer, and offering to reminisce for the benefit of anyone who'd listen. Dogs fetched, goats ate the weeds, ducks laid eggs, and cats supervised.

Commerce appeared to be booming. Best of all, there was no sign of the oppressive mismanagement of the previous administration. Infrastructure had been repaired, and nobody was bossing anybody else around.

'How did you do it?' Ori asked Nisaba in wonder.

The good-hearted hotelier laughed: her laughter was infectious. 'It wasn't hard once we grasped a very important principle.'

Ori and Hani leaned forward across the table, all ears.

'At first, we were angry about how badly we'd been treated,' Nisaba said. 'People wanted to storm the Town Council building, the guild halls, and the rich merchants' houses. They wanted to seize the guard stations and courtrooms and put the miscreants on trial. There were shouts of *off with their heads* and such.'

Hani nodded. 'I can imagine. What stopped them?'

'They realised that getting even wasn't fixing. They might waste all their energy and momentum on revenge and have none left for the things they really wanted – things like fresh food, schools, fair trade, cleaner streets. . .in the end, common sense won out.'

Gili and Jonah joined them. Gili had some thoughts of her own. 'There was another important realisation,' she told Nisaba. 'For just about forever, it seems to me, anytime you suggested that maybe it wasn't the best idea in the world to let a few scam artists run the city and take from the poor, some fool was bound to look at you with mock pity and say something incredibly stupid like, That's adorable. You actually think you can change the world! It's always been like this, and it will always be like this.' Gili shrugged. 'Somehow, we finally got over believing that. Just because fools say things like that is no reason for us to waste our lives accepting the unacceptable.'

The whole time Gili was speaking, Jonah, sitting beside her, was gazing at her with the adoration angels reserved for celestial harmonies. The formerly scruffy prophet had undergone a transformation: he was neat, clean, and appeared to be in his right mind for a change. To Ori and Hani's surprise, he hadn't spouted any nonsense the whole time they'd been with him. They considered this a considerable achievement on the part of his talented wife. Ori and Hani weren't really surprised to find that there had been a wedding in their absence, but were sorry to have missed the festivities.

Nisaba was thoughtful. 'Jonah, we're really glad you came here, you know that? You really started something and we're grateful.'

'Me?' Jonah was startled. 'I didn't do anything at all!' he protested. 'It was all you folks!'

Gili cocked her head. 'I think it was your story that convinced them,' she said. 'You were so set in your ways, so determined to uphold a belief system that taught you to despise anybody you regard as other. But you came, anyway. You went through a lot and you changed your mind. If you could, we could.' She squeezed his arm. Ori thought Jonah might pass out from sheer happiness.

'This is the best news we've heard in a long time,' said Hani, and Ori nodded. Then they ordered lunch.

****

Leaving their friends to their various pursuits, the two incognito angels went on a stroll around Nineveh – a much more pleasant pursuit than it had been before.

'I can't get over the difference,' confessed Hani. 'And all it took was good will and a little common sense.'

'Common sense,' commented Ori. 'Not always so common.'

From that mysterious somewhere where he always was, Prajapati agreed.

Looking out from the city walls, Ori and Hani could see the roads stretching out from Nineveh to other places in Mesopotamia: Wassukanni, and Halab beyond; the ruins of Akkad; far south to Warka; but not to Babylon, which no one could find because it had become legendary – a scary bedtime story for children. Gibil and the other kids had done their work well.

'What's that?' Hani pointed in the direction of a tiny village a couple of hours' walk from the city gate. It didn't look too prosperous. There was no traffic headed that way, either.

'That's new,' said Ori. They decided to check it out.

****

The 'inn', if such it could be called, looked like what Hani termed 'a real dump.' Although the badly chipped sign outside advertised 'luxury accommodations', there wasn't much sign of luxury to be found. In fact, the place looked distinctly shabby. Other signs advertised 'nightly entertainment, high-class' and 'gourmet dining', although the few customers sitting glumly under the table awnings seemed to be unimpressed with the thin, warm beer.

'This place wasn't here before,' said Ori. 'And we haven't been gone that long, maybe a few months?' Hani nodded. So how did a place this new get to looking this rundown? they both thought.

It's a mystery about shabby motels, said Prajapati. ***Also public housing projects. It's the same throughout***

spacetime: the intent to commit criminal neglect somehow moves faster than plain old timeworn.

The proprietor of the place surprised them. Hani and Ori instantly recognised him as the 'witty' city councillor who had made jokes at Jonah's expense. What was he doing running a seedy inn? He was even wearing the same ornate robe as before. Only now, the garment was fraying at the hem and cuffs, and there were a couple of stains that cleaning had failed to get out. 'Come down in the world' is the phrase that leapt to mind. His carefully coiffed hair, ridiculous in these surroundings, fooled nobody.

The innkeeper, however, was as expansive in his manner as he had been as a city executive. He stood in the doorway and welcomed his two guests with a regal and condescending air. 'Come in, come in! Delights await you here at the Maranineveh! I am your host, Kingu. This is a very high-class establishment, which I'm sure you will appreciate. Come on in!'

Kingu led the way into the dark lobby, which was filled with elaborate but badly scratched furniture. 'You notice those fancy lamps?' He pointed to the terracotta oil lamps hanging from the ceiling. They were given to me by the king of Erech. He's a good friend. He said to me, Mr Kingu, I really love what you do for the hospitality industry over in Nineveh. I'd like you to have these tokens of my appreciation.' Kingu laughed. 'I can't help it, I'm popular. People like Kingu.'

Hani, trying to keep a straight face, said, 'With all this popularity, would you happen to have a double room for us for tonight?'

'Oh, yes,' said Kingu hastily. 'I can always make room for discriminating guests. We'll put you up in the deluxe suite reserved for visiting dignitaries. I can tell you're important people from...'

'Warka,' said Ori hastily, before Hani could make up anything more outrageous. After all, Ori had documentation as a scribe of that city. 'We're on a sort-of fact-finding mission for the temple there.'

'Of course,' said Kingu, impressed. He took a small bell from his robe and rang it, and a servant materialized beside him. 'Take these guests to the deluxe suite, and make sure they get one of my special cocktails. You'll like the suite,' he confided to Hani, who was still struggling with facial muscles. 'It has an *on-suit* bath and water closet.'

They followed the bell-hop upstairs to the 'deluxe suite', which turned out to be a largish room containing two beds, a chaise longue that was missing some of its stuffing, and a dust-covered table and chairs. The boy hastily dusted these off and pointed to the inside door.

'That's the *on-suit*,' he said with an eyeroll. 'We have to call it that. It's in the contract.'

'You did well,' Ori assured him, giving him a coin. The bell-hop opened the curtains and the door to the balcony before withdrawing.

As soon as he'd left, Hani let out a guffaw. 'His name is Kingu?' Hani gasped. 'He's well-named!'

'Kingu' was Sumerian for 'unskilled labourer'.

Ori sighed and surveyed the room. 'This furniture has definitely seen better days, and in a better place.'

'It could have stayed in a better place,' commented Hani, 'if its owner had had better morals.' Hani, too, explored the room, noting that the table wobbled and the carpet was frayed. Then the inquisitive angel looked into the 'on suit', and let out a howl of laughter that made Ori jump.

'You. Have. To. See. This,' Hani gasped, pointing.

Ori looked.

The *'on-suit'* did, indeed, have a bathtub, as advertised. Also a water closet. The rest of the space in the room was taken up by piles of tablets. Tablets with writing on them.

Ori picked one up and read, 'Treaty of Nimrod with the leaders of Nineveh. . .wait, here's another. . .campaigns in Assyria. . .the Epic of Gilgamesh?' Ori looked at Hani in astonishment. 'He's taken the records and library of Nineveh and. . .'

'. . .stored them in a bathroom!' they both finished.

'That has to be a unique event, even for humans,' was all Hani could choke out, gasping for breath. Fortunately, the bell-hop reappeared with two 'cocktails' – which turned out to be a mixture of beer and citron juice, which wasn't half bad.

Chapter 40: A Night Among the Stars

When Ori and Hani came downstairs at Maranineveh for what was advertised as 'dinner and live entertainment', they marvelled at the collection of diners. Arranged around the mismatched, scuffed, low tables were equally scruffy couches where diners reclined to eat. There was certainly enough food: the tables were covered with dishes. Some of the food was familiar: bean paste, cucumber in yoghurt sauce with garlic and dill, barley cake and, of course, beer. But some of the dishes puzzled Ori. Did Maranineveh specialise in exotic food?

'Get a load of the picture on the wall,' whispered Hani. 'What in the infernal drum solo is he eating?'

Indeed, it was a puzzle. The gaudy (tasteless) painting showed a diner ingesting, with obvious enjoyment, something in a long barley roll, end foremost.

Kingu appeared at Ori's elbow. He noticed the two 'dignitaries' staring at the picture with expressions he naturally mistook for admiration.

'Great picture, eh? I had War-holi of Halab paint that for me,' said Kingu. He poked Ori in the side. 'He owed me a favour, if you take my meaning. I managed to get him to leave out the cats. Nasty things, cats. Don't you agree the painting dresses up the place?'

Hani asked, 'Er, just exactly what is the man in the picture supposed to be eatin'?'

Kingu grinned. 'It's a Maranineveh specialty! That's what makes the painting so good.' He preened. 'I call it a *hot dog*. I was the first one to name them. Now everybody says *hot dog*.'

Hani nearly choked. 'Tell me y'all ain't eatin' dogs in here?'

Kingu looked annoyed. He batted away the question. 'Of course not! It's just a colourful expression. Because the barley bun is long, like one of those silly dogs they have in North Nineveh. The meat is actually ground desert vole. Fresh-caught.'

The last time angels had stared at anyone like that was when Ophaniel had tried to explain the enfolding of the N-dimensional Euclidean space through N-dimensional spheres, about ten seconds after the Big Bang – so, a long time ago. Oblivious, Kingu went on to tout the merits of his other 'specialty day lah mason', the Hamb-herder, which was a round fishcake breaded and deep-fat-fried. He urged his guests to try it. Ori made ambiguous noises, while Hani surreptitiously looked around for places of food concealment should the proprietor follow through on the threat to send either alleged comestible in their direction.

Fortunately, just as he'd steered them to a table, their host's beady eyes, always scanning the room for someone more important to talk to, lighted on an overdressed matron he mistook for Princess Gratia of Eridu. So Kingu left them in the relatively capable hands of the wine steward, while he hustled off to see if he could impress the princess with some creative name-dropping.

'Would you like to see the wine list, sirs?' asked the unctuous waiter whom they recognised as a former city hall official. Ori was about to send him on his way when Hani grabbed the clay tablet and began to study it, utterly ignoring Ori's frantic gestures.

Hani pointed. 'This *Shatoh de Gilgamesh* looks innerestin'. What's in it?'

'Oh, good choice, sir,' the waiter purred. 'This vintage is made of dates from the Euphrates region. Aged a full six weeks.' Paying no attention to Ori's eye-rolling, Hani ordered a carafe and two winecups.

'You'll be sorry,' warned Ori. 'You know that date wine is nasty stuff.'

Hani shrugged. 'You gotta try the local specialties, right?'

'Not if they contain ground vole,' growled Ori.

Their attention was drawn to the stage, where an ear-splitting but mercifully brief fanfare had erupted from a musician giving a squeaky blast on a small brass trumpet. Kingu took the stage, also briefly and mercifully. He held up his hands to forestall applause, although there wasn't any.

'Friends, distinguished guests, welcome to this evening's show! (Waiters, keep working!) Tonight we have some really high-class entertainment for you. I know, we always have classy entertainment here at Maranineveh, everybody says so. First off, here are the Ninevettes to dance for you. They're all really, really beautiful girls, every one a 12, if you know what I mean,' he winked in a way that managed to be both sad and lascivious at the same time. 'Give 'em a big hand!'

With that, he backed into the wings, leading the (half-hearted) applause, until he managed to trip backwards into the arms of a decorative statue. Two stagehands, looking as unsurprised as if he did this every night (which, in fact, he did), extricated their boss as the music began to play a familiar tune.

Ori groaned and Hani laughed.

'Will that song never go away?' Ori wondered aloud as Hani sang quietly, 'And they dance to the gods like the people in Akkad. . .'

'Stop that!' Ori fussed. Then the waiter brought the wine, and another the menu, and Ori concentrated on querying every single item on it to make sure it was safe for a couple of lacto-vegetarians to eat, while Hani watched the gyrations of the soloist with considerable appreciation.

'What?' Hani said when Ori complained. 'It's culture! One day it will be historical! Besides, I'm memorising the moves for future performance.'

'That's what I was afraid of,' said Ori drily. They tried the wine: Ori made a face, still not liking date wine. 'Saying the gods drank this stuff is akin to blasphemy.'

'I dunno, it's kind of fruity,' said Hani. 'I think I like it. Maybe we'll try the beer later.'

'No, you won't,' retorted Ori. 'You'll stick to this stuff all night. *Bier nach Wein, das lass' sein*, remember?'

'I understood that completely,' said Hani. 'Why is that? That Tower of Babel trick of Prajapati's was really something.'

Thank you, said a voice that was only in both of their heads. ***I try. Don't drink too much of that wine. Even angels get tipsy. I'll say good-night now. I'm going to go and play with the cats: the floor show is starting in earnest.***

'I'll drink to that,' toasted Hani as the lights focused on a single spot in the centre of the stage – where a familiar figure began to sing.

> *I wrote a letter to my girlfriend,*
> *I pricked it front and back,*
> *Signed at the bottom with a rolling seal,*
> *Next day, it came right back.*
>
> *Return to sender,*
> *There's no such place,*
> *At the bottom of the Tigris,*
> *Or up in outer space...*

Hani and Ori groaned. 'Elvipres!'

'I wondered where he'd got to,' added Hani. 'It seemed like the music in Nineveh had got better lately.'

Food arrived. Even a suspicious Ori was satisfied – there was no sign of fish or flesh, and the cucumber sauce was actually tasty. It almost made up for the singing.

> *The moral of this story,*
> *Don't annoy the gods!*
> *And if you have a girlfriend*
> *Don't let her move to Akkad...*

The angels looked at each other and both reached for the wine. Ori sighed, and ordered another carafe.

Elvipres sang all his 'greatest hits' – including the one about the dog, the one about the sandal...

> ... *but my sandals of sky-blue leather, do not touch...* [8]

...the song about the bad neighbourhood in Warka, the one about being arrested for catnapping in Halab...and, surprisingly, the one about Jonah:

> *It's better than the story of Daniel or Ruth,*
> *Although it is fishy, it's nothing but truth...*

'Hey, that song gets around,' commented Hani, whose musical taste was mellowing in parallel to the wine intake.

'Where did you learn that song, anyway?' Ori asked.

'Gabriel. Horn players know all the good ones.'

Finally, Elvipres reached his grand finale – the one for which his stage show had become famous in the less-discriminating venues. We refer, of course, to his stirring 'Mesopotamian Trilogy', the song medley that managed to be maudlin, patriotic, and depressing, all at the same time. It began with what was usually an upbeat, peppy song about life on the Tigris – only now, slowed down to a dirge. Elvipres sang dolefully:

---

[8] 'nig-na-me si-ib-ak-ke-en, e-sir kus-za-gin-gu ba-ra-tag-ge-en.' Professor Simo Parpola, Helsinki, 2001.

> *In Nineveh we lived in style*
> *'Til Mama got et by a crocodile,*
> *Look away, look away, look away, to the Tigris...*

'Is this stuff affectin' my hearin'?' mused Hani.

> *Hush, little baby, don't you cry,*
> *There'll be pancakes in the sky by and by...*

'Wake me up when this is over,' begged Ori.

After what appeared to the angels to be millennia, the finale reached its apotheosis.

> *Glory, glory, jubilates,*
> *My enemies have drowned in the Euphrates...*

Everybody in the dining room stood and sang along. Most had tears in their eyes.

Hani and Ori struggled to their feet, not wanting to be conspicuous. They stood there silently while the entire assembly sobbed audibly and sang 'as we go rolling on!' The fact that they were both swaying gently in time to what Elvipres called music was taken by those around them as a sign that even foreigners were moved by the plight of the former rulers of Nineveh.

In actual fact, both angels were fairly drunk.

This was probably good, in a way: neither was tempted, as they might otherwise have been, to yell at these people that they had NOT been hard done by. That nobody in Nineveh missed them. That the place was better off without them. That, in fact, all they appeared to be good for was sitting around a run-down resort hotel, feeling sorry for themselves. If they had said all this, they might have felt better, but it would have done no earthly (or heavenly) good. People like the former rulers of Nineveh appeared to be ineducable.

As soon as the song was over, the crowd broke into thunderous applause. Ori and Hani clapped politely, and then sat back down for the inevitable encore about the blue sandals. Feeling slightly dizzy, they both declined dessert and went outside for some fresh air.

The night sky above Mesopotamia was, as always, a deep velvet blue-black. A dazzling array of stars made the heavens magic. Hani took a long look and inhaled deeply the scent of night-blooming flowers. 'No wonder everybody on earth is always makin' up stories about the pictures in the sky.'

Ori stretched, staggered a bit, and then giggled. 'Yes. There's at least one dog up there, and a hunter, and some queen on a throne, and sea creatures and a horse and. . . '

'. . . US!' finished Hani, launching into the night and seeming to aim for the brightest star. Ori shrugged and followed. Together, the two shook off alcohol and the lingering tones of cheap music, both of which had left a bad taste in their mouths.

Chapter 41: Cruising Down the River

Cruisin' down the Tigris
On a Sunday afternoon...

... sang Hani as they lounged in the back of a reed boat. Their friend and host, Nukhu, laughed as he poled the boat through the reeds and into a clear channel.

'Is it Sunday?' asked Ori lazily.

Hani laughed. 'Nah. It's Ninurta, Saturday. Cruisin' down the Tigris on Ninurta afternoon...'

Ori sighed. 'I wish...'

'Hush!' said Hani. 'You can't make a wish on Ninurta.'

'Why not?' asked Ori, puzzled.

Hani shrugged. 'I dunno. It's a rule, or something.'

Nukhu had heard all this and shook his head. 'You two can do whatever you want. There's nobody around but me – and I know you're gods.' He winked.

'Just how do you know that?' demanded Ori with a sharp look in Hani's direction. That angel blushed and Nukhu grinned.

He pointed to the little goat kid in the other end of the boat – bow or stern, nobody could say for sure, the boat tended to turn around to suit itself, but was completely watertight. 'You see that little rascal? He's called Arrow, because if he weren't tied up he'd be heading straight for where he could do the most mischief. While we were loading at Nineveh, Arrow kept trying to head-butt your friend. Of course, that's not so easy to do, even for a goat. Not when the party in question can rise up and hover in the air. That was one confused little goat.'

Ori sighed. 'I told you, no wings.'

Hani held up hands in protest. 'And I didn't use none, neither. It may have escaped your notice, partner, but them wings ain't gotta be visible to be functional. It's a nice trick, that.'

Ori thought about it, and rose a few feet into the air, still in a cross-legged seated posture – then had to grab for the railing as the boat threatened to glide out from under the experimenter.

From the other side of the boat, Arrow bleated in what sounded exactly like a loud snigger. Ori, Hani, and Nukhu laughed, too.

'I have never met a human who laughed as much as you,' Hani told Nukhu. 'What is the secret of your good humour, friend?'

'I've seen some things,' said Nukhu thoughtfully, 'such that if I hadn't been able to see the funny side of them, they might have got the better of me. Know what I mean?'

Ori nodded. 'Like the time when somebody mistook me for a – something, er, someone I wasn't. It was maddening at the time, but I suppose it was kind of funny.'

'*It ain't necessarily so...*' drawled Hani. 'It's about time you saw the humour in that story. Say, Nukhu, have you ever seen a carp flood?'

Nukhu laughed. 'Carp flood? Oh, yes. And every other kind of flood, too. Do you remember the Gilgamesh flood story? The one about Utu-napishtim?'

Ori's ears pricked up. 'I've heard that one, yes. Where the god warned him and his family, and they built a big boat like this one and put all the animals in?'

Nukhu nodded. 'That's the one. That pretty much happened to me once.'

'Tell,' demanded Hani, bright-eyed.

Nukhu looked out at the river, which wasn't doing anything particularly interesting other than appearing to spawn the occasional duck or heron, and decided to go into story-telling mode.

> 'I used to be a house carpenter, a long time ago, way upriver in Hamazi, in the foothills of the big mountains. I was a young man then. Not married all that long. The children were small. I liked it there, and I liked the work. Hamazi was a nice town, not too big, not too small, good garden soil, government not oppressive. Never too many obligatory offerings to the gods. . .no offence intended.'

'None taken,' said Hani in a dry tone, ignoring Ori's eyeroll. 'Nobody wants all that stuff, anyway.'

'Life was good in Hamazi. It would have been better if it hadn't been for my mother-in-law. Dinni, bless her heart, was a really annoying woman. I wish I could say, 'She meant well,' but I don't really think she did. It wasn't just that I wasn't good enough for her daughter – by which she really meant, I wasn't good enough for her and she'd expected her daughter to marry somebody who would support her in the style she wanted for herself. My wife Abi could have married up, d'ye see? A shopkeeper might do well, buy a bigger shop, even move into the merchant class. But a plain old carpenter? Not much money in reed houses. Not enough to satisfy Dinni.

Like I said, it wasn't just that. Sure, Dinni was disappointed because she wasn't as rich or successful or popular as she wanted to be. But as far as she was concerned, if she couldn't be happy neither could anybody else. She carped at Abi morning, noon, and night. The house wasn't clean enough. The food didn't suit her. The kids were turning into a bunch of ignorant savages like their pa. It went on and on. I was thoroughly tired of her, my wife was, too. As for the kids, they'd play outside until after dark just to avoid their grandmother.'

'That's sad,' said Ori, and Hani agreed. 'So then what happened?'

'As it happened, the local priest of Elil – he's the weather god, but of course you know that, you probably know him personally. . .'

'Oh, him, yeah,' said Hani, deftly dodging a jab in the ribs. 'Big fella. Sort of a windbag.' The little goat let out a bleat of seeming agreement, and Ori gave up. Nukhu seemed not to notice as he steered around a sandbar.

> 'As I said, the local priest of Elil was a good one when it came to weather patterns. He announced to everyone who'd listen that his calculations of trends and the meteor shower we'd had, plus the granddaddy of all giant fish nightmares, had led him to the scientific conclusion that we were in for a millennium flood. Not just a century flood, mind you: one that only happened once in a thousand years. The sort of out-of-control rainy season full of gullywashers that change the course of rivers.
>
> Sell up, said the priest. Invest in transportation, he advised. Take your wives, kids, animals, seed corn, and furniture and pack it all up in something that floats. He was very convinced of this. I for one was convinced of his meteorological expertise.
>
> Besides, I was young. Talk of moving stirred up my wanderlust. I began to wonder what was downriver, you know?'

'Brother, I hear you,' said Hani. 'I allus like to see what's over the next rise myself.' Ori agreed.

> 'Abi and I talked it over. I started gathering materials for a boat and talking to some boatwrights. After all, I had the reed-weaving skills. The kids helped. I made a deal: traded some carpentry work for pitch. Abi sewed bags and filled chests. We made a game of it and sang as we worked.

In the meantime, I stored away grain and hay and beer and accumulated a bit of livestock, goats and ducks and a couple of cows and a pair of donkeys. Financing the move turned out to be easier than I'd thought: people who didn't believe the priest were eager to snap up waterfront property and would pay top shekel for bottom land.

All of this didn't sit well with Dinna, my mother-in-law. She had no intention of moving, she said. She was happy where she was, she said. This was news to me: I'd never known her to be happy anywhere. But just about then, she developed an interest in one of the local widowers. He had a little brewery and his own tavern and he was paying her some attention. That suited the rest of us down to the ground. While they were busy gossiping and complaining all day, the rest of us could work undisturbed. We put some effort into the thing.

Pretty soon, we had ourselves a nice boat: a living area, sleeping rooms with hammocks, watertight storage areas, the works. We had stalls for the animals. I'd been talking to the rivermen and made myself a map, from the source waters clear down to where the river joined the Euphrates and beyond, all the way to the sea. I figured we couldn't get too far lost, even if the Tigris changed course.

Of course we told Dinna she was welcome to come with us – but she wouldn't hear of it. Blah, blah, fools on a fool's errand, blah, blah. Besides, she and the widower were busy bonding over how much smarter they were than anybody else. Tavernkeepers keep their ears to the ground, she insisted: they know things. And he'd invested heavily in local real estate. He was going to be a major landowner come the rainy season, which was when all of us who were going planned to pull out.'

Ori was intrigued by all the planning. Hani said, 'I like where this is going. I'm assuming the rains came down, and the floods came up?'

Nukhu laughed. 'Boy, did they ever!'

'The first few days of the rainy season didn't seem like much. Just normal rain. But I trusted the meteorological priesthood. They had science on their side. We started loading up the boat, which Abi had named Nukhu's Ark, just for fun.

To tell you the truth, by this time we were itching to go, anyway, rain or no rain. We figured we'd find out what downriver was like. So when the rain fell down harder, we loaded faster. Finally, everything was stored away. We led the animals down to the dock and settled them in. Not any too soon: by the time we all climbed aboard ourselves, the dock was almost completely under water. We untied the Ark, just in time, and started off.

The kids were excited, of course. They waved to everybody they knew as we floated past – and some people we didn't know. Some waved back, others were busy loading their own boats, and some just stared. I don't know why: it wasn't as if they hadn't seen a reed boat before. Even if ours was a bit fancy, what with the name on the side and the figure of Elil on the front.

Anyway, we were halfway through the town and on our way to passing the Sign of the Onager, which was Dinna's widower's tavern, when Abi gave a yelp.

'Oh, no! I forgot to give Mama her laundry!'

Dinna had taken to staying over the tavern – with another widow woman for company and respectability, of course, just until she could get that widower to marry her. But she'd still send a boy over to our place with her laundry for Abi to do. And Abi, bless her heart, would do it and send it back to her. She's still like that, Abi is: she'll do anything for a neighbour. Only what with all the excitement, she'd clean forgot to messenger that laundry back to her mama.

Not that there were any messengers to be found that day, anyway: they were all too busy trying to stay dry. And by this time the Tigris was rising – and I mean, rising. The banks were flooded and water was already filling the lower storeys of houses.'

'*Well, we can make it to the road in a homemade boat, 'Cause that's the only thing we got left that'll float. . .*' sang Hani happily. Ori joined in, '*it's two feet high and risin'!*'

Two boys passed them in a *mashuf* and looked toward the singing, puzzled, as yet another heron flew past. Hani, Ori, and Nukhu waved, and they waved back.

'We got to where we could see the tavern, and sure enough, the downstairs was flooded. There were some people on the roof – yep, the tavern owner, the other widow, and my mother-in-law, waving like mad. No way we could get to them. I had an idea.

'Shumer!' I yelled to my eldest. 'Bring me a bow and arrow and some of that washing line!'

I tied one end of some washing line to the arrow, took aim at the tavern roof, and fired. The arrow stuck in the thatch, nice as you please.

'What in the world are you doing?' yelled the tavernkeeper.

'Delivering your laundry!' I yelled back. 'Send that arrow back this way!' He got it. He yelled for one of his brewery men to come up with a bow. They passed the line around the chimney pole and fired it back at us, hitting the flagpole I'd had the foresight to install. We tied it all together and had us a wash line.

'Hand me the laundry!' I called to the kids. So they did, while Shumer rowed against the current to keep us in range as long as he could. We passed sheets and tablecloths and handkerchiefs and Grandma's nightie. We pinned 'em up, they hauled away, and when the next bit of line became free, we sent the next item. Just when we about couldn't hold her any longer, I added the piece duh resistance: a set of Dinna's drawers, beet red. She saw 'em coming and almost died, I could tell. She tried to wave it off, but the widower was bent on his heroic rescue of his beloved's belongings and didn't pick up the signal. The drawers arrived safely. Then we cut the rope.

The last time I saw my mother-in-law, she was shaking both fists at me, while the tavernkeeper was looking at a pair of red drawers with a bemused expression. We floated on out of their lives and didn't stop until we reached Parthosas.'

'And I bet you laughed all the way,' said Hani.

Nukhu nodded. 'Like I said, you've gotta be able to see the funny side of things.'

Hani and Ori sang Prajapati's song. Nukhu learned it and sang along.

> *I was born about ten thousand years ago,*
> *There ain't nothing in this world that I don't know,*
> *I saw reed boats out of Hades floating down the wide Euphrates,*
> *And I'll whup the guy who says it isn't so.*

Chapter 42: Rain Falls on the Just and Unjust

'Hey,' said Hani. 'I felt drops. Looks like the wet season is beginning.' Sure enough, rain fell on them, softly and straight down. Hani and Ori decided that for right now, they liked it. They left the little goat protected by the shelter and sat out in the soft precipitation, talking. After all, it didn't rain that often in spite of all the stories – most flooding was caused by melting snow in Nukhu's native mountains.

As they travelled along they waved to various people on the bank. Most of them waved back. They passed foot travellers, travellers with donkeys, the occasional camel, and once even a man and his son followed by a large herd of ducks. The little goat called to the ducks and they quacked back.

Occasionally, they passed a village. Most of them were set back, away from the river in case of flooding. The flood banks were good, rich soil, and farmers from the villages were out ploughing and planting. Hani and Ori noticed the greening of the landscape as they rode along: wildflowers began to spring up.

Hani sang:

> *A long time ago, when the earth was born,*
> *Enlil the god, he planted corn,*
> *Planted wheat and barley and a little rice,*
> *And soon the whole river valley looked real nice.*
>
> *I got green cucumbers, and long-necked gourds,*
> *And cauliflower and onions, and squash, of course,*
> *Chickpeas and lentils, but, sad to be tellin',*

> *I just ain't got no watermelon.*

'What in the netherworld is a watermelon?' Nukhu wondered aloud. Ori threw figs at Hani, which shut the angel up because you can't keep singing vegetatively anomalous songs with your mouth full.

'AtleasIdidnsaynuthinboutsneks,' mumbled Hani between juicy bites.

Ori sang:

> *Everyone 'neath their vine and fig tree,*
> *When the heat of the day is spent,*
> *Will blend their voices in harmony,*
> *And sing to their hearts' content, and sing to their hearts' content.*

Hani stopped eating and joined in.

> *And they'll beat their swords into plough blades,*
> *And their spears pruning hooks will be,*
> *And they'll study peace, and war will cease*
> *From the mountains down to the sea.*

'Nice thought,' commented Nukhu. 'From your mouths to the Creator's ear.'

Beats Wholly Satisfactory, *at any rate*, commented Prajapati.

They floated downriver with the current, tying up to sleep at night. After a couple of days, the boat and the Tigris joined the Euphrates. A day after that, they dropped off the little goat, which appeared happy with its new home (and some fresh greens). They also picked up a passenger.

'Meet Shubshi,' Nukhu introduced. 'He's known in these parts as the Righteous Sufferer. There's even a poem about him.'

It was true: the old man looked like he'd been through, if not a war or two, the next-best thing. Thin and wiry, with grey hair and beard, Shubshi presented the world with a face like two leagues of bad road. Shubshi looked back through twinkling eyes of blue and didn't seem to care a bit.

Ori said sympathetically, 'I suppose with the title of Righteous Sufferer, you've seen some things, sir?'

Shubshi settled in amongst the bales of cargo, resting his back against a roll of carpet. He laughed gently. 'I guess you could say so. But the poem that's going around gets a lot of it wrong. Besides, it's basically pro-Marduk propaganda.'

That Marduk. If he was a real god, I'd go clean his sundial.

Hani was drinking beer when Prajapati said that. Hani snorted a noseful of beer. Ori pounded Hani's back and said apologetically, 'I'm sorry. My friend takes these, er, turns.'

Nukhu winked at them in a way that made Ori suspect the boatman might have very good inner hearing.

'Please tell us about it,' encouraged Ori as Hani wiped away tears of joy. The old man gazed off across the marshes, thinking. Then he began his tale.

'The poem is all about me thanking Marduk for delivery from my troubles, but that's not it. It's more about me finally coming to my senses after a lifetime of superstitious self-involvement.

I used to be one of the most successful grain merchants in Warka. I had a seat on the Council. Everybody asked my opinion about everything: what to invest in, and when, what I thought about the intercities political situation, which wrestlers I backed, simply everything.

And I loved the attention. My family did, too: my wife could get the most influential guests at her soirees. The kids were automatically popular. Even my servants were snootier than all the other servants.

I owned the nicest house in town, up on the hill behind the ziggurat. Terrific view. My country estate was full of well-irrigated date palms. We dined well.

I didn't brag that I knew famous people: famous people bragged that they knew *me*. I was living the life of Sargon in Eden, if you get my meaning.'

'I think I do,' said Ori.

'Sounds like you were busy and happy,' commented Hani, now recovered.

'You'd think so, wouldn't you? As I said, I loved the life. Mainly because it made me feel important. People depended on me: employees, relatives, local government, artists, the community. . .it was nice to be needed.

> But I worried all the time. What if my predictions about the grain market didn't pan out? Suppose a friend invested on my say-so and lost his shirt? That's a lot of responsibility. What were they doing over in Ur? Should I tell the Council to be worried? What was the weather going to be like this rainy season? There were a million things to think about. I'd toss and turn at night. My wife got her own bedroom – said she needed "her beauty sleep".'

Shubshi shrugged and grinned a rueful grin at the memory.

'I imagine you had other worries, too,' said Ori. 'Like bandits on the roads.'

'And burglars and muggers in town,' put in Hani.

'And plant diseases and locust plagues in the fields,' added Nukhu, who was listening while steering the boat.

Shubshi nodded. 'And that's when things began to get really bad.'

> 'You see, I was raised to be a pious temple-going person. I always paid my tribute to Marduk on time. I celebrated all of the major holidays, and even most of the minor ones. I gave alms in the names of the gods. I knew all the words to all the hymns.'

Hani sang:

> *All creatures who on Earth do dwell,*
> *Where bright Euphrates river runs,*

> *Sing to Marduk, and know right well,*
> *Here is a god who gets stuff done!*

It was Ori's turn to choke on a fig.

'I haven't heard that one before,' said Shubshi.

'Pay no attention to that one,' said Nukhu. 'He'd joke with the creator himself. But go on with your story, please.'

'As I said, I was really religious. And the point of religion in Warka was that everyone believed. . .'

'Don't tell me,' said Ori, 'let me guess. That if you were nice to the gods, they'd be nice to you?'

Shubshi nodded. 'That was about it. Obviously, if you were very pious, made offerings, attended all the ceremonies, and prayed, the gods would favour you. So nobody was surprised to see that I was the first to arrive at the ceremonies, and the last to leave the temple.'

'Because you were really blessed.' This from Hani.

> 'At first I thought all the devotion was really paying off: my company made record profits. My wife's irises won the flower show. My son got accepted into the temple school. But then, things started not to go so well.
>
> A caravan got waylaid by robbers.
>
> My bookkeeper embezzled 600 shekels.

A blight struck my orchards.

That was bad enough. My neighbours were already looking at me sideways. My wife was angry with me because of all the gossip. But then came the worst blow.

I came down with a horrible skin rash that spread to my arms and face.'

'Oh, no,' said all three listeners with instant sympathy. Ori added, 'That's really bad. I'm sorry to hear that.'

'Your sympathy is appreciated. Of course, you know that a visible skin rash is about the worst thing that can happen to a socially active businessman in Warka. In the first place, everybody shuns you. It's almost impossible to do any business at all. And once word gets around, nobody wants to associate with you in any way, shape, or form.

And then, of course, there's the discomfort. Which is minor compared to all the wailing, commiserating, and useless 'help' I got offered by well-wishers who were hedging their bets in case I got better.

If I had a drachm for every piece of useless advice I was offered, I'd still be a rich man. Also, these 'comforters' kept hanging around my wife, talking and eating me out of house and home.

Then they sent for the medical experts.'

Hani looked curious and Ori explained, 'Exorcists.' Ori had transcribed enough tablets to know all about it.

> 'Yes, the exorcists came. They applied poultices. They advised me that the cause was something sexual.
>
> My wife stopped speaking to me.
>
> I denied the sex part. Then they claimed I'd slighted this or that obscure god. We went nearly crazy and close to bankrupt with gifts to most, if not all, of the 3,600 deities. And yes, every one of them had a priest, priestess, seer, seeress, or acolyte who needed a bribe. . .a devotional offering. This was time-consuming and expensive.
>
> Now, I could have dealt with a financial setback or two. I could roll with the punches if I lost standing in the community. I didn't even mind the boils – I knew they'd go away eventually. But letting everybody down like that made me nearly frantic. Besides, if I couldn't keep the family in their accustomed luxury, what good was I? I began to question my own existence.
>
> I prayed and prayed and prayed. I prayed to every one of those 3,600 gods. And you know what. . . ?'

'Not one of them answered you,' said Hani simply, refilling the old man's beer cup.

Shubshi looked surprised. 'How did you guess?'

'I've seen them statues,' replied Hani. 'I can spot a corporate myth a league away, my friend. Them gods is phonies.'

Shubshi looked amazed. 'I don't know how you figured that out, friend, but you're right.'

> 'After months of assiduous prayer, that's the conclusion I came to. But I nearly went mad first. In fact, my family thought I was mad. They had me committed to a local temple – very private, very exclusive, naturally – where the exorcists worked night and day to figure out which god's 'hand' was on me, and what omens they could divine from my hallucinations.'

'You were hallucinating by this time?' asked Nukhu.

Shubshi spread his hands. 'You would be, too, if you'd drunk as many potions as I had.'

> 'They kept asking me if I saw a dog. If you see a dog, you're expected to die.
>
> I finally got so desperate to be left alone that I swore up and down I did see a dog. A great, big one. All black, with glowing eyes. I begged them to perform a ritual of passing for me – preferably on the other side of the temple. They scurried away to do this, with what seemed to me to be unholy glee.
>
> At last, I was left alone. No priests, no 'comforters', no exorcists, and no dog.
>
> I took a deep breath. It was now or never.
>
> IS ANYBODY THERE? I said.

And I waited.'

Hani and Ori leaned forward, and Nukhu pricked up his ears where he stood by the tiller. 'What did you hear?' asked Hani hopefully.

Shubshi's grin lit up the sky.

> 'I heard my Friend,' he said. 'The voice that doesn't want any of that. Who's not there to help you succeed in business, or get famous, or get elected to anything. And I asked Him what He wanted. And He told me.'

> 'The next day, I signed over all my business interests to my sons. I left my wife the house. I packed a small bundle and set out on my travels.' He grinned. 'I've learned a lot since then. And I've met thousands of people. Some of them, I have helped: some have helped me.'

His grin grew wider. 'And today, I've even met a couple of wet-behind-the-ears angels.'

Ori looked at Hani, startled. They both looked at Shubshi.

Then they fell over, laughing, and rolled around the deck, holding their sides.

****

Once Shubshi had got to his destination, and Nukhu had delivered his last load, the well-travelled boatman informed Ori and Hani that he was at the end of the line. He didn't need the boat any longer. He planned to head north again by joining a camel train.

'Would you like to sell the boat?' asked Hani.

****

The following evening found Ori and Hani lying in the reed boat, floating out to sea, looking up at the stars.

> *Rocked in the cradle of the deep,*
> *I lay me down in peace to sleep...*

... began Hani, but Ori interrupted. 'And the River Euphrates is deep and wide, but what, if anything, is on the other side of this journey?'

'I dunno,' shrugged Hani. 'We've sure enough covered a mess of territory. And I suspect we've done a bit of good here and there – particularly you, I think.'

Ori said, 'You, too, you shepherd-wrestler, you.' They both laughed.

'Mesopotamia has been a lot of fun,' Hani went on. 'But there's a heap of costumes up in the Paternoster. What do you reckon they're good for?'

'Well,' said Ori. 'I found a text in the library. It told people how to write fiction.'

'What's fiction?'

'Made-up stories.'

'Oh, like the one about the snake in the gard-. . . ow! That fig you threw weren't ripe!'

'Okay, yeah, like that,' Ori conceded. 'Anyway, the expert said a storyteller had to make the characters human.'

Hani chortled. 'That leaves us out, then.'

'And they can't be perfect.'

'Which, of course, we're not. Because I play practical jokes and you snore off-key.'

'I do not!'

'Let's go someplace when recording devices have been invented, and I'll prove it!'

Ori laughed. 'Okay. Finally, the storytelling expert said the character had to *want* something – because whatever the character wants is what makes the story go.'

So. . . a voice broke into the discussion, **what do you two want?**

Hani stared out at the sea, glowing in the last light of a Mesopotamian sun.

Ori stared upwards and outwards, at the stars.

'To see what's out there,' they both said.

Hani added, 'And who needs what.' Ori sighed agreement.

You shall have it, said Prajapati.

About the Author

Dmitri Gheorgheni has been the editor of the h2g2 Post since 2012 and can usually be found hanging around h2g2.com or on Twitter.

Milton Keynes UK
Ingram Content Group UK Ltd.
UKHW020851211223
434780UK00016B/579